July 21 - 2000

For Rusty —
"My real estate pal"
My book finally done!
My show biz "daze" before my real estate days!

Peace - love - soul —

Michael

# THE PARK AVENUE CHORUS BOY

By Michael Mason

CHICAGO SPECTRUM PRESS
LOUISVILLE, KENTUCKY 40207

© 2000 by Michael Mason

All rights reserved. Except for appropriate use in critical reviews or works of scholarship, the reproduction or use of this work in any form or by any electronic, mechanical, or other means now known or hereafter invented, including photocopying and recording, and in any information storage and retrieval system, is forbidden without written permission of the author.

CHICAGO SPECTRUM PRESS
4824 BROWNSBORO CENTER
LOUISVILLE, KENTUCKY 40207
1-888-285-6661

Printed in the U.S.A.

10 9 8 7 6 5 4 3 2 1

ISBN: 1-58374-007-4

I dedicate this book to my wife, Nikki,
my son, Richard, and the many mysteries of life.

## People Who Were and Are a Meaningful Part of My Life

Wm. Durfee, Don Drysdale, Elgin Baylor, Wyatt Cooper and his wife Gloria Vanderbilt, Lehman Engel, Alice Astor, Dr. Charles Monell, Dr. Carole Lewis Stolpe, Dr. Jerry Benston, Irving Silverman, Phillip McKeever, Eric Hanstein, Bill Cable, Miss Dixie Evans, Brooks Barton, Dr. Hoffbauer, Dr. Fein, Dr. James Racebaren, Dr. Robert Rothbart, Lady Nancy Oaks, Peter Gould Harig, Don and Trudy Durant, James Respondek, Billie Dove, Ruby Keeler, Betty Carey, Robert Hill, Cary Grant, Ruta Lee, Joe Layton, Jerome Robbins, Chet Starvish, Elaine Young, Mike Silverman, Jon Douglas, Bobbie Cox, Joan Irvine Smith, "Liz" Whitney, Mrs. George Randolph Hearst, William "Billie" Weinberger, Mrs. Gloria Campbell, Nora Kaye, Dame Margot Fonteyn, Michael Soames, Frederik Ashton, Van Clyburn, Dianne Cannon, Carole Curb, Mike Curb, Sima Kaye, Barbara Hutton, Lance Reventlow, "Ronnie" Schune Hartnell, Alfredo DeLaVega, Betsey Von Furstenberg, Doris Duke, Capucine, Duke Jamé de Cadaval, Didiér Milinàire, and his mother, The Duchess of Bedford, of Woburn Abbey, England, my son, Richard and his wife Stephanie, my sister Susan and her husband, Don, my sister, Dr. Marilyn Mason, my brother John and his wife, Valerie, my sister Phyl and her husband Walt, my sister-in-law, Carole Mason, my many nieces nephews, and cousins, and last, but not least, my beautiful grandchildren, Nichole, Robert, and Eric. Also, Phil Long and his wife Susan.

And a very special word of gratitude to George Kalarsarinis.

# Contents

INTRODUCTION .................................................................. 9

PART I: The Park Avenue Chorus Boy
CHAPTER ONE
Under The Sun ................................................................. 13
CHAPTER TWO
Aunt Suzanne .................................................................. 20
CHAPTER THREE
Glamour, Galas, and Gabors ............................................ 27
CHAPTER FOUR
A Breath of Fresh Air ...................................................... 39
CHAPTER FIVE
A Wish Granted .............................................................. 55
CHAPTER SIX
Cowboys and Indians ...................................................... 65
CHAPTER SEVEN
Heston vs. Meredith ........................................................ 87
Chapter EIGHT
Cry For Me, Argentina .................................................... 93

PART II: A Serious Kind of Guy
CHAPTER NINE
Bravo, Michael ............................................................... 116
CHAPTER TEN
The Rich Man's Marlene Dietrich .................................. 128
CHAPTER ELEVEN
Hello, Good Bye ............................................................ 138

CHAPTER TWELVE
Undersea Girl ........................................................................177
CHAPTER THIRTEEN
The Long Goodbye ...............................................................182
CHAPTER FOURTEEN
The Cukor Connection .........................................................188
CHAPTER FIFTEEN
Elmer Gantry Was Drunk .....................................................196
CHAPTER SIXTEEN
Thin Skin That Wiggles ........................................................205
CHAPTER SEVENTEEN
Mr. Sunoco Cola Knows Best, Gracie ..................................213

PART III: The Exorcism
CHAPTER EIGHTEEN
Half A Hero ..........................................................................225
CHAPTER NINETEEN
Let's Break Love ...................................................................234
CHAPTER TWENTY
 Marilyn And Beyond ...........................................................252
CHAPTER TWENTY-ONE
After My Fall ........................................................................265

# INTRODUCTION

When you are born into one of America's most politically and financially prominent families, you should by all standards consider yourself a very fortunate individual. I never have, nor never will. That is because I know that by a twist of fate, it could have been you — but it was me, Michael Mason, and this is my story.

My limousine was larger and longer than the one that Rosalind Russell parked in front of the Winter Garden Theatre when she starred in *Wonderful Town* on Broadway. She was the star and I was the chorus boy. My car was parked every night in back of hers. She lived at the Pierre Hotel and I lived at 820 Park Avenue. I was known as "The Park Avenue Chorus Boy."

This book is fact, not fiction, and the names I mention are and were part of my life. I tell this story with love, even if all the events I write about are not just about the good, but sometimes about the unexpected, and the tragic.

# PART I

## The Park Avenue Chorus Boy

# CHAPTER ONE
## Under The Sun

They brought me to Hollywood to threaten Robert Wagner. This was a reflection of "studio thinking" in which the studio brings in a promising, unknown young actor like me, a man who is the same basic type of man as the big star they already have under contract, like Robert Wagner, and threaten to cast the unknown kid if the star doesn't behave himself. It was nice that they thought of me as a promising young actor. Robert Wagner was not exactly a household name yet, but I guess they had gotten the vibrations early, so they thought they would get a head start at keeping him in line, just as a matter of principle. Unfortunately for the studio, R.J. didn't give a damn about threats to his career, and I didn't have any worries yet, so we became fast friends, drinking together long into the warm Hollywood nights. Few people knew at the time that R.J. was from enormous wealth. I thought he was just another good-looking guy in Hollywood who happened to live in Bel-Air with his family.

I had been rehearsing six months for a screen test. Six months. Most of the Broadway shows that I had been in rehearsed for less than three months, and my screen test was only going to last 15 minutes. My dramatic coach for the test was Natasha Lytess, a small, frail, and intimidating Russian immigrant. I was twenty and she was sixty, so she had had three times the practice of being intimidating. I was more than willing to bow out when her fangs came out. After all, she was reputed to be the greatest dramatic coach in the country at the time, since she was Marilyn Monroe's coach.

My partner for the screen test was a lovely young woman named Marla. Marla was something to look at, a combination of Elizabeth Taylor and Vivien Leigh — a dynamic body with a fragile, soft face. We met at Twentieth Century-Fox Studios every day and did scenes together from whichever play or screen-play Natasha wished to tackle on that particular morning. It was four days to go to the screen test, and the morning hours dragged as we went through *Sabrina Fair*, yet again. Six months' worth of this drivel, and I was damned sick of the whole thing. Natasha broke for lunch, and someone came over and told me that Tab Hunter was on the line for me.

"Hey, Michael," he said, "there's this party tomorrow at the Racquet Club in Palm Springs and I've got to go. I haven't had my picture taken with Rita Hayworth yet and she's going to be there. How soon can you leave?"

Tab had built his career on publicity. He was a household name before he had ever made a movie, and he wouldn't get around to making his first picture for another eight months. I told him I would get the limousine and pick him up in half an hour.

Natasha was lunching, and Marla was off somewhere, so nobody saw me when I left the studio. I picked up Tab and Harold Lloyd, Jr., and we headed to Palm Springs without me telling anyone where I was going.

I knew everyone at the studio would be furious, but I didn't care. Six months of rehearsal had kneaded all the joy out of Hollywood for me. I was a party person from way back, and all this pretend glamour had sent me screaming into the nightlife I loved, to join the parties and the stars. I was a rich kid, with talent, manners, and connections to all of the right people, and I could damn near drink anyone under the table. I had the arrogance of a lot of young men, but somewhere, deep inside me, there was a destructive time bomb ticking away, ready to make a mess of me and my career.

My screen test was being done so the studio could decide if they were going to put me in a picture with Susan Hayward called *With a Song in My Heart,* the story of Jane Frohman. I was another R.J. Wagner, a rah-rah college boy, handsome and young and on the way up. In the movie Susan Hayward was going to pull a soldier boy out of the audience and sing to him. After my screen test, they gave the part to Wagner.

Tab and I strode in casually to the Racquet Club party, slick and scrubbed in blue blazers, white linen pants, and white shirts. We looked around and spotted the photographers for *Photoplay* and *Modern Screen,* and then he and Rita saw each other. They both knew what to do and they moved like magnets toward each other, two planets circling an invisible core of starlight. The photographers were on them in a minute. Tab and Rita acted like old friends, greeting each other warmly, smiling in the sea of flashbulbs.

One photographer slid over to me. "Hey, Mason," he said, "where's your date?"

"Hey, " I said, "why take a ham sandwich to a banquet?" I gestured to the rest of the room and the not-too-slim pickin's. The photographer laughed.

"Hey, Tab," Rita was saying, "come over here. I want you to meet a buddy of mine. Linda Darnell, Tab Hunter." Tab moved smoothly forward and took Linda's hand, instantly infatuated.

"It's good to meet you, Tab," Linda said after they had been introduced. "I'm sorry but I haven't seen any of your pictures."

Tab smiled. "I'm not surprised," he said, "I haven't done any pictures."

"Not even a walk-on?"

"Not even a walk-on."

I laughed and the cameras flashed. I commandeered a bottle of champagne, drank it, and got loud and obnoxious. It was a successful party.

We partied for three days in Palm Springs, using any excuse to keep going, keep drinking, and keep being seen with anyone Tab had to meet so that he could keep his momentum going. I told myself I was celebrating. After all, I was about to have my first Hollywood screen test. The days were hot and hung-over, long and languid. There wasn't enough to do and too much time to do it in. I was waiting for the nights. The nights were cool and crisp, seen through a haze of champagne, brandy, and the chlorine of someone's pool.

We returned to Hollywood the night before I was to go before the cameras and called R.J., Debbie Reynolds, and Virginia Gibson. Robert and Debbie dated regularly and Ginny and I doubled with them. When we were together, we were four attractive kids all trying to make it big, all wanting to be stars. We all thought Ginny had the best chance to make it. She was a fine dancer and singer, better perhaps than Debbie Reynolds, and she was prettier. The studio gave Ginny her image, the sophisticated lady, and she played that part both at the studio and away from it. Debbie, on the other hand, was cute and knew how to use her cuteness to her advantage. She developed herself into a great comedienne. Both she and Ginny were workaholics, but Ginny's career, for some reason, went nowhere compared to Debbie's.

Tab and I agreed to meet them at the Garden of Allah hotel. The Garden of Allah was like a fantasy land. It was located on the corner of Sunset and Crescent Heights in Hollywood, and was a star hangout because the tourists did not know about it yet. Many of the best screen writers lived at the Garden of Allah in individual bungalows that gave them lots of privacy. In the evenings, the writers would crowd around the large bar and the stars would join them, buying them drinks, chatting them up, trying to be their friends, hoping they would write bigger and better parts for them in their next movie. Large picture windows looked out onto the lighted pool, which was shaped like the Black Sea. I saw Errol Flynn stroll by under the palm trees and pass Lana Turner, who waved at Frank Sinatra. David Niven lifted his champagne glass and Humphrey Bogart smiled at Lauren Bacall and ordered another round. A typical night at the Garden.

I told the waiter loudly that I didn't like our table and wanted to move. R.J. pretended that he didn't know me, and Debbie went to powder her nose. At the new table, I asked where our Scotches were, and Ginny headed to the ladies' room after Debbie, while Tab scratched his head. Everybody left. I ordered the waiters around for a bit, and then let them be. My method was to anger everyone at a restaurant, and then over tip excessively at the end of the evening. I always got great service this way, even though I acted like a jerk. Debbie and Ginny wandered back to the table when they saw I was through acting childish, and we drank scotch for a while. We moved on to champagne during dinner and kept with it for the rest of the night. Tab talked about the lovely Linda Darnell. Little did he know that his first film, *Island of Desire*, would star him opposite Linda.

"I don't know, Tab," Debbie said, "I've been under contract forever and I've done pictures forever, and I'm only now getting recognized. You've never done a picture and you're a big star. What's the story?"

"Don't talk to me," Tab said, "talk to Henry." Henry Wilson was the great star-maker who had discovered Tab. Wilson made Tab a star by investing in him. He bought him a wardrobe and a brand-new Thunderbird, set him up in the best hotels, got him into parties, and got pictures taken of him. And more and more pictures. And still more pictures, all of which ended up in the right publications at the right time. Henry Wilson was a whiz at what he did. He made a lot of people great in Hollywood.

Later in the evening, Greta Garbo came to take her nightly swim in the Black Sea pool. It was a ritual with her. Every night she did laps after turning the pool lights off, so that no one would watch her. She walked to the edge of the pool, dropped her towel, which revealed a one-piece bathing suit, and slid into the dark water. After two laps, the bathing suit came off and plopped in the pool gutter next to her towel. She went on with her laps. I saw Errol Flynn turn slyly, push away from the bar, and walk down to where the pool lights were, listening to her swimming sounds. When she was in the middle of the pool, he flipped the pool lights on. There was a sudden, frantic splashing as Garbo made her way back to her swimsuit.

"So, Michael," Tab said to me when we all turned back to our table, "are you ready for your big test tomorrow?"

"Test?" R.J. asked. "You mean you've got your screen test tomorrow?"

"That's right," I said. "Why do you think we're celebrating?"

"Michael," Debbie said, "you're *always* celebrating, every single night."

I winked at her. "Ain't it the truth."

"Michael, you idiot," R.J. said, "you're going to get less that four hours' sleep at this rate. It's almost two o'clock now."

I looked at my watch. "Well, it doesn't matter. I'll probably be up all night anyway."

R.J. took Debbie's arm. "Debbie, we're going. I'm not going to be a party to this. Michael, even if you don't go home, at least I'll know you're not here because of me. If I were you, I'd get some sleep. Go home and rest. You're in for a difficult day tomorrow."

R.J. was a professional. He knew when to play and when to stop, and he never would have joined me that evening if he had known I had a screen test the next day. That's why I hadn't told him.

R.J. took Debbie and Ginny home. I asked Tab if he wanted to take a quick swim in the pool and we headed out the French doors to the edge of the pool, slipped out of our shoes, shirts, and pants, and dove in. We were followed by a couple of young starlets who leapt in topless, hoping some Hollywood bigwig would see their breasts bobbing on the surface of the water and discover them. But their desperate, hopeful grins gave them away, doomed even then to be used and dismissed.

The next morning I arrived at the studio two hours late. They put on my makeup quickly and I went over to Marla's dressing room just off the stage. I put my head in and said, "Let's go. They're waiting."

"That's right, you son of a bitch, they've been waiting for hours. I've been here since 5:30 in the morning, having my hair done, and where the hell have you been for the past four days?"

She glowered at me and pushed past me out the door. She walked quickly and angrily ahead of me to the stage, but I caught up with her and put my arm around her waist, and we entered together. The stage crew watched us and collectively hooted at how magnificently beautiful she was and how late we were. I smiled at the attention and knew they were blaming *her* for being late.

Natasha was standing by the studio director. She rushed over to me, yanked me aside and said, "Michael, who do you think you are?"

"I don't know, I haven't decided yet," I answered.

"Everyone is furious with you, but there's no time for that now. Listen to me closely…"

I watched the arc lights warming up. Last moment frantic details were suddenly put into gear. The camera was moved into place. Marla was hit by light.

"Forget the stage," Natasha was saying. "You're not on the stage anymore. Work the camera."

The director was pointing at me. One of the grips was running across the set. The assistant cameraman held a tape measure from Marla's nose to the camera lens. She squinted under the lights.

"Forget the stage," Natasha whispered and pushed me towards the light.

# CHAPTER TWO
## Aunt Suzanne

When I was ten years old, my father would put me on a train from our home in Massachusetts to visit my favorite relative, Aunt Suzanne, in Washington, D.C. My mother was displeased with this arrangement, but I liked it very much. Besides, it seemed totally natural to me that a limousine took me to the Boston station, I had an overnight berth alone in a train for eight or ten hours, and then I was met at the station on the other end by another limousine. At ten years old I already perceived that we were rich and that we had an ancestor in our family that we were quite proud of — George Mason, who was one of the initiators of the Bill of Rights. But didn't everyone ride around in limousines and have magnificent ancestors? I thought so then.

Nonetheless, my Aunt Suzanne was different. Her wealth didn't impress me, we had plenty of that. Our wealth was what you would call "conservative" New England wealth — two servants ran the whole house and I had to put a jacket on for dinner. Our colonial home was tastefully furnished and we lived in quiet elegance. Not so with Aunt Suzanne. Aunt Suzanne was glamorous.

After an all-night train ride, her limousine would pick me up at the station and bring me to her front door. From the outside the four stories of her house seemed un-extraordinary. Then the butler would open the door and usher me in. She always had opera playing loudly throughout her home, and the entire house was decorated lavishly with Italian art. The first impression, walking into her home, was one that stays with me. It's theatricality forewarned of wonderful things to come.

She was a great hostess and the house was created for entertaining. She would give a sit-down dinner for 30 in her dining room and get additional footmen so there would be a waiter behind every chair. They would wear white gloves, black tie and tails, and whisk away your plate so quickly once you had laid your fork down that you wondered what you had been eating from. There were regularly seven helpers in Aunt Suzanne's home, but with each overnight guest a new private maid would be assigned, so on occasion, there were 30 servants at beck-and-call.

The main drawing room of the house had been converted into a bedroom suite for her. Fresh from the limousine, I climbed the stairs and opened the large oak door to her chambers. "La Boheme" was playing. I looked down the 85-foot drawing room with the 20-foot vaulted, carved ceiling, to Aunt Suzanne's bed. There was a huge fire going in the enormous fireplace, and there were no electric lights at all, only a silver candelabra along the dark walls with candles that were lit each morning and remained burning throughout the day. The room was different from the rest of the house, done in French décor, and white bearskin rugs ran all the way down to her bed.

She slept in a giant four-poster bed that was draped in heavy maroon velvet, set up to view the rest of the room when she wished to hold court. Now the velvet was drawn like a curtain around the bed. Her maid entered, laid an alligator makeup case in front of Aunt Suzanne, whom I couldn't see behind the curtain. She pulled the curtains further closed.

"Good morning, darling, how are you? I'll be with you shortly," she said. I sat down where I was on the other side of the room to wait. I knew that because of the curtains she could move discreetly from her bed to her bath and dressing area on the other side of the bed, so I never knew when she was in the bed or when she was in her bath. Opera music was thick in the room like dust in sunlight and I remembered that Aunt Suzanne had laughed when she talked of the many servants who had left her because they couldn't take listening to Verdi, Puccini, and Rossini all of the time. I had grown to love the music and knew every aria from "La Boheme."

The curtains parted in her bed and Aunt Suzanne said, "Come down and talk to me, Michael." I made the long walk on the bearskin rugs to her bed and sat in a chair that was set up for me.

She was propped against forty thousand pillows, smiling a welcome smile. Aunt Suzanne was in her late 60s, but she still looked young and vibrant. The room was dark, as she preferred the nighttime. She was fair-skinned with ruby red lips, black eyes, and black hair. She is perhaps the reason that I'm still infatuated with raven-haired women today. She lay there between the silk sheets, wearing Belgian lace, and I wondered if she had slept in that wonderful gown or if she had put it on for me.

I sat down by her and she asked me how my trip was. I told her fine as I suppressed a yawn. It had been ten hours overnight, and in the excitement, I had only dozed.

"Michael, it's time you learned about your family. I think you are old enough to know who you are and where you come from. You must *always* remember who you are!"

Then she began to tell me lovely stories, weaving pictures in the fabric of my mind, family histories all tumbling into place. She told me how my great grandfather had been the first to free slaves in this country and had kept them all afterwards because none of them wanted to leave his Virginia plantation. She told me about her father, my father's father, and then about my own father, her baby brother and the youngest child in her family. She confided in me, whispering that he was totally spoiled rotten. I was no longer feeling my weariness from the trip. She told me lovely secrets about him, about the money he inherited when he was twenty-two, and how he had gone to China for a visit and ended up staying six years. His theory of life was "don't marry unless you are ready to settle down," which is why he waited so long to get married. She told me that my father had inherited millions, and also spent millions, and oh, how that amused her. It was the first time that I had began to have any understanding, any perspective on my family. What a fine morning it was, roused from my lethargy by my Aunt Suzanne telling secrets. They were always secrets about the rest of the family. I didn't find out the secret of Aunt Suzanne's life until after she died.

She was a very proud, aristocratic Southerner. She never let you forget it and she often told me, "Make sure you know who you are." We spent our days together at museums, fine days where she wore dark green gowns, black gowns, and violet gowns. She stood before paintings that she could have strolled into and happily become a part of. She reeked of theatricality and style, and when she ordered people around in restaurants as if they were below her, I positively believed they were. I carried Aunt Suzanne with me into my life, and when I learned her secret, I carried that with me, too. She died when I was sixteen, an enormous loss to me. My mother always resented her because of her closeness to my father and the hold she had on me; I was much like my father.

After Aunt Suzanne died, my mother gathered up her rage and disdain and told me what Aunt Suzanne never had told me: "Ah, she wasn't what you thought she was, Michael. She was a Ziegfeld Follies girl!"

The hatred that my mother betrayed in that moment told me more about my family than anything else. I now understood what they thought of Aunt Suzanne's secret past. She was the family whore in their eyes, especially to my mother's side of the family. I also realized that this must have also disturbed my father, seeing his sister on stage in various poses of undress. In spite of his flamboyant earlier life, he was a conservative man.

The effect that my Aunt Suzanne had on my family paved the road to my freedom. When a man is young, he blames his parents for not being perfect, for having blind spots. He blames them for things they have little or no control over. He is unfair, but in retrospect, he must be unfair in order to escape, so he can go from being just a family member to his own life. Let's just say that many of the battles that I had with my parents came from my need to stand apart, to grow without relying on the family fortune to protect me. But money was the least of my concerns, as I had two trust funds of my own set up by my grandmother. So my escape from family money and influence was nothing more than a romantic fabrication, a way of asserting my independence without suffering. How absurd I must have seemed, taking a firm stand against my family's money and business and then driving off in a limousine with millions in my pocket.

When you are born into one of America's most prominent families, you should by all standards consider yourself blessed. Not me. Without meaning to sound hypocritical, I realize that an accident of birth does not shield you from the world's problems. But at that time, having a longer limousine than Rosalind Russell seemed pretty wonderful, too.

In college I drifted towards the theater, again directed by Aunt Suzanne's influence away from traditional family thinking. I performed the lead in a college musical during my second year. I was slowly discovering then how much I enjoyed performing in front of an audience and that they truly seemed to enjoy my singing. I understood my Aunt Suzanne better, and decided that theater was the life I wanted to lead. I didn't need the family for that. But because of my family, I understood the power of glamour, the way people looked at me on the street, and the way they looked at my limousine. Instead of ignoring my wealth and playing it down, I decided to use it in the way I assumed Aunt Suzanne had used her wealth and breeding in her Follies days. This immediately got me into hot water.

A theatrical tour manager was in the audience on the final night of the musical. He came backstage and asked me if I was interested in being a singer in a tour he was putting together in Europe. I said that I was. It was exactly the kind of opportunity

# Aunt Suzanne

I had been hoping for, and it would get me far away from my family, my home, and my past.

I asked who the star of the show was. He told me it was former Mr. America, Steve Reeves. Reeves was still a big name then. Then the tour manager said there was a problem: Steve was dark-haired and so was I. Would I be willing to bleach my hair blond to play opposite Steve? I gave that a little thought, realized that it was an outrageous idea, and agreed. When I told my family, I conveniently left out the part about the dye job.

You should have seen their faces when I told them I was taking a job touring Europe with Mr. America. It was the worst thing they'd ever heard. "Mr. America?" they exclaimed in unison, their voices rising. "That muscle-bound gladiator?"

Unfortunately for them, their horror only made me more certain of my destiny and they couldn't budge my resolve.

I went to New York, bleached my hair, and joined Reeves and his people for three weeks of partying. I kept wondering when we were going to Europe, but every night there was a new party, new people to talk to, and more drinking to do. Finally, late one night Reeve's manager pulled me over to the side and said, "Gee, Michael, we, uh, we're in a little bit of a bind, you see, and we're sort of short of money for the tour, you see. Do you think you could ask your family for $50,000? For starters?"

I suddenly realized why I was asked to be on the tour. My money had gotten me into a bad spot. It was impossible to get the money from my family and I wasn't about to underwrite the tour myself, so I left the Reeves people, dyed my hair back to its original color, and sat out the five weeks the tour was supposed to be in Europe. I arranged to have postcards sent from stops across Europe: Paris, London, and Rome. Not too many, mind you, because that would make my family suspicious. I holed up in a small hotel off Broadway so I wouldn't run into friends or family. I wore a hat with the collar turned up and wandered around Greenwich Village and the lower East Side so I wouldn't be seen in any of the "right" places.

During those five weeks I plotted out my career in the theater. I wanted to pursue both singing and acting. I figured the way to do it was to get a job in the chorus. I loved musicals and I loved Broadway. I had the bug. I went to plays and shows every other night and dreamed and plotted. I was untrained and I was quite willing to take the $75 a week that chorus jobs paid. I didn't need the money, naturally, but it was an honest wage. I thought Aunt Suzanne would be pleased.

With the five weeks almost up, I wrote my sister and told her what ship I'd be arriving on from Europe and when she should pick me up at the dock. I gave her a later docking time than when the ship was actually going to arrive. That morning, I woke up in my hotel room, packed my things, paid my bill, and went down to the dock. The ship had come in earlier that morning and the passengers were catching cabs and kissing their lovers hello. I piled my luggage onto the dock and sat down on a packing crate to wait the two hours before my sister would come. I had a bottle of Dom Perignon with me, so I looked rather festive, and drank it. I spent the time dreaming of Broadway, the lights, and Aunt Suzanne. In a way she had made my decision to be a part of the theater. I wanted to use my family background to my advantage in my career. It was then that my gimmick came to me.

# CHAPTER THREE
## Glamour, Galas, and Gabors

Sipping champagne while sitting on the packing crate, I realized that there was something that made me special and would catch the attention of both the theater world and the world at large. My family heritage and money made me unique and to pretend it didn't exist was to ignore my greatest asset, the one thing that set me apart from everyone else. Broadway was by no means tripping over its toes to cast me. They weren't exactly looking for teenagers. But I wanted to get the feel of the theater, and I wanted to work. The only way to start on Broadway was at the bottom, take a nothing part, anything that you could get your hands on. I was happy to do a chorus job. Toss in a classy address, say a Park Avenue address, and that chorus job would take on new meaning. My angle would be recognition through ostentation. I would build up my image as The Park Avenue Chorus Boy.

Now that I was "back from Europe," I could make the scene again and I partied for a number of weeks at my sister's Long Island estate. During one of the parties, I heard about an apartment opening up at 16 East 63rd Street. It didn't sound like a neighborhood where I'd find a Bohemian flat, but I decided to look anyway.

I had my chauffeur, Jimmy, drive me to the address. As we arrived on the street, Jimmy turned to me and said, "There has to be a mistake, Mr. Mason; this is not apartment house row in New York."

"Well, who knows?" I said. "Let's look anyway."

Sixty-third Street just off Fifth Avenue boasted a row of magnificent homes. I knew of it because I had been at a party there at Roger Hammerstein's home. I looked at Number 16 and thought that Jimmy was right; someone was crazy. There was no apartment there. But I'd do anything and go anywhere, so I got out of the car and went to the front door, where I knocked loudly.

The butler answered the door and I said, "I know this is ridiculous, but I was told that there was an apartment for rent here. I'm sure it's a mistake, and I do apologize for causing you any inconvenience..."

"In fact, there may be," he said. "Why don't you come in, I'll let you speak to the lady of the house."

I was escorted into a magnificent drawing room, furnished in exquisite French antiques. The predominant feature of the room above the Louis XIV sofa was a large oil portrait of the Gabor women: Eva, Magda, and Zsa Zsa, along with Mama Jolie standing off to one side. It was some seven feet long and six feet high. I sat down and looked at the four beautiful Hungarian women and waited for the lady of the house to arrive. The thought that passed through my mind was: "These people must be huge fans of the Gabors."

The butler re-entered and said, "Mr. Mason, I would like you to meet Madame Jolie Gabor."

My mouth dropped open. I knew then that I would take the apartment no matter where it was and what the price. She took me upstairs to view her "petit villa" on the fourth floor, my new home. Jacques Fath, the designer, lived on the third floor, while Jolie lived on the second and Magda had the first.

The "petit villa" was magnificent. Beautiful living room, imported Italian marble fireplace, an adequate kitchen, high ceilings, and a wonderful bedroom. French doors swung out to a terrace with a view of the lights of New York City. Still it could have been a squalid hovel with bugs and kerosene lamps and I would have taken it.

The Gabors weren't big names then. Zsa Zsa was married to Conrad Hilton and had only just begun to make a mark for herself in Hollywood. Eva had done a play on Broadway, but the publicity about them in the papers was just society fluff.

Jolie told me that I'd be invited to all of her parties, but to make sure I didn't tell anyone I was a paying guest. "Michael," she said, "you are a guest in my home. We don't treat people here as tenants, because we don't ever have tenants as such. You're here because you were referred by a mutual friend."

"What if I want to give parties?" I asked.

"*Give* your parties," she said. "Do as you wish."

I gave great parties there, but I never got to know Jolie well. While she wanted me to play guest in her home, she still didn't want to get to know the "tenants."

The Gabors gave sensational parties. Jolie had us turn all our lights on, so that the entire house was ablaze with light and looked from the outside as if she lived on all four floors. She unrolled a red carpet that ran down the steps from the front door or the brownstone across the sidewalks of 63$^{rd}$ Street to the curb. As the guests arrived, the doorman would open their car doors and they would sashay up the red carpet to enter Jolie's private world of beautiful people. There was a flurry of photographers around the arriving limousines, their flashbulbs bursting in the night, and laughter and excitement surrounded the street as the crowds crushed close to catch glimpses of the famous and near-famous arrivals.

During the first party I was there for, I sat on the stoop and took in the whole proceeding. It was a lesson in glitter and glamour and I couldn't wait to see how Eva and Zsa Zsa arrived. They were both coming from the Plaza Hotel, but God help them if they came in the same car or at the same time. They timed it to arrive 15 minutes apart so the press could admire them individually. Eva always arrived first with Zsa Zsa a quarter-hour behind. Eva played the serious actress, Zsa Zsa the clowning comedienne.

The first of their limousines pulled up and Eva stepped out in a froth of jewelry and sable. She swept up the red carpet, waving and blowing kisses. Flashbulbs lit up the entire upper East Side and, as quickly as she had come, she was gone, sucked into her mother's home, leaving but a vague memory of reflected diamond light for her fans.

Fifteen minutes later, Zsa Zsa did the entire routine again, and again the crowds and the cameras pressed close. Everyone ate it up both times. It was the first real taste of Hollywood I had: The Arriving Gabors.

The parties were very New York — high society, elegant, and demure. The crowd was peopled by ambassadors, senators, and playwrights, and one slightly displaced young man who lived on the fourth floor, entranced by it all. I learned fast, and opened my big mouth often to play the big shot.

I met Eva that night for the first time and told her who I was and who the family was. She instantly lit up and said, "Dahling, you must go to Mother's shop."

"I've been to your mother's shop," I said. Jolie ran a shop on Madison Avenue that sold only imitation jewelry. She started a trend that saw women wearing not millions of dollars in jewelry, but thousands of dollars of costume jewelry. God knows the stuff wasn't cheap. A ring from her shop could run upwards of $2,000, and it was good-looking stuff.

Eva looked at me oddly when I said that I had been to her mother's shop. "Well, why don't you, like a good boy, buy your mother and your sisters some of my mother's jewelry?"

I suppressed a laugh. It looked like I was smiling at what a fine idea that was. I said, "Yes, interesting thought." I could just imagine sending my mother imitation jewelry. She had millions of dollars' worth of the real stuff. She never went shopping unless she was wearing thousands of dollars worth of ornaments. "Oh, I think that's a great idea. She'd love it," I said. Jolie's jewelry was very loud and gaudy, and wouldn't go at all with the genteel elegance of my mother's clothing or personality. Through the years Eva never understood why I didn't buy anything from her mother's shop.

"Don't they *like* jewelry, dear?" she'd ask me.

"Ye-es . . . " I'd mutter weakly. What a terrible friend they thought I was. "But they have so much now," I'd offer as solace.

"Oh, but not *this*," she'd say and show me a bracelet or necklace.

Finally I got smart. Years later, at a birthday party given for me by my pal, Richard Long and his wife Mara Corday, Eva and Zsa Zsa both came. Eva arrived in her black Rolls Royce with her armed bodyguards, who danced around stoops and lurked in doorways. Zsa Zsa came a half-hour later, arriving in her white Rolls Royce, with her own armed bodyguards swarming all over. Eva swept in, kiss kiss, and the first thing she said to me was, "Michael, dahling, happy birthday, and, by the way, did you ever buy any jewelry for your mother and sisters at my mother's shop?"

Naturally, my reply was, "Yes."

The party was a great success.

• • •

The Astor Hotel drug store was the place to go if you were a struggling actor, singer, or dancer. It was the local hangout for those of us who were out of work. Hanging out at the Astor was part of the life, along with the moping, sleeping late, choosing a drama school, primping in front of a mirror, getting a singing coach, telling stories about the parts you should have gotten, and finding a theatrical agent. We'd sit at the counter of the drug store and read *Variety* while chatting over endless cups of coffee.

## The Park Avenue Chorus Boy

I got to be friendly with an actor from *Hellzapoppin,* Dick Clayton. Dick got out of the acting business soon after we met because he was smart. "I don't want to be an out-of-work actor all my life," he told me, bags packed, heading for Hollywood. "I want to make some money." He went to work for Henry Wilson (of Tab Hunter fame), reading scripts for Henry and Henry's clients. He'd get ten bucks for reading the script, then another five for writing an outline of the story with a recommendation. Dick survived in Hollywood for years on $15 a script. Then he became an agent. He represented Burt Reynolds exclusively. You didn't need to do anything else if you represented Burt Reynolds.

Dick was a great source for me. He introduced me to a number of people, a few of whom were to later help me in my career. He introduced me to Shirley Jones one morning over toast. Shirley and I sat at the counter and I explained to her that I was fairly new in town and knew nothing about how to even go about looking for a job.

"Hey," she said, "you'll have no trouble at all. You're tall, you're good-looking, and obviously you've got money, so you won't have to struggle like the rest of us."

Dick told me later that Shirley had some money hidden away, too, and that she wasn't exactly starving.

Shirley and I met there all the time. We were two naive people, both new in town and we held onto each other for support. She wasn't impressed with my family background, so I liked her quite a bit. We often joked about who would get cast first, who would be discovered first, who would be the first household name. She thought it would be me. Ha!

The way things worked at the Astor, when an actor had an interview, he went to the Astor beforehand to brag about the fact. Then after the interview, he'd come back and tell everyone how it went. Shirley and I often got to play that scene together because we went on interviews together.

One morning at the Astor, she told me about an audition she had coming up for CBS. She asked if I wanted to go along with her and sing a duet. I said I'd love to. We had done so many auditions, it was hard to look at any one individual audition with any real fear or hope. We were two smiling, easygoing, kids, walking together down the filthy, sidewalks of New York, risking our egos on rejection after rejection. We did the CBS audition together and it went without a hitch. It was just another audition. And nothing happened.

At least not right away.

From that audition, Shirley was given the lead role in *Carousel*. After that she went to Hollywood and it wasn't very long before she picked up the Best Supporting Actress Oscar for *Elmer Gantry*. She thought I was going to make it first.

It was after the CBS audition that Dick told me about the biggest agent in New York, Lester Shurr. Dick said he could set up an audition if I were interested. It was a bright, sunny day and Shirley's pianist came with me and sat down at the piano in Lester Shurr's office. I sang, and sang well. Lester was impressed.

"You've got a great voice. You're not an Alfred Drake or anything, but not bad," Lester said. "You're more Hollywood material than Broadway, though."

"How do you determine that?" I asked.

"By your appearance and your voice quality. I imagine it records very well," he said. "I'd like to sign you. I think we can do something. I have a brother on the West Coast named Louis Shurr and he works with a guy named Al Melnick."

I almost asked, "Who?" How was I supposed to know who these people were? How was I supposed to know they were the biggest agents on the West Coast? They handled practically everyone, from Bob Hope and Rita Hayworth to Cary Grant.

Lester told me there was something coming up, a chorus part, nothing flashy, nothing as challenging as say an understudy role, just a singing and dancing chorus boy, and would I mind taking it just for the experience?

"Hell, no!" I chimed. I was grinning like a schoolboy. All I needed now was the Park Avenue address to re-qualify my previous title.

If it sounded like I was drifting, I was. I could tell you that I wanted to be a star, be famous, be wonderful, but I had no real long-term plan. I relied on Lester, since he was the pro who should know. I knew the moves, but I wasn't sure where they would lead me to. This show on Broadway, Lester? Sure, I'll do it. Go to Hollywood, Lester? I'm on my way. If Lester didn't land me on my feet, it was going to be tough to straighten myself out.

I went looking for a drama coach because I wanted to impress Lester and show him I was on the ball. I found the Neighborhood Playhouse and Sandy Meisner. A friend, James Kirkwood, who later wrote *A Chorus Line,* told me the name of the best singing coach in New York. He was David Craig, who was married to the toast of Broadway, Nancy Walker of *Look, Ma, I'm Dancin'.* David was the kind of guy who could take an actor and make him sing or take a singer and make him act. He gave singers movements, things to do with their hands and their bodies. He turned good singers into good actors and vice versa.

I was preparing various audition numbers with David when Lester called to tell me the audition was set up. It was for a replacement chorus role in *Gentlemen Prefer Blondes.* The tryout was at the Ziegfeld Theater, where the show was playing. That clinched it. I wanted this job in the worst way; I wanted to do my first show where Aunt Suzanne had been a Follies girl.

The day of the audition arrived, a bleak, overcast, nasty day. I took a cab down to the theater rather than my limousine. I didn't want to overdo it. It wouldn't have mattered. My cab pulled up and there was a line stretching down the block — young, handsome men, singers, actors, and dancers, all praying for that break that would put them into the Broadway spotlight. I paid off the cabby and started the long walk to the end of the line, being checked out every step of the way by the competition. There were at least one hundred guys waiting to audition. I stood at back of the non-Equity line.

Let me stress here that if you are not a member of Equity, the theater actors' union, then you audition last. They first audition Equity singers, dancers, and actors; then they audition non-Equity people. By the time the poor non-union person gets there, he could be the greatest talent alive and wouldn't have a chance. Nine times out of ten, by the time a non-Equity nobody gets on stage to audition, the role has already been cast.

So there I was in line with over 100 other guys and it started to drizzle. The dreariness of the day dampened my dreary spirits until they were miserable together. I thought back on it all and realized how ridiculous this was. So the great Lester Shurr had arranged an audition for me: big fat hairy deal. The rain plunked down on my head, the line inched into the theater, and two hours later it was my turn to go on. By then I was really frazzled. I walked to the center of the big barren Ziegfeld theater with a work light over my head and a pianist by my side.

I spoke my name, gave the pianist my sheet music, and moved to center stage. I muttered softly to myself, "OK, Aunt Suzanne, this is for you, Flo Ziegfeld, and me." The pianist played introductory chords and I started singing warmly:

*"There's a far land I'm told*
*Where I'll find a field of gold,"*

Then I threw my arms wide and belted out:

*"But here I'LL STAY..."*

"Thank you," came the voice from the audience.

"Wait a minute," I growled. "I didn't wait here in line for two hours in the rain just to be told 'thank you' after eight bars. I'm gonna finish this if *you* don't mind."

Silence from the audience. I turned to the pianist, gestured for him to begin again, and I sang the song straight through and finished it.

There was silence after the final bars, then a voice came from the audience. "Michael, will you come down here, please?"

Jack Wilson, the director, was there with the producer, the conductor, and the choreographer. I was introduced around and Jack told me it was a good thing I had decided to sing the whole song because you can't really tell what anyone can do on the first eight bars. He said to report the next day to wardrobe, I had the job. I turned to go, floating out of the theater, when I felt a friendly pat on the ass, and it wasn't from a lady. I wondered if the pat represented another reason why I was given the job — with all the other performers auditioning, my voice wasn't necessarily *that* remarkable. But no, I decided it was my panache, my panache had been remarkable. Who else finished the song after being summarily dismissed? So, maybe that had gotten me the job, maybe not. Either way, I did not care. I was in. I was on Broadway. I was doing my first show in my Aunt Suzanne's theatre. I was going to be a star and take the city by storm.

I went back to the Astor and called Lester.

"Lester, I got the job."

"Yes, I know, they already called me."

"What do you mean they already called you?"

"They already called me. Did you think you wouldn't get it?"

"Are you telling me I got it because of you?"

"Absolutely."

"You're full of shit. After the first eight bars they said, 'Thank you very much, next,' so how do you explain that?"

"Oh," said Lester. "Hmmm. I could be wrong about that. Well, the point us, you got it. It pays $75 a week and you report tomorrow. You'll watch ten days of performance out front and learn the show. You'll run through with the choreographer. You've got to pick up the sheet music and learn the songs. I'm assuming you read music."

"You assume too much. I don't read music at all."

Dead silence. Then Lester's voice came through the wire. "Learn fast."

I took the score to David Craig and we worked on it day and night. I went on stage for rehearsals and they found out I couldn't read music. Luckily, these were easy songs to learn.

Ten days to learn! I was joining a show that was already established. Carol Channing was its star and it was a hit on Broadway. I was in *Gentlemen Prefer Blondes!* Me! Mike Mason.

Those ten days before I went on in front of an audience were magical. I had been in theaters before as part of the audience many times. This was different. The thrill was part of every sleepless night, every anxious spoonful of soup before dinner, every glass of celebratory champagne. I was officially a member of the show because I was cast, but during those ten days I wasn't *in* the show, so I was still an outsider. It was a heavenly limbo with no bad memories to ruin the expectations. Inside the theater, I was in a glamorous world that I had wanted so badly to be part of, but I still couldn't believe it had actually happened. I had a feeling that someone was going to flip on the house lights one day and say, "Sorry, Michael, we were only kidding you; you really can't be on Broadway."

Every day I watched the show and learned and a little core of excitement built up inside me. The lights would go down for the overture and I would think, "This is my show. I'm going to be in this show and be up there!" I would wander backstage and watch the camaraderie that had built up between the veterans, smell their greasepaint, and the fine sweat smell from their costumes that they wore nightly under hot lights. There would be a special glow in their eyes when the audience applauded them. There would be laughter when something went wrong on stage. Between scenes, with the curtains down, I watched the beautiful six-foot tall blondes being strapped into their headdresses. The headdresses were lowered by the fly system down to their heads and attached. The actresses had to hold the headdresses up with their arms outstretched when the curtains rose because those things weighed a ton.

I was in a crazy kind of ecstatic limbo watching all these things every night, dreaming about my role in *Blondes*. It was a good time.

But I remained an outsider, It never came together for me once I was in the show. These people had brought the show together from nothing. They had taken it through rehearsals and toured with it, previewing in Philadelphia, Boston, and Washington, D.C. I was a replacement, nothing more, a new screw added to a well-oiled and perfectly working machine. I hadn't been there from the beginning. I was raw, untested, and not as good as they were.

# CHAPTER FOUR
# A Breath
# of Fresh Air

The Countess Mercati was a friend of my sister, and I met her at one of those Long Island parties my sister was so fond of giving. The Countess was in every way a countess, but she hadn't been born into royalty. She was born in the United States, raised in Rye, New York, went to Europe as a stunning young girl in the early part of the century, and married the Count Mercati. She didn't have a lot of money at the time, but she had breeding, education, and the strength of will to go out into the world and get what she wanted. She lived in Europe in grand style with the Count until he died, and then she returned to live in New York. She moved into the St. Regis Hotel, where she continued to play her role as Countess, perhaps more so than before. She lived with her secretary, her chauffeur, and two maids in a suite of rooms at the St. Regis for 25 years.

When I met her, she had gray hair died blue, was 70 years old, carried a gold cane to help her walk, and wore high-necked dresses with lace at the neck and wrists, yards of pearls, and huge diamond brooches. She rode around in an ancient Cadillac limousine. Her chauffeur followed her wherever she went, and carried her two small dogs — a couple of pugs, the type that look like small bulldogs. She spoke with a strange Italian accent even though she wasn't Italian.

She would go to Carnegie Hall and sit on the aisle because she had difficulty walking and had become annoyed with restless children who were brought by their parents and allowed to run up and down the aisles. "Children should not be at the symphony, it's past their bedtime," she'd say as she stuck out her cane to trip them as they ran by. I always wanted to say to the dazed and confused children lying in the aisles, "You've just been tripped by the Countess Mercati."

The Countess and I decided to dine together in the city one night, the first time I had socialized with her outside of my sister's Long Island home. We agreed to meet at her favorite restaurant, The Maisionette, a very chic restaurant inside the St. Regis Hotel. She told me she would meet me at 8:00 PM. I arrived promptly, asked for the Countess Mercati, and the maitre d'hotel assured me that she would be along shortly and not to worry because she was always late. I said fine, sat down at a table, ordered a bottle of Dom Perignon and an order of caviar, and started alone.

A uniformed butler, all in black, wearing knickers, leather boots, and a cap came over to my table carrying a heavy silk, gold-brocaded folding panel screen, which stood five feet tall.

"Are you Mr. Mason?" he asked.

"Yes, I am," I answered.

"The Countess will be with you shortly," he said and proceeded to put the ornate screen around my table.

"Excuse me," I asked, "what's this all about?"

"The Countess *always* dines in privacy," he said, and then turned on his heels and left. He returned five minutes later, escorting the Countess into the dining room and we had our meal behind the screen. I learned during subsequent meals that she always dined behind the screen, no matter what restaurant she went to, so that none of "those peasants," as she referred to them, would gaze upon her as she feasted.

That night she told me about an apartment that was open at 820 Park Avenue. I was already a chorus member in *Blondes,* and

I knew I would have to see the apartment because I wanted the Park Avenue address.

The following day I drove up to 820 Park Avenue, which was quite elegant and posh — it had an awning, a doorman — a typical chic Manhattan apartment building. I knew just from the outside of the building that I would take it. Senator Lehman lived there, and Arthur Murray and his wife had an entire floor. It would be difficult to leave the Gabor household, but Park Avenue was important to my image. And what the hell, eight was my lucky number. I took the place and officially became the Park Avenue Chorus Boy.

Through this all, I attended Sandy Meisner's classes in acting. I met Marlon Brando in class, but got to know him better later on through Wally Cox. I didn't know much about Brando's successes in 1947. Along with Jessica Tandy, Brando had been in *A Streetcar Named Desire,* on Broadway which had won the Pulitzer Prize and the Drama Critics' Circle Award. Cox and Brando were roommates in Greenwich Village and Cox was in awe of Brando. I didn't see why, but then I didn't know much about his *Streetcar.* Brando just seemed like a guy with muscles. I was, however, in awe of Wally Cox. To me dramatic stage actors were a dime a dozen, but a comic actor had to have a special talent. I wanted to be better friends with Cox. Brando and Cox were always riding their motorcycles up and down Broadway and into alleys, whipping around, scaring the hell out of the rat population and knocking over garbage cans. Once in a while I'd try to get them to ride with me in the limousine, but they wouldn't bite. Imagine the scene: here are two guys on motorcycles, one a weight-lifter from the local gym, the other a tiny comic with glasses, and then there's me along side of them, impeccably dressed, sitting in my limousine, trying to coax them in with caviar and champagne. They'd blow me off and go riding away in a clatter of broken mufflers and blue exhaust, while the limousine tried to follow them through the alleys. How odd it is to look back on those days. To me, Brando seemed to be just another guy in a T-shirt.

Things were moving along in *Blondes* now. I was on stage, confused at times by the newness of it all. There were moments when I'd forget the harmony of a song and mouth the words while mimicking the guy in front of me until I caught on. Other cast members showed me some resentment. Snide comments were made like, "How did *you* get in?" It took me a while to make friends in the show.

As time passed, I got more comfortable in my role and relaxed a little. Then one night I stumbled into fame, of sorts.

The "Bois de Boulogne" scene was in the second act and all the male and female singers came out from the wings at opposite sides onto the stage. We sang a quaint little French song and were dressed in berets, shirts, and baggy corduroy pants as young French boys and girls. The audience got a chance to see the individual singer/dancers and we got a chance to do our own little thing and shine on stage for a brief moment. I had to rush to make the costume change for the song, and because sometimes I didn't wear undershorts, I'd be yanking my corduroys up over my bare derriere. I think in those days I referred to underwear as "those hopelessly limiting bits of clothing suitable for un-toilet trained children and old women." That night I hadn't bothered with them. The corduroy pants for the number had buttons instead of zippers and I yanked them on and ran for the stage. The choreography called for hands in pockets. And I sang as I sauntered right up to center stage, checking out the audience as I belted out my solo.

A roar rose from the audience and I thought to myself, "Channing's doing something behind me again." I ignored it and finished my solo in ignorant bliss. I got offstage after the number and the tech crew was weak with laughter, weeping and holding their sides. I asked why and one pointed to my fly. I looked down and saw I was unbuttoned. I put my hands in my pockets while I was on stage singing, and my fly had parted wide open. There for all to see was my male genitalia, the corduroy separated in a wide oval, framing it. I turned red and grinned. I had been so caught up in the song on stage, I hadn't even felt the fresh air.

The mail that came for me after was phenomenal. It came from both men and women and was my first introduction to a subject that was taboo in those days: homosexuality outside the theater.

One note I received right after the show was from a wealthy man named Don. I ignored the note at the time, but was introduced to him later that night at the Stork Club. He was heir to $80 million and lived like it. The "gay set" that mingled with the Café Society group was extremely conservative, not flamboyant or flashy, and almost always had a date, some showgirl, in tow.

"Rumor has it," Don said, "that you did it on purpose."

"Absolutely not," I said, but I realized that some people would believe what they wanted to believe. "Look," I said, "just forget it. Who cares? It happened and that's that. If you want to believe that I did it on purpose, fine. I'm telling you it was an accident. Waiter, where the hell's the bottle of champagne I just ordered?"

We got to talking and became friendly. He invited me to a dinner party the following Saturday night, after the show. I said, "Well, who's going to be there? More than you and me, I hope."

"Oh, yes," he said. "I usually have friends over, Tennessee Williams…"

"Go on no further," I stopped him.

"Pardon me?"

"You said Tennessee Williams will be there? That's all I need to hear."

"No, but I'm having six or eight people…"

"That's fine," I said. "I'll be there, OK? I'll be there right at midnight, after the show."

I arrived at Don's on Saturday night at midnight and directly in front of me, another limousine stopped and the chauffeur got out and opened the rear door. There emerged a lovely lady, so stunning that normally I would have given her more than a cursory glance, but I was on my way to party with Tennessee Williams. What I did notice was her green satin dress, enormous diamond pins in her hair, and an enormous Cabochon emerald necklace surrounded by diamonds, which matched her eyes. She carried a white mink coat over her arm. Ruby Keeler often told me that a coat of that importance was referred to as a "Great Coat." Well, maybe I did pay a little attention, but I didn't recognize her, not at first. I moved past her into the lobby. She came in with her chauffeur. The chauffeur said to the elevator man, "Penthouse, please," and she and I got on the elevator together. I took a good look at her face then, since we were going to the same party, and recognized Paulette Goddard. So I introduced myself, weak in the knees, and together we rode up to the closest thing to heaven money could buy.

We got off the elevator together and entered the largest apartment I've ever seen in New York City. It had marble floors, eighteen-foot high marble columns (to this day I don't know how the building foundations supported so much marble), a view of Central Park, and palm trees that were fifteen to eighteen feet tall. Discreetly hidden behind each palm was one member of a seven-piece string ensemble. Don had hidden the ensemble behind the palms so that when you looked around the all glass and marble room, you were totally surrounded by clear, sweet, invisibly played music. The candle flames swayed with the closing of the elevator doors behind us, then stood straight in place where they decorated a long glass dining table.

Sitting on a white sofa was Tennessee Williams and his blond boyfriend. Across was Constance Collier, talking to Tennessee. The entire setting, the view of Central Park, the candelabra, the gold place settings — it was the most lavish dinner party I had ever been to in New York City.

## A Breath of Fresh Air

Don introduced me to Tennessee by saying, "Folks, I'd like you to meet and old buddy of mine, Michael Mason, the Park Avenue Chorus Boy."

Tennessee laughed. "What a great title for a book," he said.

Paulette was thick with diamonds that night, but then she always liked to wear diamonds. A week later, when she met me for lunch at the Plaza Hotel with Constance Collier, it was raining and she had put diamond clips on her raincoat to hold both the front *and* the back slits together. I said, "You've got headlights and taillights, they can see you coming and going."

"Yes," she said, "isn't it delicious?" To Paulette, anything with diamonds was delicious.

Tennessee was holding court, being impressive. Paulette and I sat down with them and were soon called to a dinner dripping with caviar and champagne. Don was trying to impress Tennessee and me, which is something you can afford to do if you have eighty million dollars. So I decided that I would show them. I would out-impress them both.

Pearl Bailey had introduced me to a jazz club in Harlem, the Cotton Club, and after dinner I suggested we go up there to hear some good music. Everyone thought that it was a pretty good idea and agreed. Tennessee rose and put on his black cape lined with red satin, his top hat, and his cane with a gold handle. Paulette put on her floor-to-ceiling white mink, Constance Collier put on her Russian sable, and Don put on his Italian dinner jacket. We glowed with ostentation and money. Paulette christened us the "sexy six."

We arrived at the Cotton Club and I told the owner who I was. He recognized me because I had been there with Pearl a number of times. We got a great table and listened to Louie Belson, Pearl's husband, play far into the night. Belson was a drummer and composer who had played with the bands of Benny Goodman, Harry James, and Tommy Dorsey. Later he would go on tour with Duke Ellington.

## The Park Avenue Chorus Boy

The next morning we were in Dorothy Kilgallen's column, in a blurb that said: "Michael Mason, the Park Avenue Chorus Boy, was seen at his favorite haunt in Harlem with Paulette Goddard, Constance Collier, and Tennessee Williams. Could there be a part in the future for the Park Avenue Chorus Boy in one of Mr. Williams' plays?"

There was to be no part. I hit it off badly with his blond boyfriend and insulted the kid. I decided not to follow up on a friendship with Tennessee because it would have caused jealous repercussions with his friend. Nonetheless, I liked Tennessee very much.

In those days, I was dating a woman named Robin Roberts. It was while I was out with her that I met Pearl Bailey. Without even trying, Robin Roberts looked the way Hedy Lamarr looked in the movies. Unfortunately, Robin's voice was not as beautiful as her face. On the street people would come up to her, ask for her autograph, and go away unhappy because they'd have a slip of paper that read "Robin Roberts." I finally told her, "Keep the tourists happy — just sign, 'Love, Hedy Lamarr' and send them on their way." She took on the role with great style. Unless she opened her mouth.

Once, when we went to El Morocco together for drinks, we sat near Humphrey Bogart, who was dining with Swifty Lazar and a drinking pal of Bogart's named Billy Seaman. He and his friend had bought two large stuffed pandas that night at the Stork Club and had brought them to El Morocco as their dates. Robin took one look at Bogart's panda, turned to me, and said, "Oh, I'm going to get that."

"Robin, don't go get that, leave Bogart alone," I said, but Robin was not one to be trifled with when her mind was made up. She could smell free publicity. She headed over to Bogart's booth. She looked so much like Hedy Lamarr that Bogart smiled until she got close and then he realized it wasn't Hedy Lamarr at all.

"I want your panda," Robin said and reached for it. Bogart answered her by giving her a shove and she fell right on her ass in the middle of El Morocco. The photographers caught it all. She figured this was her big chance, sued Bogart, got a lot of publicity, and was known forevermore as the "panda girl." Which brings me full circle to the first night I met Pearl Bailey.

It was closing time at El Morocco a few nights after the Bogart incident, and I had been making a lot of noise, being arrogant and demanding service. Pearl was in the next booth with Louie Belson, and she turned to me and said, "Quit making so much noise. Come with us; we're going to this neat little deli."

"Deli?" I said. "I don't want to go to a deli."

"Don't be such a snob," she said.

So we went to a delicatessen and Robin and I sat around feeling very bored and very sorry for ourselves because we were very bored. Pearl talked to Lehman Engel, who would later conduct the music for *Make a Wish*. Pearl kept wincing whenever she hear Robin's thin, whiny little voice. Finally Pearl called a waiter over to the side and ordered a number of sandwiches in a big bag. The waiter brought the bag over a few minutes later.

"Who's the bag for?" I asked.

"It's for you," Pearl said. "Come here."

I leaned close to her and she said, "Get that awful voice away from me or I will go mad and never speak to you again. Take these sandwiches home and have breakfast in bed."

I took Robin's hand and she asked, "Where are we going?"

"We're having breakfast in bed, honey, compliments of Pearl Bailey."

Robin was always good for laughs. She called me once and said her favorite singer in the whole wide world was in town and would I take her to see him? I told her sure, absolutely. She said that it would be Friday night, a big opening at the Latin Quarter. The Latin Quarter in New York was a big, jazzy nightclub a la Las Vegas, all done up with show girls, nudity, and the Star Spangled Banner. It was a fun place, larger than the only other club like it, the Copacabana. The Latin Quarter was right off Broadway in midtown Manhattan.

"Billy Daniels is going to be opening," she said.

"Billy Daniels?" I asked.

"Oh, yes, he's my favorite — oh, God he's wonderful," and I got to listen to her gush on and on about the "Old Black Magic."

"OK, Robin, OK," I said finally.

"And he's just mad about blondes."

"What the hell do you care then? You're about as blonde as a penguin."

"Oh, just never mind. Will you pick me up Friday evening?"

"Yeah, the limousine will pick you up and we'll go on from there. Do you want to have dinner first?"

"No, no. There won't be time for that."

"What do you mean, no time for that? He won't go on until 9:00 or 10:00."

"There won't be time," she said. "And I'll explain it to you later." Bang went the phone.

Friday night the car picked me up and we went over to her hotel. I arrived at 8:30 and had the front desk ring her room. No answer. What is this all about, I thought. I asked, "Is Miss Roberts in?"

"Well, we haven't seen her lately," the clerk said.

"What do you mean you haven't *seen* her lately?" I demanded.

"I know she went out this morning, but we haven't seen her all day."

"That's strange. Did she leave a message for me? I'm Mr. Mason."

"No message," he replied.

So I stood and waited around, thinking it was very peculiar. Finally, I said, "You'd better check her room."

They sent someone up to check her suite. He came back a few minutes later. No Robin Roberts.

I waited another 15 minutes. A gaggle of paparazzi clogged the door and a blonde beauty came floating in. I thought, Jesus Christ, what is all this? The lady was in a white mink down to the floor, diamonds, and platinum blonde hair. I looked again. It was Robin.

She had spent the entire day getting her hair stripped and bleached blonde. It took eight hours. They took her black hair from black to brown to orange to tan to green and finally to brownish blonde, and after that it still took another three hours to get it platinum. She did not want to wear a wig. She wanted to *be* a blonde.

"What have you done?" I cried.

"He likes blondes. Tonight, I'm a blonde."

It was weird. I didn't even recognize her and I kept making side glances at her. Even her makeup was different. Away we went to the Latin Quarter. Front row center. I was in black tie with the blonde beside me, Hedy Lamarr gone platinum.

Billy Daniels, big, black, and handsome, came out and saw this glow of blonde hair, white mink, and jewelry up to her elbows and did his entire show to Robin. I loved it. Attention just recharged my batteries, anyway. He kept nodding to her and she kept toasting him with the glass in her hand, then we'd order more champagne and make more toasts. I made a gesture to him like "Will you join us?" and he smiled and nodded.

After the performance and a standing ovation, Billy Daniels made his way off the stage to our table.

"Who are you?" he asked her. "You're incredible, both of you. Two beautiful people."

"Thanks," I said. I congratulated him on the show and we sat and chatted a while. We hung around the club until his next show, sat through it, and by then I told Robin I had to leave. I knew she wanted to be alone with Daniels.

"I'll take a cab back," I said. "And you take the limousine."

She beamed. She was going to use my limousine and chauffeur and take Billy Daniels out on the town until the wee hours of the morning. She didn't tell him she wasn't really a blonde. She kept the hair going for almost two months and the romance blossomed. Afterwards they became good friends and the constant touching up the hair became too much, so she dyed it back again. Anyone else would have gone out and bought a platinum blonde wig, but Robin said, "Oh, no, wigs come off and I don't want this to fall off when somebody's hanging onto it."

Robin had other little tricks that made her unique. Rather than pay incredible prices for expensive evening gowns, she'd buy a negligee from Saks or Bonwit Teller. She'd get them with lace, chiffon, pleats down the front and very low-cut. She'd wear them with nothing underneath, and we'd go out dancing. They did look like elegant evening gowns, but they didn't cost very much. A similar evening gown of that caliber would cost $1000 or $1500. So she had a wardrobe of different colored negligees that she didn't wear to bed, but out to the Stork Club or Copacabana. She loved the idea that someone would be trying to filter through the chiffon and lace to see if there was anything on underneath. There never was.

Someone might say to her, "My God, that's a gorgeous evening gown."

"No, it's not," she'd say. "It's a gorgeous nightgown. I'm ready for bed the minute I go out."

• • •

During this time in New York, I was meeting many people I later re-met in Hollywood. One who would gain international admiration was Audrey Hepburn, who was on Broadway doing *Ondine,* her first Broadway show, with Mel Ferrer. I saw her do the show and then had dinner at Sardi's with her and Lehman Engel. At the time I thought, "What a cute little ballet dancer."

She was odd-looking, though, with a wide forehead, eyes too big for her face, and a mouth that didn't quite seem to fit her chin. She was intrigued with the idea of going to Hollywood, but she really didn't seem to care too much about it. She was a ballet dancer and she wanted to stay a ballet dancer. This was her first speaking part on stage, and she was terrified by it all. But she had a wonderful stage quality. She was birdlike, and Broadway was almost too big for her. She'd come from the Corps de Ballet right into this speaking role of Ondine, who was herself a nymph-like little creature. Hepburn was mythical on stage and had a floating quality about her. She was very shy offstage, and carried that with her wherever she went. Years later, during the making of *My Fair Lady*, she told me that back then she never even thought she would go further than being a ballet dancer.

• • •

Meanwhile, I was still working in *Blondes*. After meeting Tennessee Williams and his boyfriend, and even after receiving many notes from men, I was still pretty naive about the gay community. There were three straight male dancers in the show who were living together. I knew them a little, but they were uptight and a bit stuck-up. One day a fellow who wrote to me after the "crotch unveiling" asked me to do him a favor. There was an infamous gay bath house in New York called the Everhardt Baths, which was the basis for the movie *The Ritz*. So this guy came up to me and said, "Hey, Mason, you know all those square ass holes that you're working with, those phony square singers? Would you put on this robe when you put on your makeup tonight at the theater? They'll get a real charge out of it."

"Why?" I asked. "What is it?"

"It's just a plain old white terry cloth robe," he said, "just put it on — would you do me that favor?"

"Oh, well, all right," I said.

So that night I sat down at my makeup table in this white terry cloth robe that read "Everhardt Baths" on the back and started to do my makeup. The three dancers came in joking and chuckling. The robe stopped them dead in their tracks.

"Well, look at Mr. Innocence over there. Have a good time, Mason?"

"Yeah," I said. "I always have a good time."

"Last night, huh?"

"Fabulous time last night," I said. I thought they meant at El Morocco, where I had been the night before, drinking and partying as usual. I didn't know that they were talking about the Everhardt Baths, and if I had, I wouldn't have known what the insinuation was. "I had a great time last night."

"Oh, really?" It was a big joke on me, but it gave them a whole new Michael Mason to contend with.

As the week went on, my crotch incident brought in more and more mail. Finally Carol Channing noticed me carrying a stack of letters and asked, "Do you have a fan club?"

"No," I said.

"Well, what is all this mail?" she asked.

"Well, I guess you didn't hear what happened the other night," I said.

"No," she said, "what happened?"

I told her. There was a long pause I could have driven a truck through as she looked at me deadpan, looked at the letters, and looked at me again. Then she fell down laughing. From that night on, I teased her unmercifully, deliberately walking out of my way to make sure I passed her with a handful of letters. "More fan mail than you got tonight, Carol," I would call out.

"You nasty little boy."

Carol was so nearsighted that when she wanted to read a bulletin board, she'd have to come right up to it, inches away, to be able to make out the words. Whenever she wanted to speak with someone in the cast, she'd walk up close to them, touch their faces with her hands and say, "Is that you, Edwin? Michael? Gladys?"

One rainy night in front of the theater she had a raincoat and hat on and was waiting for a car to pick her up. A cop came along and said, "Hey, buddy, move on. No cruisin' around the stage door."

"I beg your pardon," she said in that husky voice of hers, "I'm Carol Channing."

"Yeah, right, honey, that's what all you fags are saying this year. Get moving." And she did.

Carol's idea of a good time after the show was to come over to my place at 820 Park Avenue with a few other cast members, unwind with champagne or beer, have a late supper, and talk about the show and how we felt it had gone that night. Some nights we'd hang out at Chinatown Charlie's, next door to the Ziegfeld Theatre.

Nancy Andrews, who was understudying in the show, asked if I wanted to sing with her at a nightclub. She would leave after curtain calls and go down to Number One Fifth Avenue.

"After the show?" I asked. "You are cutting into my fun and games."

"It's a good experience for you, Michael. Good exposure, too," she cajoled.

She was right. Since I was wearing a tuxedo on stage for the finale anyway, I'd just leave the makeup on, take off the coat, put on a dinner jacket, jump into the limo and go down to Number One Fifth Avenue.

Then came the night my mother and father decided to see the show. I'd been trying to get them to come to New York, figuring they'd be impressed with their son on Broadway. They arrived from Massachusetts, checked into the Plaza, and I met them for drinks before the show. I left early and told them I'd see them later at the theater, and that we'd have supper after the show. I didn't know how my mother would react, but my father was a man who had been all over the world many times, and surely his cosmopolitan history would help him enjoy the show, and maybe even get my mother over the hump. The man my Aunt Suzanne described should be amused by *Blondes*.

It was still early in the first act and I was on stage with a bevy of beautiful, buxom blondes wearing champagne glasses on their breasts and a bunch of grapes in a triangle between their thighs. I was dancing and singing up a storm, in a frenzied excitement whipped up by my parent's presence, and I could see them in the audience, third row center. I was singing "Bye, Bye, Baby," and the girls were all dancing and we were all grinning, when my father stood up, waved, took my mother by the arm and walked right out of the theater. Bye, bye, baby. It finally caught up with him that *his* baby was wasting his life singing in the chorus of some asinine show, even if it was the toast of Broadway. He later called it the most embarrassing thing he'd ever seen in his life. *His* son, on stage, in *Gentlemen Prefer Blondes?* It was a shocker. He wanted me out of the show immediately. "Change your name," he said upon hearing that I wouldn't drop out, "or I'll disinherit you." I told him to go ahead. He didn't disinherit me, but he never came to see another show I did, ever.

# CHAPTER FIVE
# A Wish Granted

Things were moving now, inexorably spinning towards Hollywood. My life had found its own roller coaster track and I could afford to buy as many tickets as I wanted and ride it out until it crashed or flew off to heaven.

Lester wanted to put me in a new show so that down the line he could take me out of it and send me to Hollywood. The show was *Make a Wish*. Gower Champion was coming from Hollywood to do *Wish* with Nanette Fabray and Franklin Pangborn. Lester wanted Gower to discover me. By this time Shirley Jones had been discovered in much the same way. They had put her in *Carousel* and after its run, had sent her out to Hollywood to be a star.

*Blondes* was a stepping stone in Lester's schematic design of my career. It had given me invaluable experience, but would soon go on tour. Lester told me not to tour with *Blondes*, but rather to give my two weeks' notice before the auditions for *Make a Wish*. My new role was a pre-arranged thing; the power of the agency had come into play then. Gower Champion was told to hire Michael Mason, a client of Lester Shurr's, and he did and that was that.

In the meantime, Lester called his brother on the West Coast and told him he had a new client with terrific Hollywood potential. Louis Shurr came out to New York on a business trip not long after that.

"My brother, Louis, is coming out from the West coast tomorrow," Lester said one morning, "and I want you to meet him."

"Fine," I said. "I'll have my limo pick you two guys up at your office and I'll take you to '21.'"

I purposely dressed conservatively, in a blue blazer, striped tie, button-down collar, and no cuff-links — the rah-rah college look. I knew that was the image that Hollywood was buying, and I wanted to impress Louis Shurr that I was not the flashy, flaky Broadway character he had doubtless heard about.

It all went off as smoothly as a hot knife through butter. Louis was very taken with my veneer and said I was definitely Hollywood material. He told me he'd handle me when I got to the coast, would arrange a screen test, and get me going once the show with Gower Champion was finished. It was all just a matter of time.

Later, Lester asked me what part I had been playing for his brother. I told him I was playing the nice guy, the clean-cut all-American boy. That was the part I wanted to play in Hollywood. Lester was impressed. "You certainly got away with it, Michael," he said without sarcasm.

But for all the Hollywood promises and buildup, I was still a chorus boy. My career may have been arcing toward some wild, final goal, but I was only just beginning to get an idea what that goal was. *Make a Wish* gave me my first direct taste of Hollywood stew: a little beef here, a hunk of potato there, pepper to taste, and a whole lot of water to drown yourself in.

And I was drownable, too. I could easily fall for the glitter and glamour side of the business, the style with no substance routine — sometimes I practiced it myself. I thought I'd get off on the "right foot" with *Make a Wish,* so after leaving *Blondes* with a week to go before rehearsals, I decided to follow the sun. Being the George Hamilton of my day, I took off for the Bahamas to soak up a good tan. I had my own special method to ensure fast tanning: I mixed baby oil with iodine. It gave me a smooth tan with an intense color. I should have patented it the "Park Avenue Tan." I walked into rehearsal dressed in white linen, my skin dark as the ages, and turned everyone's head. Half the cast needed neck braces after that day.

Gower Champion was a conservative, shy man — except when he was working. This was an important Broadway show for him, he had something to prove. He had done *Lend an Ear* in 1948, originating the show in Hollywood and bringing it *and* Carol Channing to the Broadway stage together. This show was to originate on Broadway, so it was more respectable. His wife, Marge, was possessive and came to all rehearsals, sitting in the back of the theater to watch every move he made. She sniffed out any rival, boring in on any eyes, male or female, who coveted her property. If you showed interest in Gower, you would have to have been ready to duck. Marge was there to swoop down and claw your eyes out.

Gower brought on the wandering eyes of Broadway, too. He was tall, slim, handsome, and moved in that graceful, catlike way some dancers move. After all, he and Marge had been the toast of MGM, one of the greatest dancing duos of their day. He was very hard on the Broadway dancers. He had a lot to prove; the Broadway crowd thought that anyone from Hollywood was second-rate, so he took no nonsense from anyone. The main targets of Gower's dictatorial excesses were Harold Lang and Helen Gallagher, the two lead dancers in *Wish*. What Marge and Gower were to Hollywood, Harold and Helen were to Broadway. They were a fine dancing duo, very highly respected Broadway regulars. Gower had his work cut out for him to prove that *he* was the best dancer around. During rehearsals, he rode Harold and Harold rode him right back. Antagonism built up between them and set off a chain reaction of bitter fights that would soon infect the cast, crew, and production team alike.

Gower was an easy target for the Broadway people. He took a lot of heat, not all of it undeserved, for underestimating the strength of Broadway and overestimating Hollywood's ability to ride rough-shod over it. His production numbers were too much Hollywood, all intimate moments designed for the camera. Cameras could come in close for shots of all that small movement, blown up one hundred times on screen for the viewer. This kind of choreography didn't work for the stage, which required grand gestures and obvious motions. Every action of the actor or dancer must travel over the footlights, over the orchestra, to the back rows of the theater. Winks, grins, and sneers had no place on a stage. For that reason Gower was severely criticized for his Broadway work throughout his career, except for his last production, *42nd Street*.

He was soundly criticized for one particular production number that ended *Wish's* first act, the Circus Ballet. It was a disaster on stage, although up close, a work of intimate genius. Only a Hollywood director could have created such an elaborate piece, ultimately designed to smell the hot breath of a close camera. On stage it was confused and meaningless. It was conceived as the full center ring of a circus done as ballet. Dancers mimed animals, freaks, and acrobats, creating individual circus moments of great power. Gower dressed the dancers for circus acts — two guys in a horse costume were ridden by a pink-plumbed, featherladen woman, clowns bounded on stage, elephants lumbered, and trapeze acts flew overhead. The designer, Raoul Pene DuBois, went crazy designing it, weaving the most enchanting fantasy out of his dreams. Gower approved it all. A miraculous, elaborate costume contrivance, totally wasted on stage because it was too damned busy.

Somebody was paying for it and the bulk of that burden fell on the shoulders of a certain gentleman from Philadelphia. This gentleman did not get along with *Wish's* producer, Harry Rigby, perhaps falling prey to the atmosphere created by Gower's feud with Harold. One night Mr. Philadelphia brought an early end to the Circus Ballet.

One talented, muscular, handsome blond dancer — a pet of Gower's, and incidentally, the dancer around whom Gower had designed the ballet — was to swing above the circus ring as a trapeze artist. Naturally Harold was angry because if anyone was going to be half-naked at the end of the first act finale, it should have been him. This dancer wore nothing but a dance belt, a piece that covered the crotch that was painted the color of his skin. The gentleman from Philadelphia arrived to survey this notoriously difficult Circus Ballet he had been hearing so much about. He entered the theater during the rehearsal while the blond dancer was suspended from a crane in the ceiling, slowly spinning upside-down. The gentleman took one look at the circling, bare-assed kid, turned to Gower and Harry Rigby and said, "Get that flying asshole out of my show!" And that was the end of the Circus Ballet.

Before we opened on Broadway, the show was taken out for preview showings in Philadelphia and Boston. They were having trouble with the script, so they brought in Abe Burrows of *Guys and Dolls* fame to clean it up. The stars got new material and new jokes every day. Burrows wrote all night and threw the new pages on stage the next day, then watched the stars go crazy. The only seasoned Broadway professionals were Harold, Nanette, and Helen. With all the others being Hollywood stars, unaccustomed to learning things rapidly, Franklin Pangborn and Melvin Cooper were thrown in a spin, not unlike lint caught in a whirlpool. Abe Burrows, on top of everything else was writing the hardest material to perform well: comedy dialogue. The changes were made so fast that no one's feelings were spared. The new material may have been great, but it made all the Hollywood people grumble and created a wider split between the Hollywood and Broadway performers. Money poured into the show like mad — at the time it was the most expensive musical ever produced on Broadway, costing $385,000. The joke circulating around town was "You'd better make a wish that the money comes in." When all was said and done, *Make a Wish* ended up losing a fortune, but we all made *Life* magazine with a great photo layout and much praise for Gower.

It was a good show for me, though. I got close to everyone in the cast and got to see a show built from the ground up. I was with the show through all the changes and was baptized by fire. We worked 24 hours a day in those rehearsals on the road to get the show together, with scenes being changed nightly, both lines and choreography. It was the first time for me, and the first time is always fun.

Perhaps to protect herself from all the chaos, Nanette Fabray played the big star role during the show. On an Actor's Equity preview before opening night in New York, her wardrobe, which had never been right all along, was still annoying her. Throughout rehearsals she had picked her costumes apart verbally and had thrown temper-tantrums about it. So on that preview night, she simply refused to go on stage wearing anything in the wardrobe. There was nothing anyone could do to change her mind. *Make a Wish* was a period piece set in France in the late 1930s, and she went on in street clothes. It was very unprofessional and the reviews were bad. New York street clothes were totally out of place because she was playing a little orphan girl. No amount of imagination could make up the difference between French orphan and Saks Fifth Avenue chic. She made her point with the producers.

Franklin Pangborn, however, went over big and was the favorite of audiences. He was recognized from all his amusing butler roles in movies, and even though he had a small part, he always got the biggest hand when he went on.

The Beaux Arts Ball was created to replace the Circus Ballet as the close of the first act and it was ready in time for the New York opening. It was a Parisian Ball attended by students, played by the chorus. We were dressed wildly, wearing as little clothing as anatomically possible. We were clowns, showgirls, jugglers, weight lifters, muscle men in leopard skin, magicians — whatever Gower and DuBois could dream up.

I was a gladiator, given a rather skimpy costume. At the height of the number I strolled down a center staircase to the "oohs" and "ahhs" of the audience, the costume was that good. The first time I wore it I felt naked on stage. I was poured into a slender pair of bikini shorts, leather sandals, leather belts crossed on my chest, and topping it off, a plumed headpiece that rose about three and one-half feet above my head. Over this I wore a silver leather cape, about 15 feet long, that trailed behind me with a red satin lining.

Harold and Helen played two Americans visiting Paris and they wore simple sailor suits to the ball, the only normal costumes on the whole stage. Both Harold and Helen were poured into the pants of the sailor suits, so that they would (and did) bulge. Especially Harold.

Throughout Harold Lang's career, everyone believed that he padded his jock because of the size of his bulge and the way it hung out in front, even in ballet costumes. It was always right there, straining the costume material, aching for air. So he carried a reputation as a guy who used padding the same way some women padded their bras.

On opening night, Harold joined the Beax Arts Ball in his tight sailor suit with his crotch obvious. I was at the top of a two-story high platform, close to the lights where it gets very hot. I was in my gladiator costume and makeup, carrying wads of Kleenex with me so that before the curtain rose, I could dab myself under my armpits and on my brow. I waited too long, still dabbing as the curtain was about to rise. I didn't know what to do with the big wet wad of Kleenex in my hand, so I dropped it. It fell straight down, plop, on the stage next to Harold as he was doing knee bends, limbering up.

He looked up at me on the platform.

"You son of a bitch!" he yelled. You did that on purpose!"

"Hey, please, I didn't. I had to get rid of it. What else was I going to do?" I pleaded.

Then the curtain went up on this lavish set with everyone dressed, or undressed, to fit the occasion of the ball. I started to make my walk down my staircase to the stage floor. Harold was hesitating, trying to move gracefully into his dance number with Helen. He was so nervous and keyed-up he turned and did a larger split that usual. With his tight sailor pants, his tight sailor pants split as he split. His bare derriere cracked through his pants and he had to finish the number that way. That night Harold's ass became as famous as my crotch had been in *Blondes*.

Later in the run of the show, after the Beaux Arts Ball had ended, we all came offstage for intermission when the stage manager caught me and told me to go down to the stage door because there was a gift waiting for me. He said that according to the guy at the door, it was an incredible thing. Curious, I obliged. The gladiator cape flapped behind me as I descended the staircase. I was used to wearing the costume by this time, even if I did look a trifle naked, and I wanted to see this gift that was left me before I changed. My friend, Hugh Lambert, who later married Frank Sinatra's daughter, Nancy, had overheard the stage manager and followed me downstairs in his muscle-man outfit, which in itself was a scanty bit of covering, not for the fainthearted.

We arrived at the stage door. The doorman looked us up and down and said, "Here." He handed me a brass plaque with an embossed inscription: "To the greatest gladiator of them all — Make a Wish."

"*This* is the gift?" I asked. "This thing you guys have been carrying on about? This is a piece of junk."

"No, no," the doorman said. "Open the loading dock doors."

Hugh and I went over to the loading doors, two wide steel doors that were made to take truck deliveries of sets and lumber. The muscle man in leopard skin tights and the gladiator in a silver cape and leather jock unhitched the doors and swung them wide.

Out there in the alley in the rain, water beading up on its new finish, outside against the filthy brick alley was a gorgeous Chevrolet convertible. The roof was white, the interior was red leather, and the body was silver — the colors were chosen to match my gladiator costume. I leapt off the loading platform down to the car and walked in the rain, getting my costume soaking wet.

"Who sent it? Who's it from?" I asked.

Hugh stayed up on the platform to keep dry. "I don't know." He turned to the doorman and asked, "Who's it from?"

The doorman shrugged. "I don't know either, Mason, but you'd better come in out of the rain or the wardrobe people are going to be pissing razor blades."

I racked my brain. Who could have sent it? Don? No, not his style. The Countess Mercati? Unlikely. My parents? Not on your life, not after that night in "Blondes." But who? I stood there, dripping with rain, a soaked gladiator admiring his new present and wondering who his Santa Claus was. I wouldn't find out until more than a year later.

I drove that convertible everywhere. I was very obvious, bold, and ostentatious in my silver car. Whenever anyone pointed out that fact to me, I simply related a favorite story my Aunt Suzanne told me. She was wearing an enormous 15-carat diamond ring, and someone commented, "Don't you think that's a little ostentatious?" Aunt Suzanne smiled and said, "Darling, I always thought so, until I had one."

I came in out of the back alley and Hugh tossed a towel at me. "Let that be a lesson to you, Mason," he said. "You take your clothes off in public, you get big cars."

From that night on I drove the silver Chevy from 820 Park Avenue through Central Park to the Majestic Theater. I parked behind Gower and Marge Champion's Cadillac convertible, and tipped the doorman to look after it. When the cops came around on horseback, the doorman said the Cadillac was Gower's and the Chevy was Marge's. I never got a ticket.

On closing night, I gave the cast party, just as I had given most of the other parties for *Make a Wish*. The money people

## The Park Avenue Chorus Boy

were all at each other's throats and they refused to throw any parties. That left it up to the Park Avenue Chorus Boy. The gentleman from Philadelphia didn't come because Mr. Rigby was going to be there and they didn't get along. Gower showed for a while, but Harold was there, so he left early. Nanette Fabray wouldn't come because Helen was there, and they tried not to share the same oxygen in a room. Somehow, though, the party was successful. Harry Rigby went on to become a big producer. The gentleman from Philadelphia went back home, where he should have stayed in the first place and just mailed in the checks. The play lasted ten months and I was sorry to see it end.

My next move had been planned long before. The drifting currents were sweeping me to Hollywood.

# CHAPTER SIX
## Cowboys and Indians

Aunt Suzanne used to say, "Anything west of the Mississippi River is cowboys and Indians."

I didn't think I was out of control. It seemed natural, trusting Lester and Louis, leapfrogging from *Blondes* to *Wish* to Hollywood. In retrospect, I was treading water as the current swept me downstream.

I left exactly two days after *Make a Wish* closed. I loaded up my silver convertible with personal things, my chauffeur loaded up the limousine with the maid and everything else and we drove in tandem across the United States, from one coast to the other. I kept the top down all the way and greased up with baby oil and iodine to ensure arriving in California with a jungle tan. We stretched the trip out, stopping along the way to visit friends.

Our longest stop was in Las Vegas, where Helen and Harold had flown out to join Rosemary Clooney on stage at the Thunderbird Hotel. It was party time all over again for ten days in the most exciting, noisy, wide-awake city I'd ever seen. I had never even heard of Las Vegas before Helen and Harold told me they were going to work there. Imagine my surprise, driving in from the desolate desert to the neon palaces of gambling heaven.

Hallucinate is a word that goes well with Las Vegas, no matter how you come to her. I had seen gambling in the casinos of Europe, but never on such a massive scale as in Las Vegas. These were gambling cathedrals. They were the size of football fields!

Thousands of people were dropping their coins into one-armed bandits and throwing chips onto green felt to be swept up by the house.

The gambling didn't entice me; I wasn't a gambler. The slot machines amused me because they were something new, and roulette was fun for an hour or so. I certainly could afford to gamble if I had wanted to, but it never really interested me. I remembered one incident in Europe, watching a drunk pal of mine, Peter Gould Harig, of the Gould banking fortune, lose $30,000 in one night. That sobered me up to gambling quick. Of course, it didn't sober him up. He was so bombed he couldn't remember it the next day. I picked up the remainder of his chips that night and made him back about $12,000.

Harold, Helen, Rosemary, and I were out partying one night in one of the casinos and I was formally introduced to slot machines. I thought, "My God, this is fantastic! Put in one dollar and ten come out!" It wasn't long before I realized how quickly those single dollars could add up to hundreds as you wait to get the ten dollar payoff. I gave it up.

Harold by that time had already gotten bored with gambling and had gone over to the bar to talk to some of the showgirls. He was drunk and left $850 in chips with Helen. She gave them to me, told me to cash them in and not to give the money to Harold because he was too drunk. I cashed the chips for $50 bills and put them in my pocket. The night wore on and everyone got tired. At about 4:00 am we all headed for home. I decided not to go all the way back to my hotel, so I crashed at Harold's. We stumbled into his hotel room and before going to sleep, I purposely laid the $850 in fifties across the dresser.

The next day Harold saw the money. "What the hell is *that* all about?"

"That's what you won last night, you jerk," I said.

He couldn't remember winning anything. "I won that? I was drunk and I did that? Let's start now!" So we went back that afternoon and gambled and played the machines and he won another five hundred dollars. I won about one thousand dollars. The irony for me was that although I rarely gambled, when I *did* gamble, I could never lose. I never lost at the track, either.

Many years later, at the 1969 Kentucky Derby, Peter Gould Harig and I were Saul Silberman's guests, Saul being the owner of the Tropical Park Racetrack in Miami. Saul lost one million dollars a year gambling at his own track. I had a great time that afternoon hanging out with Cathy and Darren McGavin. We were in the box next to the then-President Nixon. Saul Silberman was a wild man and Nixon was fascinated by him and his entourage, the strange group of people that we were. Saul had on his huge diamond tie pin and large diamond cuff links. His runners were going back and forth at the snap of his fingers, placing $10,000, $15,000, and $20,000 bets. Nixon thought we were crazy, but his secret service men were having a ball.

Peter and I decided we were going to pool our betting money. "All right, Peter," I said. "No money hangovers tomorrow, OK? What we'll do is just place out little $100 bets."

"Well," said Peter, "what horses do you want?"

"I don't know. Why don't you choose the horses?"

We were watching Saul, who had lost close to half a million the day before on The Oaks, the pre-Derby Day race. We could only imagine what he was going to win or lose on the Derby Day itself. Saul heard us pooling our betting money and said, "OK, California Kid, what *are* you going to do?"

I was on the spot. "California" gave me an idea, though. "All right, we'll just bet straight across — win, place, and show — we'll pick all three money horses."

"Uh huh," Saul grunted.

"Yeah, " I answered, "I'm gonna pick the number one horse, the number two horse, and the number three horse — win, place, and show."

"Oh, you are?" Saul inquired.

A guy from the press was listening. "How are you going to do that, Michael?"

"Very simple. I have a unique method," I said mysteriously.

Well, my unique method was this: I took "Majestic Prince" to win because it was a California horse, "Arts & Letters" to place because a friend's son, Steve Galloway, was in art school in Los Angeles, and "Dyke" to show, for all of my lesbian friends.

And that's how they came in — one, two, three — Majestic Prince, Arts & Letters, and Dyke. It blew them all away. No one could figure out how I did it. I had tried to explain it to the press the next day, too, although I stumbled over the part about why I had chosen "Dyke" to show. Poor Saul couldn't handle it. He lost that day, too.

That first trip to Las Vegas included an introduction to Beldon Kettleman. Rosemary told me that she wanted to introduce me to one of the "greatest guys in Las Vegas." Beldon owned the El Rancho Vegas, which was *the* place to stay in those days. His house, a huge Spanish hacienda, was on the grounds of El Rancho. We drove up in the limo, watched by armed men behind every tree.

"What the hell's going on?" I asked.

"He's a very big, important man," Rosemary said. This was the part of the West I was unaccustomed to. Here were people who needed gunmen to protect their homes. Here were the cowboys and Indians that Aunt Suzanne was speaking of, only she had meant it figuratively. We went onto the property, and at the front door, all of us had to sign in, including Rosemary, who was a star in Las Vegas, knew Beldon well, and who had been on the cover of *Life* magazine. No matter, Rosemary had to sign in, too.

Beldon Kettleman was quiet, handsome, and unassuming, not at all the flashy Las Vegas personality I had expected.

The Sands Hotel was opening across the road that night. Beldon said, "Let's go over to the Sands and give them a break on their opening night, what do you say?"

*A Wish Granted*

We jumped in a limo just to cross the street and entered the Sands. Again the effect of the size and scope of the gambling glitter house astounded me. I watched as greedy thousands played the waiting machines. I watched as the house dealers smiled and swept up losing chips. I watched as waitresses preyed on the people, distracting them with free booze and food. It was all so fast and furious, like being in the middle of river rapids and going down for the third time, that I almost missed her. She blended into the scenery so perfectly that it took a second look to see Chi Chi, one of the showgirls from *Gentlemen Prefer Blondes* had just come in on the arm of a high roller. And because I was so taken with seeing her and talking about old times, I almost missed the real high drama of the night.

Beldon was over at the crap tables and I kept my eye on him while talking shop with Chi Chi. I noticed that he went into his coat pocket, pulled something out, and laid it on the table. He was there less than a minute, nodded to the others, and moved away, definitely on a mission. Now I watched more closely. He went over to the roulette wheel and stopped there. He went into his pocket again and I realized he was betting large amounts of money. The roulette wheel spun. Beldon grinned, and they swept his money away! Why was he grinning, I wondered, as he wandered over to where I was with Chi Chi.

"All right," he said, "we can go now."

"That was pretty quick," I said.

"It was a pretty quick quarter of a million dollars, too," he countered.

"What are you talking about?" I asked.

"I just dropped $250,000 on roulette and at the crap tables." He snapped his fingers — easy come, easy go.

"What?"

"Mason, that's nothing. This is Las Vegas. I'm giving them a break. Gotta get some money in the till for them; this is opening night. C'mon. Let's go back and have a party."

So we took the limo back across the street to the house, ten minutes and a quarter of a million dollars later.

I saw Rosemary's show many times. She was a straight pop-ballad singer and did a fine show, which included her big hit "Come On to My House." Helen and Harold came on after her and did a medley of dance numbers from Broadway shows.

During the days we went out on Beldon's yacht on Lake Mead with Helen, Harold, and a gaggle of showgirls — Rosemary rarely came — to picnic with champagne and have fun and games. The favorite exchange of the day was: "We're having a yachting party."

"Oh, can I bring anything?"

"Yes, a towel and a toothbrush."

After about ten days of this, I was getting bored and anxious to get to California.

I said good-bye to Vegas and got back on the road in the 100 degree-plus heat, convertible and limousine crossing the dessert in six hours, with me greased up with baby oil and iodine. We headed straight for the Beverly Hills Hotel where I had reserved a bungalow. My convertible pulled in first, limo right behind. The doorman was aghast — here was a shirtless kid with a deep brown tan in a convertible with red leather seats, loaded down with suitcases, followed by a long limousine with a uniformed chauffeur and a maid, also loaded down with personal effects. The doorman had never seen anything like it before. We were covered with dust from the desert, and I got out of the car and asked him, "Where's the swimming pool?"

"That way," he said, pointing. "And who are you?"

"Never mind, my chauffeur will take care of all that."

I walked past him to the pool and immediately ordered a bottle of champagne. Then perhaps, still mesmerized by the memory of rising heat waves off the highway — I didn't stop to think about etiquette or what I was doing — I stripped down to my shorts and jumped in the pool.

As I climbed out, feeling better, but still foul-tempered, some guy pool side said, "Oh, that's terrific. Just wonderful. New kid in town?"

I turned arrogantly, "Who're you?"

"I'm Mike Connolly," he answered.

"Whoop-dee-do," I answered.

"You always do stuff like this?" he inquired.

I didn't like the way he asked questions. He reminded me of a reporter. "Yeah," I said.

"Well, that's interesting. Playing the big shot. Very interesting."

Of course, he was a reporter, just my luck. Mike Connolly was *the* Mike Connolly of the *Hollywood Reporter*, one of the top columnists in town. Everyone in Hollywood reads the trade papers, or "trades" as they are called, both the *Reporter* and the *Daily Variety*. Connolly was one of the guys you went to when you needed publicity.

We disliked each other immediately, an adversary relationship which lasted until we discovered we had many things in common.

"So you're getting some good PR for yourself, right?" he inquired.

"Yeah," I said, "I'm working on it."

He asked me a few more questions, found out who I was, and I appeared in his column the next day:

"The Park Avenue Chorus Boy is in town. He's a 'Shurr' bet for stardom. Look out folks, he's off the wall."

The lifeguard came over to me and said, "Listen, pal, you usually don't jump in the pool around here in your jockey shorts, d'ya mind?"

"I don't mind at all," I said. "Have you got any swim trunks I can wear?"

"Sure," he said. I followed him to his locker and he tossed me a fresh pair of trunks. I returned to the pool to finish my swim and my champagne.

Louis Shurr and Al Melmick saw the bit in the *Reporter* and called me at the hotel. I had planned to lie low for a few days, but Mike Connolly blew my cover. Louis wondered why I hadn't been in touch with him yet, I told him I had been resting. He told me to be in his office at ten the next morning.

The next morning I put on white slacks, a blue blazer, and a white turtleneck and walked into the offices of the Shurr Agency in Beverly Hills. In the lobby, waiting for a meeting, was a gorgeous blond with an exquisite figure, dressed in red with a high-necked collar and long sleeves.

"Hey, how are you?" I asked quickly. I contemplated sitting in her lap and proposing marriage.

She smiled impishly at my headlong approach, sidestepped sweetly and said, "Hey, I'm fine."

"Are you waiting for an interview?" I asked, amazing myself with the deftness and subtlety of my tangled tongue.

"No, I don't need an interview here. I'm already under contract."

"Well, I'm Michael Mason from New York." Ah, the quick and witty chorus boy slobbering over a pretty girl.

"I'm Barbara Eden," she replied.

"So, what are you doing?" I asked.

"I'm under contract to Fox Studios; they're trying to make me a movie star," she said and laughed at the presumptuousness of it all.

"Hey, I think they've got a good one," I said. "You'll do it."

We talked for a while, but I realized that she was forbidden fruit. You didn't ask someone like Barbara Eden for a date, not on a first meeting.

## A Wish Granted

I went in to see Al Melnick and Louis Shurr, and they told me I was to do a screen test at Twentieth-Century Fox Studios, working with the drama coach, Natasha Lytess.

I was put under a one-year contract to Fox, and if they liked my test, I was on my way. The agencies were strong enough in those days to tell the studio to put me under contract to do a screen test. It was simple and straightforward, and very magical for a hard-working Broadway singer like me. I never had to do anything, which may have been one of the reasons I didn't take it as seriously as I should have. I had taken Broadway seriously, but that was hard work. This was handed to me on a silver platter: "Here you go, Mason, here's a contract, a coach, and a screen test. Go out there and do it good. The next step is movie stardom." It was all just a little too easy. Or was I beginning to feel that I shouldn't do well, because I hadn't earned it myself? Maybe I knew I wasn't paying my dues.

I stayed at the Beverly Hills Hotel al little while longer, then moved to the Voltaire Apartments at Sunset and Crescent Heights, behind Schwabs. I think part of this change was to get me near the big star hangouts so I could play movie star more often. Schwabs was right there and Garden of Allah was across the street. The fun and games became the number one priority for Mike Mason, wealthy, handsome, talented Park Avenue Chorus Boy — now *there* was a kid who was going to be a movie star. Everyone thought so.

Each day I rode out to the studio to be "groomed" for my test by Natasha Lytess. She worked with both Marla English and me, independently on some days, together on others. We did scenes from every light comedy play imaginable. Natasha also served as studio spokesman to me. Through her I learned what their intentions were by watching the kind of things that she did. She was the one who introduced me to R.J. Wagner.

Marla and I had been rehearsing a scene from a play when R.J. stopped by. I knew it wasn't just a casual visit when Natasha stopped the rehearsal and led R.J. over to me by the arm.

"Michael, I want you to meet Robert Wagner," she said.

"My friends call me R.J. And I've heard your name." He knew I was his studio threat.

"Yeah, I've heard yours, too," I said. I also knew I was his studio threat.

"Who do you know in town?" he asked. I tried to sum it up quickly in my head; he was being awfully nice for a guy who was supposed to be under the gun with me as one of the bullets. So the studio obviously wanted us to meet because Natasha had made a production out of the introduction. What did R.J. really want?

"Very few people," I replied. "I only know a columnist, Mike Connolly. Oh, yeah, and I met Barbara Eden . . ." I wondered if he was being my pal now so he could get close enough to slide a knife in my back. Keep your friends close and your enemies closer, they say. But he was acting pretty straightforward.

"Well, I'm going with a girl named Debbie Reynolds and we have a little group of friends. Why don't you join us and double-date some night? There's a gal I know under contract to Warners, Virginia Gibson, and I'd like you to meet her." It sounded good, very good. "That's assuming you like redheads. . ." he added. That did it. He was offering friendship; the redhead clinched it.

"Great," I said, "love it."

Natasha stood by, gnashing her teeth in frustration. She was annoyed, as would be the studio executives later, because R.J. and I had hit if off so well. Here I was, the big threat to R.J.'s career, the guy who was supposed to keep R.J. in line, the actor who would step into his role if R.J. was a bad boy, and we were suddenly going to go out and be buddies. The studio would have drooled gleefully if sparks or bitterness had transpired between us, and reported savage and intimate details in the trade and gossip magazines. But there was no conflict between us and no competition. I spent my non-working days and all my nights partying, usually at the Garden of Allah. R.J. spent most of his

A Wish Granted

days at the studio studying, always thinking of his career. I went to work whenever I had to, but I wasn't what you'd call dedicated. Still, I had everything going for me, so I was sure stardom would be mine, no matter what. It had happened for others.

R.J. , Debbie, Ginny, and I were a foursome around town, to be seen at the Garden of Allah, Ciro's, Mocambo, Ah Fong's, all the hot spots. Little by little I was getting to know people in Hollywood.

I wasn't the only guy getting the screen test treatment. The studio had R.J. doing one test after another, first with this starlet, then that starlet, until even he was getting a little sick of it. R.J. lived with his parents in Bel Air and had been discovered at a party at the Bel Air Country Club by Henry Wilson. Wilson sent him down to the studio the day after the party and told them to put R.J. under contract. They did and screen tested him to death the whole first year he was with them.

There was a fear growing inside me that I wasn't as good as some of the other people who had been in the business longer. As Gower Champion had discovered going from Hollywood to Broadway, the transition wasn't easy. They were two very different worlds. I didn't know what it was like to act in front of a camera — I didn't even know how a camera worked. On stage, gestures are large and the voice is loud and controlled. In the movies, everything is done differently. You can whisper and the microphone will pick it up. If they want a voice to be deeper, they can turn a dial. I was aware enough of my ignorance to be unnerved by the technology. That year in Hollywood, I never quite got the hang of it. It wasn't that I couldn't have figured it out, it was that I didn't bother to take the time, perhaps because I was afraid, either of failure or finding out that I wasn't as good as the other actors. As I spent more and more time rehearsing for my screen test, I began drifting further and further away from a working actor's attitude into a frivolous movie star game. If Broadway was hard work, then Hollywood was play. You can't goof around on stage – you're there and the audience is in front of you, and you either perform or die on stage. In film, you can always do another take. But there was something else I didn't learn about film that first year. Good film acting depends on developing a personality in front of the camera. The camera is so intimate that actual acting can look false. A natural personality carefully planned and executed is what film acting is all about, and is what makes the audience feel comfortable with you. You don't need to be a great actor if you photograph well. If you can remember your lines, you will do all right.

R.J., Ginny, and I collected ourselves and went to what was my first feature film premiere, *Singing in the Rain*. The stars were Gene Kelly, Donald O'Conner, and Debbie Reynolds. The Egyptian Theater was a zoo that night, famous stars in bright lights, parading for the throng of screaming fans. I got a huge kick out of it, and I met half of Hollywood that night. We were marched from the Egyptian to a studio-rented limousine to a late dinner dance, and I found myself across the table from Elizabeth Taylor. Here in the flesh was my aching heart's desire and I couldn't even muster a word. I was dumbfounded and in tongue-tied awe of this woman. Here was God's masterpiece of raven-haired delight; a young Aunt Suzanne. She soon realized that I was gaping at her and it was all I could do to apologize and introduce myself. Later, she had these words of wisdom: "Michael, you are a darling. You will be very successful in this town if you can only leave New York behind you."

That night, I met Tab Hunter as well as David Niven and Errol Flynn. It was a night for me to gush uncontrollably, and I invited everyone for lunch the next day at the Polo Lounge. I was amazed that 24 people showed up, including Tab and Errol Flynn. I was finding my way into Hollywood movie star society.

One day, R.J.. and I were driving down Sunset Boulevard on our way to visit Ginny at Warner Bros. On the street there was a big sign which read "Phil Hall Buick," a major Buick dealership on the West Coast in those days, In the window was a beautiful lemon-colored Buick convertible with a black leather interior.

"Hey," I said, "I'm going to buy that before we go to the studio and surprise Ginny."

"You're off your rocker," R.J. said. "What do you mean you're gonna buy that?"

"Right now — I'm gonna buy it now. Why not? This is an old car," I said, referring to the silver Chevy. "At least a full year old."

I pulled up in front of the dealership and parked opposite the yellow Buick in the window. I walked up to the salesman and said, "Hey, I want that car in the window."

"Yeah, you and everyone else out there in comedy-land," the salesman said. Then he recognized R.J. and looked at me again, wondering if he should take me seriously.

"Look," I said, "I want that car and I want it now. I have to be at the studio in 45 minutes, and I'm in a hurry, so hop to it."

R.J. began to move away from me, walking as nonchalantly as possible over to look at other cars. "Why do you need to have it *now*?" he muttered, talking as if to the other cars. "They need time to check your credit."

R.J. kept wandering around, pretending he didn't know me. "Mason, when you're through making noise, just let me know so we can go," he said. He looked at the price of a hardtop coupe and winced.

During this incident, a man named Phil Long, who worked there, came out to see what was going on. Phil was the brother of actor Richard Long, which is how he knew R.J.

"What the hell is the big noise about?" he asked R.J. "R.J., who's your funny friend?"

R.J. shrugged and grinned. "Go ask *him*," he answered, hitching his thumb toward me.

I told Phil in my best blustery baritone that we were going to the studio in my new yellow Buick to pick up Ginny, and, if he wanted, he could go with us to dinner at the Garden of Allah.

The Buick people noodled around for a while, conferring in little knitting circles, picking up telephones and setting them down again, until one of the dealers walked over and handed me a set of keys.

I drove the Buick off the showroom floor, got to the studio on time, picked up Ginny and, true to my word, returned to pick up Phil to go to the Garden of Allah,.

I waved a sad farewell to the gladiator Chevy. It had been a fine gift, but I might have felt sadder leaving it behind if I had known who had sent it to me.

Later, I found out how lucky I was to have traded in the Chevy. The yellow Buick saved my life. R.J., Debbie, Ginny, and I were at a party up on Appian Way that Tab was giving. Had I still been driving the little Chevy convertible, R.J. and I would have been dead. We were leaving the party and we started hollering to Ginny and Debbie, "C'mon, let's go! We've got another party to get to." I backed the Buick up and the rear wheels went over the edge of a cliff. It dug into the ground, heavy car that it was, as the drive shaft lodged in and settled there. We got out of the front seat and left the car literally teetering over a straight 500-foot drop. If it had been the Chevy, it would have been over the cliff and long gone. We left the car there, called my driver, and had him pick us up in the limo.

We returned in the cold light of morning and there was my car, still teetering. The guy in the tow truck who pulled it away from the cliff kept his door open for fear the weight of the car would pull his truck over the side. They had gone to the trouble of clearing everybody out of the way down below.

We drove around in the Buick more often than the limo. Every time R.J. got into the limo, he would say, "This is so corny it hurts," and I would snicker because he had a limo from the studio at his disposal any time he wanted it.

We were in the Buick the night I met Johnny Stompanato.

# A Wish Granted

It was a typical night, making the Hollywood scene. R.J. and I had met at Ah Fong's, and then had gone on to Ciro's for a drink. It was dull at Ciro's that night. I told R.J. that we should go to the Beverly Gourmet Restaurant, because it would be more lively and they had a piano. R.J. had never heard me sing, and I felt like showing off. I wanted to impress R.J. with my voice. We sat ourselves down by the pianist at the Gourmet. He and I got to talking, and since you can't put a nightclub singer next to a piano and expect him to be quiet, I started to sing along with him. He asked if I knew "My Funny Valentine." I had used it in my New York club act and I sang it with him. Halfway through, I felt a hand on my shoulder. I finished the song and looked up at an absurdly handsome fellow who said, "Sing it again, kid, it's my song."

"Take off — I don't sing for strangers," I said.

He gave me a bad look and walked away. R.J. nearly fainted. He said, "Jesus Christ, you just insulted Johnny Valentine!"

"Who the hell is Johnny Valentine?" I asked.

"Johnny Stampanato, Mickey Cohen's right arm. He's a wild man with a reputation a mile long, He has notches on his gun. He could be a star, but the studios are afraid to touch him."

I looked over; he was sitting with Lana Turner and two other beautiful women. I figured I had better do something fast. I told the pianist, "Listen, play 'Funny Valentine' again if you know what's good for me."

He graciously started the song again and I stood up and sang. I walked over to their table and gave it all I had, without a microphone, without lights, without a stage, just me singing "My Funny Valentine" for Mr. Valentine himself. He kept a somber expression almost all the way through, but I gave it such heart and passion that he finally cracked a small smile. I did the whole nightclub sell and finished to a round of applause from the crowd, and I loved it. So did Stompanato.

"Hey, you're great," he said afterwards.

"Thank you, and I apologize for my big mouth," I said.

"No problem, no problem," he assured me.

They invited me to sit down, and R.J. joined us. After a while, Stompanato invited us out to his Malibu beach house. Both R.J. and Lana declined.

"I have to work in the morning," Lana said.

"And I have another in a long series of screen tests," R.J. said. "We're working people, you know."

"Unlike *some* people, right, R.J.?" I said.

"You know it, Michael," he said.

"Well," Stompanato said, "it's just you and me and these two lovely ladies, Michael."

We ordered another bottle of Dom Perignon. I had the market on Dom Perignon in those days, or so I thought. Years later, I learned differently. I was in Rancho Mirage at Wally's, and I ordered Dom Perignon. When they said they didn't have any, I was outraged — the best, most expensive restaurant in the desert not have any Dom Perignon?

"Mr. Mason, you don't understand," the maitre d' said. "Elizabeth Taylor was here last week. What she didn't drink, she took with her."

Stompanato, Lana, R.J., and I worked our way through the last bottle before Lana and R.J. left to get some sleep. I told Stompanato that I would follow him to the beach in my car. He would, of course, take the two women with him.

I followed his Rolls Royce down Sunset Boulevard, lagging a little. I wondered what I was getting myself into. Here was a man with the reputation of being a very tough guy and I was trailing along to his beach house. What in God's name was I doing? I pulled in through enormous gates, nodding to the guards protecting Stompanato's home

The women made themselves comfortable in the living room and Johnny was sitting at his mirrored bar alone, staring out at

# A Wish Granted

the surf. Soft music was playing and the light from the roaring fireplace licked at the back of his jacket. I walked over, poured myself a scotch and asked if he was all right.

"Sure," he mumbled.

I asked if he would be more comfortable with his jacket off. He stood up. I helped him out of it and saw two leather straps crisscrossed over his back. He turned around and saw the straps were attached to holsters, and in the holsters were two .38's.

I smiled the only smile I could arrange at the moment. "Loaded?" I asked.

"Naturally," he said.

"You, uh, want to put them to bed for a while?" I inquired.

"Not a bad idea," he answered. He turned and headed for his bedroom and I followed with his suit coat in hand.

He got out of his suit and into a terry cloth caftan. He saw I was a little shaken up by the guns. After all, I had really made him mad the first time I sang "My Funny Valentine." He reached into his closet and tossed a silk robe at me. "Relax, kid. Put this on," he said. He walked out to the women in the living room.

I followed him out a few minutes later, wearing the silk robe. There, lying naked in front of the windows of the glass-lined room, was Johnny Stompanato, flanked by an exquisitely naked woman on each side. They were stretched across white bearskin rugs, the type Aunt Suzanne had in her bedroom.

Early the next morning Stompanato's house man, fully dressed of course, walked in over us, dozing naked on the white bearskin rugs. "Breakfast in one hour," he proclaimed.

I woke up with a jolt, got to my feet, and ran out the door straight for the Pacific Ocean, digging my heels into the cool, sodden sand, and then crashing, arms wide, into the surf. I came up spitting salt water and seaweed. I found I had company.

"So how did you like your first beach party, kid?" Stompanato inquired.

I had to admit I liked it.

Years later, I saw Lana Turner just before things went sour between them. They were about to go to Acapulco together, which is where the change happened, and Lana told me before they left that she loved him, was happy, and wanted to marry him. When I talked to Johnny, he echoed her sentiments. He was going to give up his old business and make an attempt at being a leading man in the movies. They seemed happy and very much in love.

Then, in Acapulco it all went to hell somehow. They came back and it was bad — and then came the murder. We heard about it in lurid detail. Johnny Stompanato left Lana's bed in the middle of the night while she was asleep, crept down the hallway and slipped between the sheets of Lana's seventeen year old daughter, Cheryl. Lana woke up groggily, saw that Johnny was gone, and went down the hall to investigate. She heard noises in Cheryl's room and opened the door, finding Johnny having sex with Cheryl. A bad scene ensued with Lana running down to the kitchen, and Johnny and Cheryl, both naked, following.

What happened next is a subject of debate. Supposedly Cheryl took a butcher's knife and, because he had raped her, stuck it into Stompanato and killed him. When the police were finally called two hours later, Cheryl took the rap, claimed self-defense, and served no time as a minor.

Johnny had lived one hell of a life. He was a big, tough man with all the women he wanted, all the money he needed, always surrounded by an entourage. His "front" was a pet shop on Westwood Village, his "business." He had all sorts of cute little animals — puppies, kittens, parakeets — and in one corner in a cage he had an ocelot. It was the only thing in his store to remind people that he was a tough guy. An ocelot is a beautiful animal. It is an oversized cat with a leopard's coat, which has been known to cause a person great bodily harm. When I saw the ocelot in his store, I thought of my convertible with the yellow and black, which closely matched the colors of the ocelot. I wanted to take the kitty for a ride.

"Hey, Johnny," I said, "you gotta let me take that cat into Hollywood and do the whole number."

"Yeah?" he said, "the last one who did it was Gloria Swanson. That cat is dangerous."

"So what? Who cares? I will control it," I said.

"Well, wear leather gloves in case you need to sock him in the jaw. His teeth are still sharp and his nails aren't clipped, just filed."

The chain was heavy and the collar around his neck was wide. I put the ocelot in the back seat with a friend of mine and we drove to Schwabs. I whipped into the parking lot and everybody congregated around us. Sid Skolsky, the biggest columnist in Hollywood, was there, which assured me of great publicity. Mike Connolly came later and I walked the ocelot into Schwabs. It was behaving rather nicely because Johnny had given him a tranquilizer, but everyone stayed back until one publicity-starved actress came near and said, "Oh, Michael, what a cute little kitty-cat. Oh, she's darling," and proceeded to reach out to pet the cat. Well the cute little kitty-cat bared its teeth and went into a hissing, guttural, snarling rage. The starlet went screaming out the front door.

• • •

By this time I had been in Hollywood for six months rehearsing for my screen test. Six months of *Sabrina Fair* and *The Philadelphia Story*. Six months of preparing for a screen test that would run fifteen minutes on screen. Six months of play time because I was bored. Six months of hanging around Tab, Harold Lloyd, Jr., R.J., Debbie, and Ginny. Six months of meeting and partying with Hollywood.

We hung out a lot at Farley Granger's beach house. This was not long after Farley had made *Strangers on a Train* for Alfred Hitchcock. Shelley Winters was a close friend of Farley's and was always there. She was slim, even skinny in those days, a gorgeous pinup girl. The group included an ex-baseball player, Larry "Bud" Pennell, and a host of others. I first met Katy Thalberg at one of Farley's parties and we dated often. I didn't know she was Norma Shearer and Irving Thalberg's daughter. I also dated Jean Styne, daughter of Jules Styne, and Judy Spreckles, daughter of Kay Spreckles and the Spreckles candy fortune. Kay would later become the last Mrs. Clark Gable.

Because Farley's beach house was host to so many parties, he devised a method to deal with the potential guests. He had a flagpole on the roof of his house, and if the flag was up, come on in, it's party time. If the flag was down, just keep on walking.

Six months passed. I did the screen test, after the late night at the Garden of Allah. It was a couple of weeks before we could see the results. Then one day, Natasha, Marla, and I were sent to a screening room filled with big studio executives, who were waiting to see my work, I had no idea what to expect and, at that point, I didn't care. I wanted to get back to New York and do some real work. I was tired of Hollywood. But I was sorry that I hadn't paid more attention to what I did in those six months.

I settled down in my seat and waited for the lights to go down, It had taken two full days to shoot the screen test, and things had not gone smoothly. My late entrance that first morning was partially to blame.

The lights went down. The first piece of film to roll was my personality test. The personality test was not a scene, but an intimate setting where they asked you questions about yourself. You were supposed to relax and be yourself, totally natural, while you impressed the studio people with your screen persona. There was one camera very close to my face and I sat on a high stool in front of a blank wall of a sound stage. Very relaxed. I looked directly into the camera, the black hole of cinema, and I answered the disembodied voice of Natasha, who stood behind the camera and asked the questions. I couldn't see Natasha because she was back there behind the intimate setting., behind the lights with the cameramen, the director, the assistant director, the sound man, the boom man, the grips, the technicians, the studio heads, and whoever else wanted to watch the test. Very intimate.

And then the questions. They asked where I was from and what I had done. I was supposed to laugh and come on funny and casual while telling little anecdotes about myself.

Natasha: Well, tell me a little something about yourself

Me: Who, me? Jeepers, Tash, uh, where can I begin...OK, well, let's see, I'm from Massachusetts... well, New York, really, although my Aunt Suzanne is from Washington, D.C..."

At least on Broadway when you were auditioning they let you sing a song or read from a script. Why couldn't there have been someone there behind the camera to say, "Thank you, NEXT!"

I talked about New York and the shows I was in. I told a few stupid anecdotes, tame ones, mind you, about *Gentlemen Prefer Blondes* and *Make a Wish,* and I told them about Sandy Meisner and the Neighborhood Playhouse. I left out the Park Avenue Chorus Boy and the more lurid tales. I didn't want them to think I was crazy. In retrospect, I think I would have come off better if I had told them about my wild background.

I resented answering questions about myself as an actor. They asked me what I had done and I drew a complete blank. "What do you mean, what have I done?" is what I *wanted* to say. "Who are you looking for; what kind of man would you like? I can give you a choice: you want a rah rah college boy? Here it is. You want the arrogant snob? Here you go and I'll throw in a side order of haughty butler if you would like. You want a raging wild man or a brooding Dane — what do you want? Are you interested in me? Or do you want to pull me into some false sense of security, draw me out so you can compare me with all the other actors you have real respect for? I know, I've seen what sort of people you think of as actors."

Instead, I fumbled around on screen for a while, trying to think up ways to answer the questions so I wouldn't expose myself.

The key to a good screen test is to let go of your immediate feelings. You have to think about the *later* audience, the audience in the dark theater watching the test. Don't think about the audience right there behind the camera. Who cares if you look like an ass to them. What counts is how you look later on. The only thing that mattered that day was how the camera saw me.

I wasn't used to playing to an audience that wasn't there, I was used to immediacy, instant gratification, applause. I had trouble making the separation in my mind. I felt like a fool sitting on a stool in a sound stage in front of a black wall, talking to a black hole. So I didn't play the camera. I played the immediate audience for the applause. The camera made me look foolish. I was still a kid from Broadway, where nothing was ever recorded for posterity.

And then there was my face up there on the screen. I was wearing too much makeup and looked 15 years old. I don't know why I looked so young on camera. R.J. was my age and he photographed like a man in his early 20s. I photographed much younger. Perhaps it was bone structure. But there I was, my head ten feet across, a giant shape with eyes, nose, and mouth, gesturing wildly as if I was on stage. It's one thing seeing yourself in home movies, but here I was, filling up a whole wall with my foolish drivel. Every little thing stood out.

I wanted to get back to New York. I slid further and further down into my seat. My personality test was over. Then I got to see the scenes Marla and I did together – the best scenes of two days, edited together. Oh, God. I slid even further down into my seat. And further. Oh, boy did I want to go back to New York.

# CHAPTER SEVEN
## Heston vs. Meredith

Lester called. "I heard about your test," he said.

"Yeah," I replied, "I laid a bomb."

"You were *terrible*. Get your ass back to New York and get back to work. You can work on the stage. I'll put you in anything I can, even summer stock. Maybe you can do Hollywood later, but for now, you photograph too young."

That was a kindness, saying the reason I should return to New York was because I photographed too young, One agent said it was because I had "mean eyes." Of course my eyes were mean. I was so upset about the six month screen test, my feelings were coming through my eyes.

I wasn't sorry to leave Lotus Land. Back I went to 820 Park Avenue, laden with Hollywood anecdotes, some fabricated, some just stretched for the New York people. The New Yorkers who believed my stories thought I was a big shot. I created wonderful scenarios about how I had told Hollywood where to go and how I turned down a contract. It sounded great, everything the New York stage actor *should* do with all those Hollywood phonies.

Lester arranged a show for me in Bermuda. It was the first job that opened up, a summer stock show that nobody ever heard of before or since. It was a forgettable show called *Stock in Trade* and I was a featured singer.

I boarded a plane with a group of people I had met through past shows and laughed and boozed it up on my way to Bermuda. We stayed at the magnificent estate on Bermuda called Bel Air and life went on, not much different from the way of life had gone on in California's Bel Air just a few weeks before. I shared the manor with five other actors and actresses. The heat was intense and the humidity vicious — we'd lie on our backs on the floor to keep cool and stare a the ceiling where cockroaches carried on interminable battles with spiders. The ceilings were fourteen feet up, but we could see them well enough and kept tally of the battles: Roaches 17, Spiders 15. There was no respite from the humidity which was clinging to us between the rains. Our clothes built up thick mildew and I started checking my armpits and behind my ears for growths. I'd try to combat the humidity by laying my clothes on the railing of the veranda, but they stayed wet no matter what I did.

The show went on for months and we were all good, but so what? What difference could that make in a small review? I was anxious for something new, something more challenging. Nothing was coming up in New York. The sun was nice, but you can only bake your skin for just so long. I had flopped in Hollywood and I wanted to show the world that I was not just a flash in the pan. I needed to get moving again. I had seen where the currents could take you when you had no control over your own career, and this time in Bermuda was becoming seductively similar to my Hollywood days. Time to take things firmly in hand.

Fate stepped in with the person of Charlton Heston, coming to Bermuda to do a production of *Macbeth*. This would be my first step back into the big time, back into the real world of the theater. I would soon discover that it wasn't Shakespeare's *Macbeth* he was doing at all, but Burgess Meredith's version. This would take me out of the real world of the theater and put me into the twilight zone. But all in with good time — first I had to get into the show.

Our show was over by the time Heston arrived. I delayed my trip back to New York to meet him, but then most of the review cast were staying on anyway to soak up some more sun. Heston arrived and checked into the Miriana Hotel next to the theater. I made point of being there the day he arrived, walked up to him, and introduced myself. He made the point of looking at me wide-eyed, not unlike, "Who is this jerk?"

"You don't remember me," I said. ":I met you at a party at Louis Shurr's house with Norma Shearer."

This was not a total lie. We had both been at the same party and I bumped into him once while rushing towards the bathroom. Whether he remembered or not, what was he going to say, no?

"Of course, Michael, how the hell are you?" he asked.

"I'm fine, Chuck," I replied. "Good to see you again. I understand you're doing a great production of *Macbeth*. I have heard wonderful things about it.." I had really not heard anything about it.

"Yes, that's true," he said.

"My show is over now, as you probably know — I've been down here doing the lead in *Stock in Trade*.

"Oh, sure," he said, "know it well."

I smiled. Sure, Chuck, sure. "I'm not really ready to go back to New York yet, so I thought you might be able to use a little help. Why don't you put me in with your show?"

"OK, come around tomorrow and I'll introduce you to Burgess Meredith and Nancy Marchand, our Lady Macbeth," he said.

Bingo.

The next day I met everyone and was given a copy of the script. I flipped though it quickly, expecting to see Shakespeare. *Some* of it was Shakespeare, but much of it was Meredith. Burgess Meredith had rewritten *Macbeth* and created his own version, one that Heston loved. Nancy Marchland was a fine New York stage actress with enormous grace, talent, and integrity. Not only did she not know that the play had been altered before she signed onto the role, but it was beyond her comprehension that anyone would even *think* to rewrite Shakespeare.

"How dare he do that?" she raged. "Had I known, I would have never signed on for the production!" Nancy was to spend the bulk of the show in with a near rage, fuming over the "new" lines she had to speak as Lady Macbeth. It wasn't a problem of learning the lines; it was the bad taste of bastardization that hurt, the desire to say the real words at the last minute — something, anything to heal the hurt of seeing Shakespeare so wounded. There was little left of Shakespeare when Meredith was through with it. He had whittled it down and sucked out the beautiful language. No one was immune to his touch, not even Mason, the Park Avenue Chorus Boy, in with the role of Donalbain, the son of Duncan, the king of Scotland.

Heston brought out the full Paramount wardrobe, trunks full of brocaded satins, furs, and leathers. It looked as if he had taken a giant suction machine and emptied the racks of clothing at both Western Costume and Paramount Studios. Heston's trunk full of costumes arrived in Bermuda and the island tipped sideways because of the weight. They had to change the ballast so we wouldn't slide off into the Atlantic.

The production was extravagant, of course. What else do Hollywood people have to do on stage but be extravagant? There was a cast of 120, an army of 40 men, and 35 horses, which actually tramped across the stage. Sounds crazy until you realize the production was performed at Fort St. George.

Fort St. George, at one end of the island, is an open-air fort, a setting Shakespeare himself would have loved, the almost perfect location for *Macbeth* imaginable. First, the show was performed at night, the darkness casting deep shadows, hiding secrets in with black, gloomy passages. The witches knelt around a true burning fire in with the opening scene, up on a parapet, flames warming their wrinkled cheeks, their voices crackling in with the dark, thrown down shadowy holes to echo against the stones. The doorways were lit with torches, licking the walls and scorching the sky, and scene areas were hit with spotlights. The horses came on with plenty of room to spare and they weren't inhibited in the least — though we had to trudge through horse manure for the rest of the night. The fort was high up over the ocean, which broke on the rocks down the other side of the walls. The wind blew and it was lovely, eerie, and fine. In spite of all the changes that Meredith made, there were great moments: Nancy Marchand and Charlton Heston gave shining performances, the setting was grand, and the mood could turn truly eerie when the winds blew at precisely the right moment during a performance,

They seated three hundred to four hundred people a night in with the bleachers at one end of the fort, facing the ocean. The audience's entrance and exit were through this chamber, down that room, and up the stone stairs, further adding to the spookiness and mystery of that other world that was *Macbeth*. It was breathtaking,

But they had chosen Bermuda for other reasons. Everyone could relax and have a good time while they were there. We rehearsed on the beach, water up to our necks, as mangled Shakespeare carried over the waves. If it was particularly hot, Burgess would take a little stool out in with the water and let the ocean lap around his legs.

Heston and Meredith had many personality clashes and were at it all the time over little things. Heston had an ego that made him think he *was* Macbeth. Every part he took on, he became the character. The New York actors suffered quietly from both the alterations in with the play as well as Hollywood flare-ups between actor and director over the interpretation of the character of Macbeth. Heston learned his lines well, but took his own liberties with the part. Burgess would watch Heston's performance and blow his stack, wanting it done *his* way. After all he *was* the producer, director, and writer.

During one scene I had with Heston, I was to come on and say, "What is amiss?" Heston was to reply, "You are, and do not know't. The spring, the head, the fountain of your blood is stopp'd." No, that was Shakespeare. In Meredith's rewrite, after I say "What is amiss?" Heston then says something like, "You are, the house of Dunisane is afire..." Nonetheless, that evening I was late getting on stage and Heston was left standing there, ad-libbing. He was looking around, wondering where I was, when I realized that I had blown it and ran toward him, hollering "What is amiss?" as I ran. He stage-whispered furiously, "You are, you son of a bitch, you're late!" It was the only humorous side I ever saw to Heston.

Heston and I would walk down the streets of Bermuda and he was often accosted. He was tall, extremely handsome, and women followed him in droves. When an attractive young woman would come up to him and ooze, "Oh, Mr. Heston, Can I have your autograph?" he would reach in his pocket and pull out a picture. He didn't smile or say hello, he just handed her the picture which had "Best wishes, Charlton Heston," written on it. He went right on walking, and by the time the poor girl knew what happened, he was a block away.

*Macbeth* ended. I returned to New York in the middle of October. Lester said there still wasn't much to do, but *Wonderful Town* was coming after the first of the year and I would audition for that. I took a deep sigh and looked around me, wondering if I wanted to spend autumn in New York. I could play the Park Avenue Chorus Boy. I could go back to El Morocco and the Stork Club. I could start a new love affair, take classes and singing lessons, and just generally keep in shape for the *Wonderful Town* auditions. I could walk the streets of New York in the evening, drink too much, dance until some ungodly hour, then make love and sleep till noon.

I decided to sail on the S.S. Argentina to Buenos Aires.

# CHAPTER EIGHT
## Cry For Me, Argentina

The S.S. Argentina was part of the Moore-McCormick Line, sister ship of the S.S. Brazil, and one of the classiest tour ships afloat. The Argentina made a 34-day cruise from New York to Buenos Aries, stopping in Trinidad, Barbados, and Rio de Janeiro.

I had stumbled blindly into things plenty of times, luck turning ordinary circumstances into bonanzas. But luck was usually a step apart, a bold flash of intuition that picks the three money horses at the Kentucky Derby for all the wrong reasons. Taking this cruise was more than luck; it had the clean cold taste of irony to it, mixed with the awkward sensation of destiny. The plain and simple fact is, I met a woman. I had never seen her before, did not know who she was, and therefore couldn't know she would be sailing on the Argentina the same time I was.

But she knew me and had known me for some time. It was a few days later when I found that out, when she realized I was on board, she arranged for us to meet that first night at the Captain's table. It would have worked brilliantly, a master stroke of subtlety, to be introduced casually by the Captain. I was far too busy being seasick, heaving my guts over the rail, then falling back into the deck chair to wait for the next lurch. We moved out of Long Island Sound that night into the Atlantic Ocean, where it was cold and choppy. I was un-elegant, ghostly green in my cashmere coat and scarf. The chief purser and two sailors hauled me out of the lounge chair in the middle of the night; I was freezing to death as my empty gut tried to relieve me of the dry lining of my stomach. I missed her dinner party and ruined her surprise.

The following night the sea was calmer and so was my gut. I had managed to swallow fractional amounts of food on and off during the day and was becoming quite the pro by supper time. I was the recipient of numerous warm, friendly, clever remarks like, "Why, Michael, what a fast learner — you look like you've been using a fork all of your life," and "Gee, Mike, don't worry about cleaning your plate. . . " I sat at the Captain's table and took the comments with a pasted-on grin, secretly noting the offenders' names for later extermination.

She entered. She was nineteen years old, a blinding sight in diamonds and sapphires, violet gown with violet eyes to match, framed with a two rows of long eyelashes. A small, sculptured body. God, only nineteen. She burst into my head with bells and whistles. A creature of true beauty. "Captain," I said, leaning left, "who is that woman?"

"Ah, Mr. Mason," he confided, "that is Maria Estelita"

"You may find this a bit odd, but do me the favor of introducing me. In fact, if you were to do it right now, I can't say that I'd mind. I would like very much to meet this Maria Estelita," I said.

"Very well, Mr. Mason," he said. Surely at that moment there was a twinkle in his eye, but I would have missed it anyway, as I stared, entranced by Maria.

A note on love at first sight: it doesn't exist, never happens, not to anyone... that's what they will tell you, and they tell you that because it's never happened to them. Well, let me tell you that they're wrong. I know it happens, because I lived it, sailing on the S.S. Argentina, on the way to Buenos Aires, gazing at Maria. It was love at first, second, and third sight. I was stung with Cupid's arrow, struck and stupefied.

The captain introduced us, calling me Mr. Mason. I asked her to dance so we could be away from everyone else and I could

## Cry for Me, Argentina

talk to her alone. The orchestra was playing a slow number, and she moved effortlessly into my arms. I was pleased with her directness and said so.

"Thank you," she said, "but you will find me even more direct that you would expect, Michael."

I pulled back and looked at her. "How did you know my first name? The Captain didn't mention it," I said.

She smiled the first of her many devilish smiles and said, "I've been following your career."

Instant panic. Where had I met her before, what shameful thing had I been doing, what trouble had I gotten into then, and what trouble was I getting into now?

"What do you mean you have been following my career?" I asked, waiting for the bomb to go off.

"You intrigued me. You are very handsome, you know. But perhaps I am being too forward? Perhaps you don't like pushy women?"

"No, no, not at all," I said, "please be pushy."

"I was in the audience when your fly was open," she said, matter-of-factly.

Boom, there it was. "I see," I managed. It was worse that I had imagined. I quickly tried to think up an excuse.

"Yes," she said, "I saw you in *Gentlemen Prefer Blondes,* but that was only the first time. I saw your nightclub act at Number One on Fifth Avenue twice, and then I saw you in *Make a Wish.* My bodyguard didn't like *Make a Wish* very much, though."

"Why didn't you tell me?" I asked.

"I thought your feelings would be hurt to know my bodyguard hated the show," she replied.

"No, I mean introduce yourself. Why didn't you come up to me?"

"I couldn't. I am seldom away from my duenna," she said.

South American women of a certain class always have a duenna with them, an elderly female companion who keeps them in line. Maria also had a bodyguard because of the wealth and political prestige of her family.

"Your gladiator costume was very cute, you know. Your silver cape with the red inside. You were gorgeous."

A small crack of dawn broke over the gray matter of my brain. "So you liked me in that. . ." came out from my mouth.

"Oh, yes," she sighed. "Did you make a wish?"

And then the dawn became a full symphony of enlightenment and I knew who she was. "You, it was you?"

She nodded.

"You sent the car!"

She smiled. "Well, I had to do something, Michael."

"But isn't a car a little extravagant?" I asked.

"Certainly not. It was very cheap, that American car. Only a little more than pocket money for a day in New York." She smiled. "I didn't go hungry, I can assure you. Remember where I come from, Michael."

"Where?" I asked. "Argentina, you mean? Buenos Aires?"

"You do not know? The Captain did not tell you?" she inquired.

"Not exactly," I confessed.

"I cannot say too much, but we are related to the ruling family."

"The Perons?" I asked.

She nodded.

More enlightenment, What I didn't know then, she filled in later. Here was a woman who was part of a rich, powerful family and she was practically a prisoner to her duenna and bodyguard. She went to New York many times with the family and stayed in an apartment at the Waldorf Towers. Maria could go the theater as long as her duenna and bodyguard were along. When she actually became attracted to someone in the show, she was forced to hide her excitement from everyone. She sat in the theater, wanting to scream out her ardor, wanting to turn to the person beside her, wanting to point and giggle. But she was Maria Estelita and no one must know, so she surpressed her schoolgirl crush and sent me a car instead.

"Why didn't you leave a note in the glove compartment of something?" I asked.

"I couldn't," she said. "I was never allowed out alone."

I wanted to ask her how she managed to choose the car, pay for it, and have it delivered if she wasn't out alone. I decided to save those questions for later. I didn't think of those questions again until it was much later, and by then it was too late.

We swayed to the music in silence, her hips pressing gently against mine, her fingers curling a lock of my hair at the collar. My body went electric through her small, delicate touches. My nerve endings were screaming with a stinging raw energy, clashing with her cool assured persona. She moved her fingers to my ear lobe and touched it in a way that was so innocent, yet so devastatingly sexual, that I pulled her close and tight and kissed her hard on her lips. She gasped, but didn't struggle. Then came another rush of enlightenment, and I realized that with a bodyguard and a duenna, she was still a virgin.

In time our mouths moved apart and I saw the dream in her eyes. She lay her head up in the crook of my neck and we wove ourselves together, swaying to the music. Where I stopped and where she began was indistinguishable. Ecstasy was a shallow pool compared to my pleasure that night.

"We have to get away alone," I said to her.

"That will be difficult," she said. "But not impossible. I looked around and saw both her bodyguard and duenna watching us like emotionless cats, following us with their eyes, ready to pounce on a single missed beat. "Although perhaps tougher than I thought," she confessed.

We danced together again and again that night, and I fell more deeply in love as each breath passed between us. And then it came to me, the simplicity of it astounding me — why hadn't I thought about it instantly?

"Maria, I would like to meet your parents," I said.

"What?" she asked as if I were insane.

"Set it up for tomorrow afternoon. We'll have drinks," I said confidently.

We parted that evening with little more than a slight, promising kiss. I did not sleep at all that night, my body and soul yearning for her.

Waiting for four o'clock the next day was like waiting for reviews after opening night. I was filled with a mixture of dread and ecstasy. I spent the day wandering the sun deck, practicing my most impressive stories, and testing my voice so it didn't rise above a soprano. I worried that I had misinterpreted Maria, that by now she would have forgotten me and was meeting new handsome young passengers and they would be sitting in deck chairs sipping hot chocolate and holding hands. "Enough, Michael," I told myself, "don't torture yourself."

Four o'clock came and went. No Maria. 4:10. I practiced crossing my legs. Ankle over knee. Knee over knee. 4:15. Spot on the trousers. Precious seconds to wipe it off. Then wait again.

They entered and came over to my table, Maria leading. All the strength in my soul overcame my desire to take her into my arms. I put on my most gracious, most sincere, most Aunt Suzanne manners and greeted them warmly. I could see that my initial appearance, my dress, and my manners sold me to her father. Somehow I had expected it to be the other way around, with her mother easier to win over than the father. Maria introduced me as Michael Mason of Virginia and Park Avenue. They didn't act impressed, but they didn't seem disturbed either. Nothing was mentioned about Broadway or my shows. As far as they were concerned, I was a rich young man travelling alone because I needed a rest.

I made an excuse to go to the bar, giving them a chance to make initial comments to Maria and each other. I told the waitress to come over in a few minutes and to put the drinks on my tab. I returned to the table and deliberately sat next to Maria's mother. I knew this was the big test. Mothers are always looking for something wrong with the young men their daughters fall in love with. You can never be sure what, it is always something obscure they find wrong, something that they learned the hard way, long ago, with the first man they ever loved. Mothers always remember that one thing, and look for it in other young men. If I showed her one thing, it had better be a good thing.

The cocktail waitress came over. Should I order liquor or play the teetotaler? What type of woman was Maria's mother? Surely in Argentine society she had seen it all. But did the party life sicken her or amuse her? I went with my instincts.

"If no one minds, I thought we might order some tea," I said.

I turned to look at Maria's mother, and her expression gave nothing away. I moved closer to her and took a big risk. I said intimately, in a stage whisper, "It's very early for champagne, wouldn't you say?"

That did it. The frost melted and she smiled, inched closer to me and said in her own whisper, "I always wait until six o'clock for champagne."

I could see that Maria was impressed and I knew I would get along magnificently with her parents. We talked until six o'clock and then ordered a bottle of Dom Perignon. We parted to change for dinner and reunited at eight o'clock.

After dinner Maria and I were told that if we would like to leave them and go for a walk on deck in the moonlight un-escorted that it would be all right. We excused ourselves with much graciousness, calmly walked away from the table, and scooted out the door as fast as we could. As we left the dining room hand in hand, for the first time that night, I dared to admire her black chiffon dress and her diamonds and emeralds.

We went out into the cool misty evening to be alone for the first time. There was a rainbow ring around the moon from the mist, which dewed on Maria's face. We held hands for the entire walk up to the empty sun deck, stood apart from each other, and admired each other. Suddenly and simultaneously, we magnetically fell into each others arms and kissed deeply.

The kiss began somewhere passing the coast of South Carolina. When we finally came up for air, we were opposite Fort Lauderdale. She told me she was a virgin, which I had previously assumed. I took a worried step away from her. Was she telling me not to go any further? Her hands took my hands and brought them to her breasts. I felt awkward even though *she* was the virgin. She seemed to have control over the moment. Her fingers ran down my sides, down my hips, and brushed against my crotch. I was dying.

The ship doctor is a very social fellow. It is part of his role. All ships make sure that they hire attractive medical help. Many a young woman travelling alone will make a point to have a medical complaint in order to see the good doctor.

It took me a while to locate the doctor and figure out his game on board the ship. Maria and I needed a place where we could be alone. It had to be secure, because I wanted to be with her for a long time in order to do things right. We couldn't use her stateroom, that was clear, unless we wanted her duenna and bodyguard to join in. We also couldn't use my stateroom in case somebody saw us going in or coming out.

After a few days watching the doctor making his house calls, I had a thought. There was one woman in particular he would see every day for long periods of time. It was Mata Monteria, the flamenco dancer who did a show every night. She had been in Hollywood as a stand-in for Rita Hayworth. She and the doctor were a couple. I figured out my approach to him. I went up to him late in the afternoon the third day as he sat at the bar. I sat beside him and ordered a drink. He raised his eyebrows and said, "So, young man, I see you have quickly made a conquest."

I laughed good naturedly and waved it off. "Ah, but not one as wise and experienced as yours."

His expression changed. "Mine?" he asked.

"But I'm a discreet fellow," I said.

"There is nothing to be discreet about, my friend," he said, leaning forward, "How did you find out?"

I shrugged. "I've noticed that you rarely use your cabin."

"You have been coming to my cabin?" he asked.

"No, no, you don't understand. Maria and I need a place to go. Since you are rarely in your cabin, we thought perhaps we could . . . "

The doctor threw his head back and laughed. "All you had to do was ask. You didn't need to learn my secrets," he said.

I shrugged. "I like to protect my flank."

We made an arrangement to use his cabin whenever he wasn't there. Generally that entailed finding him somewhere on board the ship, getting his key and going there. We rather liked the arrangement, since it made us feel mischievous.

I got his key and went off to find Maria. She was on the promenade deck, wearing white chiffon, leaning over the railing looking forward. The wind whipped at her face and threw her hair back behind her. I stood and looked at her for a while, unwilling to intrude on her mood, her concentration. She was so lovely and free in that pose, freshly tousled in the breeze, young and mysterious in chiffon. Then she let go of her scarf and it flew back to me into my hands. She turned to run after it and there I was.

"Oh, Michael, there you are. Did you catch it? It must mean something," she said.

"It does. You didn't lose your scarf," I said.

"You are so romantic," she teased.

I sniffed the perfume on the scarf. "Very nice."

She took the scarf from me and tied it back around her neck. "And very expensive," she added.

"As much as my car?" I asked.

"Nearly."

I held the key up in the air. She grabbed it, ran for the door and started clattering down the metal stairs. I had already told her about my plan with the good doctor. I ran after her as she laughed and turned down the corridor to the "B" deck. I was close behind, but not in any hurry to catch up. When I turned down the corridor to the doctor's cabin, she was already there with the key in the lock. I walked slowly down the hallway as she got it open, squealed with glee, and slammed the door shut behind her. I made a fast grab to catch the door, but I was too late. I didn't want to make a scene in the hallway, so I knocked lightly. "Maria, Open the door please," I said.

I heard her say something inside but it was muffled and I couldn't make it out. "Maria, come on, open up. There are people walking out here."

A fellow in a riding outfit turned the corner, saw me at the door, looked confused, and then went back the way he came. I stood away from the door and tried to look nonchalant. When he was gone, I was quickly back at the door.

"Maria," I pleaded, "don't play games."

"In a minute, Michael, just be patient." Then she laughed. "Patient. In the doctor's cabin," she said. She loved to make silly jokes.

I leaned against the wall, starting to get angry waiting.. Then the door opened a crack. I pushed the door wide open.

I had never seen the inside of the doctor's cabin before. It was enormous — his bedroom on one side with a large double bed, his examining room on the other side with and examining table and other medical paraphernalia. Maria had turned the lights down low and was standing barefoot, wearing one of the doctor's white jackets. I knew she had nothing on underneath. A stethoscope was around her neck and she was twirling the end in a circle in front of her.

"Close the door, Michael," she said.

I did.

"Now, she said, still twirling the stethoscope, what seems to be the problem?" she asked.

I reached for her waist. "You seem to be the problem. I can't get enough of you."

She slipped out of my grasp and turned towards the examining table. "Very interesting," she said, "sit up here."

I was confused. What was she doing? Playing "doctor?" I hadn't played "doctor" since I was eight years old. "Maria... " I said, a little frustrated.

"You want to be difficult? I'll call my bodyguard in, and he can help you to understand."

I smiled. "All right. I'll sit up there." I sat down on the table. She came closer and I reached for her again.

"I'm afraid you'll have to control yourself, Mr. Mason. The examination hasn't taken place yet," she chided.

This was the damndest way to lose your virginity I had ever seen. "OK, OK, I'll be good, don't sweat it." I figured she could lose it any way she pleased.

"All right, take your shoes and socks off," she demanded.

I undid my shoes and dropped them on the floor, and then removed my socks.

"And while you are at it," she said, "why don't you also take off your jacket and shirt."

I took off the jacket and shirt, too.

She came closer. She put the stethoscope against my chest. It was freezing cold.

"Hey!" I exclaimed.

"Calm down, Mr. Mason, the examination has just begun," she said. As she moved the stethoscope around my chest, she started undoing my belt buckle.

"Would you like some help?" I offered.

"Oh, no, this is normal procedure." She finished with the buckle, unclasped my pants, and started to unbutton me. Suddenly she tugged at the pants and shorts and then they were off.

"Oh," she said, "I recognize this little fellow, hmmmm, not so little anymore. Well, now I think we can definitely go on with the examination.

"Oh, really?" I asked. "I think it's almost over."

She pushed me back on the table and sat beside me. She decided to listen to the beat of my rising sun with the stethoscope and I managed to finally get at the buttons on the doctor's coat. It was much too large for her anyway.

The coat came away and she sat there only wearing the stethoscope. I took a deep breath and looked at her. She was exquisite. She had done a lot of athletics, which was obvious in her skin tone and the quality of her muscles, but not so much as to ruin her delicate shape. Her legs were slightly muscular and firm. Her breasts were large and firm and I wanted to suffocate inside of them. She placed her hands on my chest and leaned over to kiss me. Her breasts nestled against my chest, and I put my arm around her to press her hard against me. We kissed, without ending the kiss, I moved up around her, got my feet on the floor, carried her across the room, stethoscope still around her neck, and laid her down on the bed. I took off the stethoscope and threw it across the room, landing on the examination table. Then I turned all my attention to her.

She took to sex like a fire takes to the forest. There was nothing bashful about Maria and her pleasure. She embodied total abandon and we rocked the double bed more than the Atlantic Ocean was wont to do. The day closed over us and we lay quietly together afterwards, the sweat cooling our bodies.

I was in deep trouble now. There were only 30 days left in the cruise before she would leave the ship and it would be too hard to say good bye.

Maria took great joy in escaping from first class. Her world was made up of black ties and bodyguards, dinner dresses and duennas, and I came to realize that this cruise was one of the rare times she ever had fun. She never escaped the eyes of the duennas and bodyguards long enough to play — she had not yet experienced what life had to offer. I felt like a surgeon, restoring sight to a blind goddess, then being the first face she sees when her eyes open.

She'd slip down to her room and change into something casual, a pair of slacks and a blouse, and then hide her clothes with a flowing evening cape. Her bodyguard and duenna figured we were just out walking on deck. I would meet her at the other end of the ship by the second class lounge, and there we would dance and hoot and holler and carry on with all the other kids that were travelling on board ship for vacation. Those were the best times, when we were down there and played with what Maria called "the peasants." She loved it because she was escaping, a young bird testing her wings and flying out of the giant tree whose branches protected her. Of course her family thought she was safe. She was on board ship, she was with me, she was out dancing in the first class area near the pool. Little did they know we were downstairs in tourist class, having a ball.

We "officially" met Mata Monteria and the doctor there. We used the doctor's cabin frequently; he was using Mata's cabin. Mata was a hot-blooded Spaniard with innumerable charms, none of them lost on me. I got to be good friends with her, and years later, met her under unusual circumstances. I was in Beverly Hills in a movie theater watching a comedy and I was laughing like hell. A woman came walking up the aisle in the dark and put her hand on my shoulder.

"Excuse me, it's very dark in here, but that laugh could only belong to one person. You are Michael Mason, are you not?"

"Yes," I said, "who are you?"

"Mata Monteria, darling," she answered.

I leapt up and gave her a big hug in the aisle. Movie patrons were yelling "Quiet! Sit down! Take it out to the lobby!" So we did, walking out in the middle of the movie.

Maria wasn't oblivious to Mata's charms either. When Mata was around, Maria would press close against my side and squeeze my hand.

Maria's joy, escaping from first class to join second class society tripled during the ship's costume party. Maria decided we would slip down to second class for a while without letting her duenna and bodyguard know. This would be tricky because it wasn't like just going for a walk. The duenna and bodyguard would be at the costume party watching over us like a couple of hungry hawks. But she had a plan, of course; Maria always had a plan.

She was costumed as a Spanish girl in a black dress with a black mask and veil hanging off her Spanish hat. Her entire costume was accentuated by a diamond bracelet and necklace. I wandered in with her and greeted the captain and his staff, who were welcoming guests in a receiving line. Her duenna and bodyguard were close behind us and they moved over to a couple of chairs at the edge of the action. I felt for them — the duenna was an old woman, long ago resigned to the fact that although this job was a great rise in station for her, her payment for the job was to maintain a serious demeanor. The bodyguard was a young man, and fun was not far from his thoughts. I saw his foot tapping to the music. He wanted to dance — he already had his costume: the gangster look.

Maria and I wandered into the maze of costumed people. We were surrounded by clowns in red, yellow, and black wigs, magicians, devils, and witches. Younger women with curves wore the least clothing possible. All the costumes were magnificent, elaborate, and expensive, brought from home, planned well in advance of the cruise. I had hopped on board at the last minute — spur-of-the-moment Mason — and hadn't arranged for a costume. I went as a doctor, a costume not too difficult to procure given my proximity to the ship doctor's closet. Maria found the person she was looking for, another first class woman about her size, wearing a peasant outfit.

"Michael, wait here just a moment," she said. She and the woman went off together and I watched them go into the ladies' lounge. A few minutes later they were back. The peasant girl took my arm. "Let's go," she said.

"Beg your pardon?" I asked, moving to the other Maria in the Spanish outfit. "Sorry, honey, this dance is already taken."

The peasant girl squeezed my arm. "Michael, it's me. Come on, we're going to second class."

I watched the Spanish woman disappear into the crowd and saw the bodyguard, foot still tapping, looking after her. I looked at the peasant girl on my arm, in a little ratty and beat up costume, and saw my Maria's eyes under the mask.

"I think it will work if you fooled me," I said, "but aren't you worried about one thing? What about the diamond necklace and bracelet?"

"What is she going to do? Throw them overboard? Come on, don't worry about it. If she throws them overboard, she'll have to go overboard after them," she said.

"It might be worth it to her," I said.

Maria dragged me away.

Down in second class the party was considerably different. First class was demure and the people were more intoxicated with their costumes than with alcohol. Second class was wild. In many cases, no one cared whom the person danced with or kissed was. The music was loud, the dancing frenetic, and the costumes were much crazier, more inconsistent, and not always identifiable as a specific person or profession. Second class costumes were cut and pasted together, relying more on makeup and glitter, pulling odd pieces of clothing together to make whatever costume could be made. We were four decks below the first class party on "A" deck; second class was on "D" deck and it was there that the fun was happening.

We moved through the ruckus and found our way outside. People were shooting off rockets, and flares crashed and gleamed. We carried our drinks away from the mayhem, wandered in between lifeboats, found a quieter spot and sat down. I looked over and saw, a few feet from us, a completely naked couple. They had obviously thrown their clothes overboard in a fit of passion. She was on her back and he was on top of her, grinding away. They moved to the rhythm of the music, and she had her eyes wide open, watching the fireworks explode over her head.

I turned to Maria and said, "I hope this isn't her first time, because if it is, she's going to expect fireworks every time, and is she ever going to be disappointed."

Maria laughed and the man looked up and said, "What's so damn funny?" The woman kept looking at the sky.

"You'll never know," I said. I grabbed Maria's hand and we headed to a quieter place.

We refilled our glasses and settled by the pool. Near us were two men, one in a sailor costume and one in a baseball outfit, who were sitting at a table eating spaghetti and meatballs from a large bowl. They were drunk as lords, putting down beers as fast as their throats would open to let the brew flow in. As they drank, the spaghetti slopped over them, turning their clothes redder and redder. Pretty soon they started discarding clothing soaked with tomato sauce, dropping them on the deck. More drinking, more spaghetti, more stained clothing. Before long, they were down to nothing, stark naked slurping spaghetti and guzzling beers.

Then the one who had been a sailor looked at the other man and saw that he was naked and free of the spaghetti sauce, so he dug his hand into the bowl and slapped some on the baseball player's body. The baseball player smiled, scooped sauce out of the bowl and did the same. Pretty soon these two naked men were not naked at all, they were totally gooped up with spaghetti sauce, meatballs on their shoulders, long white strands of noodles hanging off their noses, their elbows, and their penises. The spaghetti men laughed, turned and leapt into the swimming pool.

That was it for Maria. She no longer wanted to stay in the second class party. I took her back to the first class party, where she changed back into her Spanish outfit with the diamonds and spent the rest of the evening on my arm, staying near the duenna and bodyguard.

The costumes that everyone brought doubled for carnival in Rio. I knew Rio was going to be a fun, amusing place and I wanted to be totally ready for it. The ego of Michael Mason came bursting out all over. I wanted the best suntan I could muster because we were going to the Copacabana Beach Hotel and wear white dinner jackets. I went to the uppermost roost on the highest deck on the ship on the day we crossed the equator. I had the baby oil and iodine going, wearing only bikini shorts. I fell asleep. The entire left side of my body, from head to toe, was completely burned. I ended up in bed for two days recuperating from a fever of 103 degrees.

I recovered in time to see the most beautiful harbor in the world, Rio de Janeiro, Brazil. The one-hundred foot Christ statue on top of Corcovado Mountain stood two thousand feet over the bay, arms outstretched, the sun hitting it, the shadow of the cross was falling across the water as the ship's bow cut through it. Maria and I were given free reign in Rio and I hired a limousine and chauffeur. We did the town right, with her bodyguard following in another car.

We left Rio and moved into the last leg of the trip, to Buenos Aires, and we knew the end was coming. I had reservations at the Plaza Hotel and she lived near there, but we knew once we got to Argentina, it was going to be over. We were so much in love that I almost proposed, but I knew it was an impossible situation. She was Argentinian and a Catholic; I was a New York Protestant. That really meant nothing to me, but it was important to her family. Add to that her social position, then mix in her age, and there was nothing to discuss. We could not get married.

The last days on board ship it was harder to get away from everyone. We had made too many friends and everyone wanted to socialize. We could find little time alone. We looked for breaks in conversations to slip away to the doctor's cabin for one last embrace, one more intimate kiss, one more tender bout of love making. But each time was tougher and tougher to get away. The last time, we finally ran away from a crowd of people as the boat was about to dock.

When we arrived in Buenos Aires, I was invited to a party hosted by Maria's father for the Perons. To this day I am not sure how Maria's family was affiliated with Peron's government. I knew her father was a relative of some sort, was closely allied with Peron and had an estate which was a great deal like a European palace. This was the zenith of Peron's power as dictator, and Eva Peron was still alive, with great power of her own. There were soldiers with bare bayonets on every street corner of Buenos Aires, including the front of the Plaza Hotel. The rich in Argentina were super-rich and the poor were dirt-poor. It was something I couldn't adjust to. I was brought up in a country with many levels in the class system, but the differences in America are just not carried to such extremes.

For Juan Peron to come to a party given by Maria's father meant that her father was extremely important. To give you a feel for the size of the estate, they had twenty-four full-time gardeners for the hundreds of acres spanning the estate, magnificent pools and guest houses, two tennis courts, a huge horse stable, and forty-five servants on staff around the clock. I could only begin to imagine the way the Perons lived in the Royal Palace.

About an hour after the party began, there was a hush that sifted through the crowd, then great fanfare and flourish as Juan and Eva Peron entered. She looked like an empress, beautiful, laden with jewels and white satin.

It was a fully formal event — women in full-skirted evening gowns, great music, with wonderful waltzes. It reminded me of the American South before the Civil War. The ballroom was easily twice the size of the ballroom of the Beverly Wilshire Hotel in Los Angeles, and much more lavish. These galas were given once every two weeks. The butlers and footmen acted as waiters and wore black tie and tails.

Maria walked me over to where the Perons were and introduced me as a member of New York society. Juan Peron and I made small talk about New York and Rio de Janeiro. Eva was at his elbow, as she was at all times. There wasn't a word spoken to or by him that she wasn't privileged to hear, and she would interject if she felt it was necessary. She was a strong woman.

She said to me, with a glint in her eyes, "I'm sure you have made Maria very happy." She had been a singer and dancer before she married Juan Peron, and I was dying to return the glint in her eyes with one of my own and tell her what my real background had been, but of course I did not. Nonetheless, she saw two attractive kids just off the boat after a romantic cruise together, and she knew damn well what we had been up to. Maria was grinning ear to ear as she and Eva communicated silently. Juan Peron and I continued to make small talk about cities we had been in and the respective weather, and then Maria and I moved on.

A few days later the S.S. Argentina was ready to leave. We had to say good bye. There were no more places to go, to hide and be alone, to kiss and make love. It was all over except for the waiting, the separation, those last desperate, anxious moments, staring at each other, making wishes.

I left her that last night. I returned alone to the ship, which was to sail at midnight. I told her not to come down and see me off, but as the ship eased away from the dock, I moved up and down the railing, searching through the faces of waving people, pushing other passengers aside, desperate to see her smile again. We pulled further away from the dock and I moved progressively to the stern, then stood alone, staring at the lights growing small. An enormous black limousine with a motorcycle escort screeched onto the dock. Maria threw open her door and ran to the edge of the dock. She raced along it to the last plank and stood there. I saw her take her scarf off her head, the one I had caught on deck the first time we made love. She held the fluttering scarf in her hand, then set it free. It drifted away from her, off the dock, into the water. She just stood there watching the ship disappear. I never knew why she arrived so late, too late for a proper good bye.

It took a long time to get over her. My father had told me years before, "Never let possessions possess you."

Maria and I didn't correspond. We had decided that it was best not to.

The ship without her was terrible. The doctor held my head and poured brandy down my throat. Then the brandy turned to tears and ran down my cheeks. The doctor became a very good friend.

I left the ship when we arrived in Rio. I was becoming an insufferable bore, drinking and moaning about losing my Maria. I went into nightclubs and sang sad, lonely love songs, and made the other patrons cry. I was in good voice, but it did me no good. One night I sang at the Gloria Hotel, and the midst of a quiet song, there was a hooting from the back of the room.

"Boo! Hiss! Rotten, stinks terrible, awful! Get him off!"

I recognized that voice and stopped my song in the middle, running to the back of the room.

"Don!" I cried. Good old eighty million dollar Don. My old pal. He was in Rio on his private yacht.

I hitched a ride back with him to the Bahamas, then flew to New York, spending the last of my blubbering days over Maria, at sea. When I got back to New York, I was through sniffling. I was ready to go back to work and New York was ready for me. *Wonderful Town* was about to be cast.

# PART II

# A Serious Kind of Guy

# CHAPTER NINE
## Bravo, Michael

Back on Broadway! I was home — I came back with some experience under my belt, a little wisdom under my hat, and a touch of extra weight in my heart. Time to knuckle down, get a little serious, and make a little headway. I was tanned after the succession of sun situations: California, Bermuda, and South America. I would now pale under the indoor lights of Broadway; the makeup and the cold cream stripped away layers of lovely bronzed skin.

They cast me in *Wonderful Town*.

First the vital statistics: *Wonderful Town* was adapted from the play, *My Sister, Eileen*. Lehman Engel was conducting, Rosalind Russell was starring, and Edie Adams was Eileen. The story concerned two sisters from Ohio who come to the big city, find a basement apartment, and deal with New Yorkers for the first time in their lives.

I was hired to understudy Jordan Bentley in the part of a football player, a part called "The Wreck." It was an ambiguous situation for me, where on the one hand I hoped to go on and be discovered; on the other, I dreaded the idea of doing Jordan's part in front of other people. I was badly miscast. I didn't look anything like a football player. I was lean, trim, and had none of the bulk needed to fill in the gap between actor and role.

In the limited rehearsing I got to do, my comedy scenes were good, the song was easy (and stupid — "I can pass that football"), while the numbers with the chorus were great. The big question was this: how do you play football without a little natural brawn? With any luck, I'd hang out backstage of the show, doing walk-ons here and there and filling in with the chorus. I felt, just wait till the next show; in the next show I would be cast right, understudying a kind, but unlucky actor who would conveniently come down with a debilitating yet harmless disease on the night the critics would be in the audience just waiting, no, just *itching* to discover a brand new star...but not in this show. Lord help me if that ever happened on *this* show.

So, wouldn't you know it, Jordan Bentley went out to play handball one morning, fell, and twisted his knee. He was out, he couldn't walk. That afternoon the stage manager called and said, "This is it, Mason. Jordan hurt his leg and you are going on tonight!"

I never even had a complete run-through. I didn't know what the hell I was doing. The nervous wreck had to play a football wreck because Jordan's knee was wrecked.

I got to the theater in the early afternoon, waiting for Rosalind so we could rehearse before the night's performance. She didn't care a damn who was the understudy for anyone but herself, Edie Adams, and the leading man, George Gaynes. What made things worse was that I already had two strikes against me with Roz. My limo was always parked behind hers and mine was bigger. Roz didn't like that at all. She would fly in bitching, "Who's damn limousine is parked behind mine?"

"Michael Mason's, dear."

"Who is that damned Michael Mason?" she demanded.

"The Park Avenue Chorus Boy, dear," came the reply.

"The Park Avenue *what*?"

It drove her nuts.

That afternoon, with Jordan out of the picture, Roz wreaked her revenge. She was called in for an emergency rehearsal to do the comedy scenes with Edie Adams and me. I was running through my song with Lehman Engel when she breezed in.

"All right, all right, where's the understudy? Lets get this thing over with. Run the lines, run the lines! I have things to do!" she bellowed.

She took one look at me with my mouth open and Lehman's baton in the air and said, "Oh, my god. *He's* the understudy? The Park Avenue Playboy? *That* is supposed to be a football player? Tennis, yes, but football? Never!"

I wanted to melt away, day-old ice cream on a sunny sidewalk. In fact I wished it was already the next day and it was all over and I was safely in my grave, buried under a pile of bad reviews. I realized that I looked less like a football player that day than I ever had before, standing in the middle of the stage in a T-shirt, a pair of shorts, and tennis shoes. She really messed me up psychologically.

Diana Herbert, who played the wreck's wife in the show, a talented and kind person, turned to me and said, "Hey, ignore her. Roz is an infamous bitch, so just ignore her." Sure. Ignore her if you can. Mr. Nervous was going on stage in front of an audience without doing a complete run-through of the show beforehand. Diana was the only person holding me up emotionally.

I was in a daze all day. I came out of it smack dab in the middle of the performance, on stage, while singing my song ("I can pass that football... ") I looked out over the footlights at the audience and thought, "My God, I'm actually singing at the Winter Garden Theater in front of 1,000 people — this is fantastic!"

I stopped singing so I could get a better look at all of them. The chorus caught on right away, and picked up where I had paused in the song. Sensing that something was wrong, Lehman looked up. He saw what had happened, threw his baton in the air, turned his back to the stage, and looked out at the audience, which got a big chuckle. I walked forward a few steps with a dumb grin on my face and got a better look at the theater and its customers. Two lines further into the song, I noticed I wasn't singing and picked up the lyrics from the chorus. I had been thinking, "Hey, Shirley MacLaine came in as an understudy in the *Pajama Game* and walked out a star — why not me?" I figured I would go from *Wonderful Town* into doing the lead for my own show.

I forgot to look down at my frame, the ex-football jock. I just didn't look like a stumbling, bumbling guy that couldn't do anything but block, punt, and tackle. I did the part for about a week and a half in Jordan's place. But I did it well. I proved my professionalism by stepping into the role and performing admirably, after that first night, that is. I didn't get any general recognition for it, but I had gained the credibility and respect of my peers. The Chorus Boy stepped in, took over, and was *good*, singing and acting for ten days on Broadway. I carried it off so well, I was later given a role in *Fanny* with Ezio Pinza and Walter Slezak. I was no longer just some jerk in a limousine. Once I overcame the two-line botching of my song, the audience rallied around me and expressed their support through their applause.

Roz's revenge was not so sweet. I found out later that Roz was greatly disliked by many, many people because of her temper and her star mentality. Granted, she had been a big star in Hollywood, but when she came to New York, she and Freddie Brisson, her husband, desperately needed a hit. She got it with *Wonderful Town*.

One night I gave a party at 820 Park Ave. I had created some enemies along the way, as everyone does, and one of them crawled out of the woodwork that night. This particular fellow, a dancer in another show, stood in my living room, at my party, surrounded by a group of my guests, and made wise-ass comments about me.

"This Mason, this Park Avenue Chorus Boy with a limousine, who the hell is he kidding?" he said. "All this family money is probably just a load of bullshit. He's being kept by some old woman or maybe some old man — he's been seen with a lot of them — old women and men. He's probably gay, too."

Roz overheard this and didn't like it. She was a notorious hater of gays, but no matter what this fellow had to say about me, she disliked his style. She came over to me and said, "Michael, who is that mouth over there? I really resent the way he's talking, and he's talking about *you*, saying ugly things."

"Oh?" I said.

I walked over to him to hear this intruder at my party. Roz followed and I sensed her standing behind me, waiting to see what I would do. I heard the dancer say, "Mason's just another gypsy, a chorus boy who got lucky through somebody. His family doesn't have money, it's all a bunch of bullshit. He's being kept, he's a faggot..."

"Hey," I said, "what is your name?"

He told me.

"How well do you know Mike Mason?" I asked.

"Very well, I have been around him a lot," he replied.

"Really? Well, I'm Mike Mason, you asshole, and let me tell you something and hear me well. I don't care what *you* think of me, I don't care whether you think I want boys or girls — all I know is that you don't fit into either category. So get the hell out of here."

While everyone else applauded, Roz stepped forward and said, "Bravo, Michael." A major victory for me.

Unfortunately there were only a few moments of Roz Russell straying from her image. It wasn't long before she was back in bitch mode. At Christmas time she did something that no one had ever seen done by a star of a Broadway show. In those days, she was probably making $5,000 a week, no small peanuts. Chorus members who made $75 a week, and were grossly underpaid, looked forward every year to the Christmas parties and gifts given by the stars of the show. It's always a fine time to be in the theater because stars were renowned for giving special presents and great parties.

During the run of *Fanny* the following year, Ezio Pinza gave marvelous presents to the cast, presents that required some thought. To each man in the show, he gave a gold tie tack the size of a quarter from Tiffany's with our initials on them. On the back an inscription read: "Warmest Regards, Ezio Pinza." It was a great keepsake and took time and effort on his part, and it was greatly appreciated. The women received a bracelet inscribed with their initials. The gifts came wrapped in a Tiffany box — the whole production was a class act, but then, Ezio Pinza was a classy man.

I also remember fondly the Christmas during *Blondes* when Carol Channing said, "Let's not have all the usual jazzy ornaments on your tree, Michael. Let's have a party and *make* the ornaments."

"What a great idea," I said.

Some chorus girls brought sequins which they used to decorate their faces in the show, while others brought wardrobe scraps and everyone made ornaments by hand. Carol brought miniature boxes of cereal, put red ribbons on them, and hung them on the tree. It was clever and made for a festive, creative party.

*Wonderful Town*'s Christmas was pure humbug out of a can. Scrooge Russell first announced that she was giving a little gathering, her Christmas party, on stage, catered by a local delicatessen.

"Gee, Roz," I heard people mutter under their breaths, "what a thrill. Let's sit on stage where we rehearse all day and act on all night and be catered by a deli where everyone eats half the time, anyway."

Roz's idea of a Christmas party was to have cheap sandwiches sent in a couple of nights before Christmas and drink beer and wine on stage at midnight after the show.

For her gift to each member of the cast, she sent her secretary out to buy milk glass ashtrays, the cheapest she could get, 15 cents apiece at the local Woolworth's. Barbara Hutton would have loved that! I related the incident to her later on, and she really had a good laugh. Barbara was famous for the gifts she gave people. I still wear a diamond ring she gave me, only because she was sorry she missed my birthday party. Roz's secretary cut postcards of New York in a circle and glued them to the bottom of the cheap ashtrays, and Roz handed them out to the members of the show. She thought it was clever. And for Lehman Engel, the conductor, she got a *bigger* cheap ashtray and a *bigger* postcard of New York City at night. His response was, "Well, the poor dear, she had bad times in Hollywood. Rumor has it they were broke and needed a hit and got lucky with this show on Broadway."

So I gave the Christmas party for the cast and served champagne and caviar, good booze and good food. A wonderful time was had by all.

I was with the show throughout its entire New York run. As the run was coming to a close, rumor had it that *Wonderful Town* was going on the road and we were all asked to go with it. I asked who would play the leads. Edie Adams would continue on, but Roz was returning to Hollywood with a new picture deal. Carol Channing would replace her, wearing a red wig. Since I was then invited to do *Fanny*, I turned the road show down.

Carol started rehearsals for the road show before the New York show ended. She didn't want to see Roz's performance — she wanted the role to have her own interpretation without being influenced by what Roz had done. I went to Carol's opening night and she was altogether different from Roz, proving once and for all Carol Channing was not a flash in the pan. Through this period, I managed to keep the memory of Maria from intruding on my every waking thought. I did party, but not quite as desperately as before. And then, one night, my patience was rewarded.

Countess Mercati gave one of her St. Regis parties, and there I met a stunning blonde who looked like Marlene Dietrich. Her name was Susan McKay and we hit it off like crazy. She was appearing in an off-Broadway play, and had enacted a no-romance policy so she could dedicate herself to her career. She had starred as Billie Dawn in *Born Yesterday*, Joan in *Joan of Arc*, and Sadie Thompson in *Rain*, to name a few of her accomplishments. I was very taken with her. It was the first time I had fallen for a blonde.

I asked her to go dancing with me later at the Stork Club, and we left the Countess' party at one in the morning. Even that first night it became clear that Susan McKay was not only unimpressed with the café society whirl, she also did not like the group I hung out with! She wasn't talking any nonsense from me. She figured me out fast and set me straight on just how much guff she was going to take, and it wasn't much. We could have dinner together once in a while, go dancing occasionally, but if I had other things in mind, I could just call one of my playmates. End of negotiations. She was just getting over a love affair and that was how things were going to be. I was sympathetic, still getting over Maria.

"When you want to shack up," Susan said, "you can drop me at home and go get one of your dollies and take *her* to El Morocco and laugh it up to the wee hours of the morning."

This crazy style of dating went on for almost a year. Everyone loved her, and why not — she was brilliant, well educated, and a beauty. On top of that, I couldn't impress her one damned bit.

Needless to say, I fell in love with her.

It was months before I found out that Susan McKay was her stage name. Her real name was Nikki McCormac and was from Chicago. She was a graduate of that city's Goodman Theatre, which may be this country's finest training school for actors.

• • •

Lehman Engel and I moved on to *Fanny*. David Merrick was producing and Joshua Logan directing. Josh was famous for *South Pacific*, which up to that time had been the longest running Broadway musical ever, going for five and a half years. Josh brought Ezio Pinza with him from *South Pacific* to *Fanny*.

Florence Henderson was hired as Pinza's daughter, Fanny. She had never done anything to speak of; she was just an innocent girl from Indiana. Bill Tabert, also from *South Pacific*, was hired as Pinza's son.

I had seen the closing night of *South Pacific*, so I was acquainted with the people I was going to work with. On "Pacific's" closing night I witnessed the most moving thing I had ever seen. On stage was a group of people singing for the last time the songs that had been their whole lives for five years. Mary Martin would sing with Pinza and tears would start down her cheeks halfway through. Pretty soon Pinza was crying, and not long after that the audience was crying, too. It may not be the best way to see a Broadway production, but it was the most dramatic.

We did our *Fanny* previews out of town and I was sorry to leave Nikki behind. She was the first woman I missed when I was away from her — well, the first American woman.

When *Fanny* got started out of town, I got a taste of what Pinza had been up to all those years. Pinza ran around with all the women in the show. His wife sat in the background and I have no idea whether she knew what was happening or not. The great Ezio Pinza, opera star, came to Broadway initially to make money, and secondarily to make women. He did both.

I was one of two understudies for Tabert. The singing role was enormous. I had been told that I was *the* understudy, and I signed my contract believing this. When we started rehearsals, I realized the other understudy, Jack Washburn, had a better range and a more operatic voice than I did, and that *he*, not I, was the actual understudy. *Then* they told me that I was only the second understudy. I was angry, but I had signed the contract and there was nothing I could do about it. Jack and his beautiful wife,

Dianne, and I became close friends. He must have had some inner demons we knew nothing about. He was a wonderful man with a great voice. He also had two delightful children, Kevin and Wendy. A few years ago, I was devastated when I heard that Jack had died.

I enjoyed watching Pinza work, but from the wings, the active chorus boy was bored. To appease me, they gave me little things to do. I played the part of a butler in one scene, and also played the part of a sailor who had some lines and some singing to do. I was doing walk-ons and small scenes with Pinza and Walter Slezak, but basically I was back in the chorus. They did what they could to make me feel better, but as luck would have it, the understudy, Jack, never went on anyway. Later, Jack took *Fanny* on the road and was excellent.

While we were still on the road in Philadelphia previewing the show, I called our family jeweler at Tiffany's and had him design a diamond and sapphire engagement ring. We went back to New York, and the ring was ready by opening night.

*Fanny* opened well in New York, and after the show everyone went to Sardi's. Everyone but me. I told the gang that I would join them later, and I took Nikki to the Plaza Hotel, where we chose a quiet corner and sat down to drink champagne and eat caviar. She lifted a fork-full of caviar up to her lips and noticed there was something other than black fish eggs there. With her fingers she scooped it out, the ring from Tiffany's. As she held the ring, still covered with caviar so she couldn't tell what it was, I proposed. She looked at the thing in her hand, rinsed it off with champagne, and I put it on her finger. Then she said yes.

We got married in January. The only way I was allowed to go on the long weekend when we eloped to Greenwich, Connecticut, was through David Merrick, the producer of the show. David said he had never been at an elopement party before, and thought it was fun and romantic. I told him I needed a best man, so he was it.

Nikki decided not to get married in traditional white, so she wore a lovely blue chiffon dress. As we went down the elevator to the limo, the doorman said, "Why, madam, you look absolutely beautiful today, radiant in fact. You look as if you are going to a wedding."

"As a matter of fact, I am," she said.

We have marvelous pictures of David Merrick in his homburg and black coat with a black velvet collar without a smile on his face. He took the whole wedding very seriously. He looked like he was going to a funeral. When he got back to New York, he put a note on the bulletin board that read: "Michael Mason is out sick. Very sick. He just got married." He brought back the remainder of the wedding cake, and the cast partied with champagne while we were at the Plaza Hotel.

On our wedding night, as we were having dinner downstairs in the Persian Room of the hotel, a magnum of Dom Perignon champagne arrived.

"What's that?" I asked.

"Compliments of Mr. Walter Slezak on your marriage," replied the waiter.

"What does he expect me to do with it? Bathe in it?"

We figuratively began to do just that when a one-pound tin of Russian caviar came over.

"What's this?" came from me again.

"Compliments of Mr. Ezio Pinza," the waiter said.

"Good God, they're going to suffocate us in champagne and caviar!" I passed out drunk in out suite at the Plaza, woke up hung-over the next morning, and realized I was married.

David Merrick sent us an odd wedding gift. Keep in mind that I never had dinner at my home unless it was a catered dinner party. David knew that. Nikki and I always dined at the finest restaurants either before or after the show. So what wedding present did David bestow? A salad bowl from Tiffany's. A salad bowl? When would I ever use it? It wasn't that I had expected him to give us a lavish gift — he simply didn't tune into the reality of the situation. David had explicitly told his business manager what to buy for us. Apparently his business manager, when given his instructions, had said, "What? For the Park Avenue kid? You're gonna give him a salad bowl?"

"That's what I always give people when they get married," David replied.

After two nights at the Plaza Hotel in New York, we decided to go to the country for a few days. What better place than Uncle Alden's 5,000 acre estate in New Jersey, only 45 minutes from Manhattan. Alden was in Europe, with Aunt Maude and Uncle Eli, and unaware of our elopement. He had wanted us to be married on the little island in his private chapel in front of his Cotswold mansion.

We reached the mansion by driving by the guard gate house, about a mile and one-half up the drive, past the stables, to a setting only found in England, an exact replica of a $17^{th}$ century English Cotswold Manor house. Every room had a fireplace, including Italian marble fireplaces in all the bathrooms. The estate took five years to build during the Depression years, and the artwork and furnishings were brought in from around the world. I called ahead to alert the servants that I was bringing my wife with me for a few days' stay.

The staff had chilled champagne waiting for us in the library, and there was a fire going in most of the fireplaces. It was a nice way to start a life together. I took everything for granted in those days. In retrospect, I know how spoiled I was and how I had been given everything money could buy. Yet, even then I knew you can buy camaraderie, sex, and friendship, but not true love.

I told David that I was leaving the show to take my honeymoon in Europe. He asked me to wait until he could find someone to replace me. In March, Nikki and I sailed on the Queen Mary to Europe for a six-week honeymoon.

# CHAPTER TEN
## The Rich Man's Marlene Dietrich

Our six-week honeymoon lasted a year and a half.

Our families were unhappy that we had eloped. I went for the grandstand play and asked my parents what there was to be unhappy about? I told them that rather than spending $15,000 to $20,000 on a wedding, we would take that money as a wedding gift so I could show Europe to my bride in style. That went over big.

I had had it as the Park Avenue Chorus Boy. I had things to do, people to see, impressions to make. I wasn't a famous actor yet. Nothing extraordinary had happened after my understudy performance in *Wonderful Town,* but I had been spoiled standing on the Winter Garden Theater stage. It was intoxicating to sing to all those people every night and gather the applause. I wanted more! I liked doing comedy and getting laughs. More! I had gotten laughs in places Jordan never got laughs. So I was packing up the Chorus Boy and shipping him off. Ever since Bermuda, I had been trying to figure a way to get rid of him. A long vacation was my current answer, maybe toss him over the R.M.S. Queen Mary and have the New Mason stroll into dinner and order soda pop. One way or another, I was tired of being invisible, so that had to be shucked, too, along with the parties and the café society and my dollies and my teddy bear. Ahem. A joke.

The Queen Mary took only four days to cross the Atlantic, and we arrived at Le Havre and then took the train to Paris. Across

*The Rich Man's Marlena Dietrich*

from us in our compartment were an elderly couple, probably in their seventies. I was always attracted to elderly people anyway, so we started chatting with them. The woman told us that they had never been to Paris before and spoke of saving up pennies for the trip. Then she said, "We're looking at the two of you — you are all of 20 years old, I'm sure, and obviously on your honeymoon. I hope that you don't mind that we were listening to your discussion about your wedding. Have *you* been to Europe before?"

"Yes," I said, "but my wife hasn't."

"Aren't you blessed," she said.

"What do you mean?" I asked.

"We've never been to Europe before and we waited too long. Here we are, visiting the most glamorous cities in the world, and we are too old to get out and really walk and enjoy them."

"And the worst part of it," said her husband, "is the dancing. I'm too old to go out dancing all night anymore. I was some dancer in the old days; you should have seen me. We have been married for 50 years. We danced a lot back then."

I wished I could turn back the clock for them, or at least loan them a couple of years.

Nikki and I checked into the Continental Hotel in Paris, promptly realized that we hated it there, and went over to the Ritz. My Aunt Maude and Uncle Eli, who were in Europe at the time, told me that I was ridiculous to pay such exorbitant rates, but. I had to have the best. I was almost housebroken, but the Park Avenue Chorus Boy still had a few hooks in me.

Aunt Maude and Uncle Eli stayed at the Continental when they were in Paris, the Dorchester Hotel when they were in London, and their apartment at 540 Park Avenue when they were home. They had been going back and forth regularly on the Queen Mary for twenty-two years. Their apartment on Park Avenue was perpetually filled with steamer trunks and boxes always in some halfway state of packing or unpacking. Aunt Maude had huge boxes sent over to Europe filled with toilet paper and Kleenex, because she could not stand the tissue in Europe. They would sail on the Queen Mary, live three months at the Dorchester, three months in Paris at the Continental, come back to the States, spend three months in Virginia, and then return to New York for the opera and ballet season. Some life-style for all those years!

Once while at the Dorchester, Aunt Maude had Uncle Eli sign a little note. Bear in mind, Uncle Eli was seventy-two years old, a multimillionaire, a brilliant man with a seat on the New York Stock Exchange. She made him sign notes like he was a little boy that said, "I will not have more than three martinis before luncheon. Signed, Eli T. Watson." It was wonderful. He got around it, though. He would say, "I only promised not to have more than three martinis *downstairs* prior to luncheon." So, he had to go across the street for a set of martinis, come back and have three martinis downstairs, and then have lunch with Aunt Maude.

Nikki and I went to the Louvre practically every other day that we were in Paris. We went to the Bois de Bologne and I was careful to make sure my fly was closed. We used my aunt and uncle's limousine and made trips to Versailles and out to the French countryside. We visited with a dear family friend, Elsa Schiapparelli. A renowned designer and the social center of attention for the "in" crowd, she was the Coco Chanel of her day and gave magnificent parties to which everyone wanted to be invited.

Scap, as we called her, lived at 22 Rue du Berri in one of the most impressive homes in all of Paris. We went to many of her dinner parties and met Ernest Hemingway, Simone Signoret, Yves Montand, and Marlene Dietrich, among others. Years later, I was to do a film with Montand.

One day Scap told me that since I was in Paris, she would throw a party for me at Maxim's. Now that sounded like a pretty fine idea. Nikki and I dressed up, went to Maxim's, and were led to Scap's table to sit down among friends. I noticed there were two empty chairs, one on either side of Scap.

"Who are your guests, Scap, who are so late?" I asked.

"It's a surprise," she whispered, winking.

About twenty minutes later, the Duke and Duchess of Windsor entered, were escorted to our table, and sat by Scap. I had to laugh. No matter how wonderful I thought the Duke and Duchess of Windsor were — after all it takes a very special man to abdicate the throne to marry the woman he loved — my first instinct had been to feel insulted. I had erroneously believed that Nikki and I were to be the guests of honor.

The Duke of Windsor was a little like someone out of a Noel Coward play, very elegant, quite grand, yet extremely straightforward and nice. The other guests were falling all over themselves to put on airs, and ended up looking very foolish alongside the Duke and Duchess.

Nikki and I wanted some privacy after Paris, so we decided to go to Madrid. We thought no one would know us there. Error number one. To begin with, blondes were a rare commodity in Spain, so we started attracting attention. Then everyone in Madrid, from the doorman to the waiters to the beggars on the street, was convinced that Nikki was Marlene Dietrich. They followed us down the streets, into shops, and through museums. The photographers went crazy, snapping pictures of "La Dietrich." We couldn't win and we couldn't escape. The limo I had rented cinched it. She *had* to be Dietrich if she were riding in a limo. Nikki finally caught on and we never went out unless she was wearing a heavy scarf over a black wig and dark glasses. After that, no one bothered us, and we ended up falling in love with the city. The people there were wonderful. We spent ten weeks there, which allowed us to relax and be ourselves.

My father, who had thought we would only be gone for eight weeks at the most, finally called and asked what we were still doing in Madrid. I told him that we had run out of money. This was, of course, false, but he believed me. He wanted me to return home and get back to business, although the business he had in mind was different from the business I had in mind. From my father's perspective, it was time to be serious, which meant no more Hollywood and no more Broadway. Time to join the family, Michael — a wife is a responsibility. My father expected me to have matured enough to understand the realities of the world, all because of a marriage ceremony.

We went back to Paris and did and redid the night life — the Lido, the Follies, and La Pan a Gilles in Montmarte, which became our favorite hangout. It was a restaurant/bar frequented by writers, artists, and actors that Simone Signoret and Yves Montand took us to. La Pan a Gilles encouraged impromptu acts: a guitarist would stand up and strum, a mime would feel his way into his act, and an actor would rise to do a soliloquy. The famous, the infamous, and the not-so-famous hung out there.

All this Paris night life made me insecure; I couldn't paint, my French was all right, but I couldn't get a job singing. What could I do? And then what was I going to do when I returned to the United States? I was spinning my wheels in Europe, digging the hole deeper and deeper.

One night we went to Ciro's with Aunt Maude and Uncle Eli. There was an 18-string orchestra conducted by a tall, white-haired man. My Aunt Maude knew I was down in the dumps, so she sent the conductor a note through the maitre d' which read: "Young Mr. Michael Mason, star of Broadway, would be happy to sing with the orchestra." When they asked me I was, of course, somewhat embarrassed, but I got up there and gave them what they had all come there for, a real show. I sang songs in Italian and Spanish, like "Torna Sorrento" and "Mata Nata." It was a real treat to sing backed up by all those strings, syrupy and dripping over my baritone. My confidence started coming back.

Every time went to Ciro's, Aunt Maude, in spite of all her money, carried in her own secret flask of Scotch. A Scotch at Ciro's was four or five dollars a shot in those days, and she refused to be taken. She would start by ordering Scotches all around from the bar so we would have the glasses, and later the maitre d' would wonder how we all got so bombed on only one drink apiece. Maude just kept replenishing when no one was looking, and she had a backup flask in Uncle Eli's pocket in case we ever ran low.

I didn't have to worry about my future for long. As we walked into our suite at the Ritz one night, the phone was ringing. Hugh Martin, the famous songwriter who had written the music with Jules Styne for *Make a Wish* was calling from New York. Hugh was a close friend of Judy Garland. Hugh had written "The Trolley Song" in *Meet Me in St. Louis* specifically for Judy, and she was, in fact, in his apartment when he placed the call. It was she who had told Hugh where I was. His call was the answer to a million prayers.

"Michael, I'm doing a show in London and need another American, a lead singer. We can't find anyone here in New York we care about. We have had a helluva time tracking you down. Do you want the job? It's a revue at the Royal Court Theater."

I leapt at it. Hugh put Judy on the phone and we chattered away for a while across the ocean, and I found myself falling right back into the swing of things. We left for London the next day.

Nikki and I decided to stay at the quaint old Royal Court Hotel directly across from the theater. We went over that day to meet the cast. The English director, whom we got to know fairly well, decided to "test" us when he first met us. He probably had an image of Americans as tough pioneer types who liked their whiskey strong, their women stacked, and their politics stuffy. He introduced himself, then told us he thought Nikki and I were terribly lovely, grand Americans. We both nodded, knowing something was up.

"Oh, I see you are newlyweds," he said.

"Yes," I said.

"So have I been, just recently."

"Oh, really?" I asked.

"Oh, yes, he's just the loveliest black boy you'll ever want to meet in your life," he said, looking straight at Nikki, waiting to see how she would react.

"Oh, how is he?" she responded. "Well, we look forward to meeting your bride some day."

It broke the ice. She hadn't been shocked or scandalized, so maybe we weren't so stuffy and foolish after all.

We particularly liked one chap in the show named James McColl, a fine actor and a nice fellow. He reminded me of Clifton Webb. He had fallen prey to the most disturbing thing about English theater, the boozing. I had been around boozing all my life, but English musical revue actors were something else, famous for their gin bottles backstage. They drank the stuff straight, then hit the stage and it was high camp from beginning to end. They would start ad-libbing and you never knew from one moment to the next where the scene was going to go. I drank *after* the show was over.

It all caught up with James, though, strolling about in his elegant clothes and spats when he didn't have a dime to his name. He got bad reviews when the show opened and went into a major depression. My reviews were good, and in general the critics liked the show, but they were cold to James. He sat one night in his dressing room in front of his makeup mirror and rather than putting on makeup, he smeared it on the mirror in the shape of his face. He painted eyebrows and a mouth on the greasepaint oval of his face, he touched up the rouge on his mirrored cheeks. Then he stood up, put on his coat and hat as the curtain went up and walked out of the theater, into the alley through the rain. It was the last we ever saw of him. He died two weeks later.

I had a lot of trouble with the American producer. He allowed his friend, Rudy, to sing songs in the show. Rudy was primarily a dancer, but apparently he had a yen to sing and prevailed on his friendship with the producer to do so. He was all right as a dancer, but definitely flat as a singer. I came to rehearsal and found one of my eight lead songs in the show had been given to Rudy. Well, no one actually told me in so many words, but the other actors pointed me toward the song list on the bulletin board. The producer had scratched out my name and written in Rudy's.

I warned the producer that I would leave the show if he kept it up. It took me a long time to get around to doing something about it. He threatened me with my signed contract while gradually whittling me down to three songs as the months passed. I may have been the lead singer according to the program, but Mr. Flat was singing my songs.

I tried to keep things low-key when it came to money. I gave up the limo, but my Aunt Maude kept what she called her "little ole' Cadillac" at the Dorchester, which was actually a Rolls Royce stretch-out a mile long. Once in a while when I couldn't resist and I needed a fix, I used it.

The British actors were living on nothing. One night, a girl in the show came in grinning ear to ear and I asked what she was so happy about. She told me she had been to a dinner party just before and had a lamb chop. It was a big deal, a lamb chop, when you lived on a few dollars a week. English actors have always lived on nothing. It was a rude awakening for me. In New York it didn't matter as much. As an actor or chorus gypsy, you were paid enough to live reasonably, if not well. But to go into an English actor's apartment, or flat, after the show was a revelation. You would find a small, tight space jammed with furniture, a few windows, and meager foodstuff crammed in a small icebox. They had to put a shilling in one meter to make sure the gas kept going, and another for electricity. One had to sacrifice to be an actor in England.

I met Princess Margaret at the Royal Court Theater. She loved the show and the people in it. The theater was a hideaway for her and she and her entourage would join us after the show for supper and dancing. Margaret was unpretentious and didn't go in for jewelry or flair. Her favorite drink was Dom Perignon, so it was natural that we drank a lot of it together. She had her limo and bodyguard, but I never got any sense of "I am the Princess" from her. She wore dark clothes with a cape and came off as a tastefully dressed woman. When she went somewhere snazzy like Claridge's she could look dazzling and fabulous, but overall she liked the creative world of art and the theater. It followed that she would marry Anthony Armstrong Jones, a talented painter and photographer; a decent, simple man. Through my family, I knew his uncle, Oliver Messel, quite well.

We toured England with the show — Southsea, Bournemouth, Edinburgh, and Glasgow. I wanted to destroy my image as a snob .Everyone knew I had money because I had been staying at the Royal Court Hotel, but I was trying my best to play it down. When we traveled, rather than taking a limo to Southsea, Nikki and I rode on the bus with the cast. The tour involved all-day bus rides on hard, wooden benches. We stayed in what were called "theatrical digs." In Bournemouth the "digs" meant staying in someone's private home. The lady of the house would fix tea and biscuits for breakfast and we would trot off to rehearsal.

By the time we hit Edinburgh, Nikki and I had just about had it with the whole routine. Getting from Glasgow to Edinburgh was a long trip that seemed even longer on the wooden benches of the bus. We thought we had broken our backs. We knew they thought we were spoiled Americans, even though we had been traveling with them for weeks. They were not likely to change their opinions of us, no matter what we did, so we were suffering for no reason.

In Edinburgh, the theatrical digs consisted of a very nice house, comfortably furnished, and the people were pleasant. We hadn't seen the bathroom anywhere when we arrived, so Nikki asked where it was. The owner of the house said, "Oh, come with me, dearie," and took Nikki far down the hall, opened the back door and pointed. "There it is, love, out there in the yard." An outhouse. We said to each other "Thanks, but no thanks," grabbed our bags, and checked into the Palace Hotel, leaving the world of theatrical digs behind.

We took the train back to London when the show came off the road. I had been trying to prove a point to the English actors, but they thought I was just playing a game. They probably were right.

Back in London, the play continued at the Royal Court Theater and I was still down to three songs. I threatened and fought, but it was no use. I confronted the American producer: "One more song taken away from me, in fact if one isn't given back to me, I'll only not appear tomorrow, I'll get sick so fast I'll close your damn show in two minutes!"

"You pampered, spoiled *nouveau riche* punk. . ." he sneered.

Well, that did it. We weren't *nouveau*, we were *anciens*.

"Listen, you miserable New York son of a bitch with your asshole Rudy friend," I said, "I'll blow you right the hell out of the theater. I'll pay the chauffeur, no, in fact I'll do it myself, I'll run my limo right through the theater and close your god damned show!"

I didn't get the song back, so I called in sick and that was the end of it.

The show had run for eight months. We sailed a week later for New York on the S.S. United States.

# CHAPTER ELEVEN
## Hello, Good Bye

Believe it or not, I had cleaned up my act; I was on my best behavior. I had spent a year and a half in Europe, and even though my temper had ended my last show on a sour note, I had been pretty good, all things considered. I had really put in an effort to handle each and every situation seriously, in an adult frame of mind.

But it was still decision time. Why hadn't my destiny appeared before me like a bolt of lightening — be a violinist, Mike, or go out and make pizzas, Mike. Should I continue doing Broadway, trying to parlay my one true asset, my singing voice, into a stage career? Or should I take the reviews from Europe, add them to the successes of *Wonderful Town* and *Fanny* and return to Hollywood where they would bend over backwards to cast me in a movie? Tough choice. It could have been decided by a flip of a coin, and it was. I took Hollywood. Hollywood always had been impressed with image and flashiness, and that's what I had for them. My smoke and mirrors on top of their smoke and mirrors.

Aunt Maude and Uncle Eli were still in Europe, so Nikki and I moved into their apartment at 540 Park Avenue while the packers worked at my place at 820, getting us ready to move to California. We wanted to entertain during our three-week stay, and 540 Park was a great placed to do it, once we moved the cartons of Kleenex the Queen Mary could not accommodate. We gave parties, but for a whole new group of people, no more café society bullshit. The group included Dame Margot Fonteyn, Freddy Ashton, Michael Soames, Oliver Messel (Lord Snowden's uncle), Countess Mercati, Barbara Hutton, as well as Lucia Chase, head of the Ballet Theater, Nora Kaye, Pearl Bailey, Lehman Engel, members of Sadler's Wells Ballet Company, and Van Clyburn, who had been discovered by Aunt Maude and the Olga Samaroff Foundation. He was then an unknown pianist from the Julliard Conservatory who went on to become one of the world's most famous pianists.

I was interested in joining the mature, sophisticated social circle and leaving the El Morocco and Stork Club sets behind. The sophisticates dined at the Newport Restaurant, the Plaza and Carlyle Hotels, the Masionette, Versailles, King Cole, and the St. Regis Roof Garden. From the café society bullshit to the Park Avenue scene. Three weeks of dinner parties, good food and good drink, black tie to say hello and good bye. After being in Europe, I was able to drop ten names every ten seconds and enjoyed playing that role, because everyone was looking at me in a different light. I had grown up to become one of them, or at least I was trying to.

Hello, good bye.

We were ready to set off for California. My entourage had grown by one, Nikki, along with the chauffeur and the maid. We again packed up the limo and were ready to make the same drive to California that I had made a few years before. But it was all new, somehow. It wasn't just that I had given up the yellow Buick and had bought a new Cadillac convertible. Considering all that had happened, this was the quietest period of my life. I was still on my best behavior. As much as I tried to get rid of the Chorus Boy, the European life and the New York scene just weren't the answer. So it was back to Hollywood to try again. I couldn't be a chorus boy in the movies, and I wasn't about to become the Bel Air Extra.

How was I to know all this quiet uncertainty was only the calm before the storm?

## The Park Avenue Chorus Boy

Our one big stop heading for the West coast was to see Nicky Hilton in Albuquerque, New Mexico. Nicky was a good friend. He managed to blow all his money doing some damn thing or another, so Conrad, his father, had exiled him to New Mexico to learn the hotel business. We stayed there a few days, then went on to California.

We had reservations at the Beverly Hills Hotel again. The doorman recognized me.

"Well, Michael, how the hell are you?" he said.

"My God, you have a good memory," I told him.

"Hey, I always remember people who tip well. You are a pain in the ass, but one thing you do, you tip well, baby. How are you? The pool is where it always was, but wear a suit this time, OK?"

Hmmm. Would all of Hollywood have as good a memory as the Beverly Hills Hotel doorman?

We checked in. Our furniture would take a few weeks to arrive, and that would give us time to look for a place to live. I called up Louis Shurr's office and set up a meeting with Louis and Al Melnick to plan my new career. Nikki and I spent two or three days resting up by the pool and getting our minds back to steady ground after the many days of driving. We enjoyed champagne lunches and started talking to the Hollywood people. I had decided to avoid the old crowds in general — R.J., Debbie, Tab, and the rest. We got together once in a while, but it just wasn't the same. I was a serious guy taking care of my career now. I was married and a veteran stage actor. I saw Mike Connolly by the pool and an old friend, Sheila Graham. I tried to show them that I was older, and, hopefully, wiser.

I called a few real estate agents and said I was looking for an unfurnished house to lease for a year. I wasn't about to by anything because I did not know what was going to happen. I wanted something, really wanted it, and that made me vulnerable; the fun and games wouldn't protect me if I didn't get it right this time. I not only had myself to answer to, I had a wife, and maybe some children some day. We found a wonderful home in Bel Air and waited for the furniture to arrive.

Nikki and I went in to see Shurr and Melnick. Louis' secretary, Gertrude, and I were friends from before and gave us a hearty welcome, so there was no immediate hint of the coming chill.

We entered the office where Shurr and Melnick were waiting, sat down and sniffed the frost in the air. Funny. I casually chatted about Wonderful Town and the Royal Court Theater. They didn't seem to be listening. The sound of hemming and hawing was loud and clear in Louis' voice when he said, "Well, we'll figure out what we can do . . . . I think we should get you involved in some classes somewhere and, uh, we really don't know what to do yet." Big smile, pat on back. We'll figure out something." And we were escorted out.

We climbed into the limo and I said, "Nikki, do you have the same feeling I have?"

"Yes!" she said. "Get yourself a new agent."

So began a very short hunt. I was no longer a "Shurr" bet for stardom. I had to change my laundry tags. I met Paul Kohner through a friend of ours. Unfortunately, he was only interested in representing Nikki. He took one look at her and wanted to turn her into another Marlene Dietrich.

"Wait a minute," Nikki said. "One Dietrich is enough, and anyway, I'm not here to be in the business. I was an actress, but I have given it up. My husband is the one."

Kohner glanced over his shoulder at me, grunted, and turned back to Nikki. At that moment I realized that I couldn't take Nikki on any more interviews with me.

Then it all started to come to me. I saw that the same warm drunken town I had played in four years earlier was taking a different shape now. The town was looking too bright, too hard-edged. Hollywood needed the haze of nearsightedness, booze, and dangerous drugs to make it appear normal.. When you have

*141*

been sobered up by marriage, Hollywood could be a vicious, carnivorous harpy.

In Hollywood you have to step carefully over the shards of other people's dreams and careers. This is Transientville, where the hundred-mile-an-hour Santa Ana winds come boiling down off the desert in the fall, and they're so hot, fast, and dry that fires seem to spring up from them in the surrounding canyons.. Then the rains come in the winter and the burnt-out land muddily slides into the lowlands and on to the freeways, while the rest of the grass grows long from its good drink so it can brown to a dry crisp during the coming parched summer and be fodder for the Santa Ana's to beat into fires again in the fall.

And of course, there is the never-ending threat of earthquakes and the constant flocking of overcooked religious cranks who turn everyone else into spite-filled conservatives with loaded pistols behind their locked doors. Then, spread that out over a huge area, give everyone a car in which to be antisocial and you begin to get the picture. No one ever asks "How's your wife?" in Los Angeles. They ask, "Are you two still together?" Transientville. The heartbeat of America, where dreams are made and destroyed..

We met Brett Halsey one day for lunch at the Beverly Wilshire Hotel. Brett and I had been friends the first time I'd come out to the west coast, and he hadn't met Nikki yet. He brought along a friend of his, a young actor named Steve McQueen. McQueen was not yet a big star, but everyone saw great potential in him. He wore a t-shirt and jeans and spent most of his time riding a motorcycle up and down Hollywood Boulevard. In fact, the motorcycle was the only thing that seemed to fit in with the image he present to the public. McQueen was never a tough guy from the street — -that was all a facade. He was a soft-spoken, gentle guy. All he cared about at the time was his wife, Neile Adams, and providing a good home for her. Brett and McQueen sat down, had a drink and we started talking about agents. I told McQueen I was leaving the Louis Shurr Agency after five years.

"Well, if you want one of the hottest agents in town," he said, "Stan Kamen at William Morris is terrific. Why don't you call him tomorrow? Tell you what. I'll call him later today or tomorrow morning and set it up."

I did call the next day, figuring that even if McQueen had been making cocktail talk, maybe I could get to talk to Kamen and get a referral. On the line to his secretary I dropped the magic words, "Steve McQueen," and the doors swung open. They set me up for a meeting at four o'clock that afternoon. I walked in and Stan Kamen already had contracts written up ready for me to sign.

"Let's pretend you haven't been in Hollywood before," Stan said. "Let's forget you were ever trying to be an actor up to now and we'll take a whole new approach. You're more mature now and obviously you've got your head screwed on straight."

I auditioned for William Morris so they could see what they had. I sang for Stan and for Norman Brokaw, another high-power agent at Morris, and they met to decide if they were going to push me for pictures, television, or the stage.

They sent me out to audition for Joe Pasternak, the head of MGM. Joe was the kind of guy you could hit right between the eyes with a great love song. So I did. I sang to him and he seemed to be enjoying it, so I just went right on singing, one ballad after another. After about seven numbers, the big tough Joe Pasternak had tears in his eyes. "I have never heard a more beautiful voice in my life," he said.

I thought to myself, "Oh my God, I've got it made."

"But there's a problem," he said.

"What's the problem?"

"Vic Damone. He's under contract. We have to use him."

"What do you mean, you have to use him? You just said I'm the greatest thing you've ever heard, better than Darnone."

"That's irrelevant. Stick with your singing, because you really are good."

And that was the end of that. I was out just as fast as I was in. No screen test, nothing. It was just a long afternoon's serenade.

I auditioned for and was accepted by the Desilu Studios Workshop Group, people under contract who met and did scenes together in between whatever small assignments they could get.

Carol Ohmart, Brett Halsey, and other up-and-coming young performers were in the group. I worked with them, studying and doing scenes, three evenings a week. During the day I'd go out on interviews for commercials as well as TV shows through William Morris, but for the time being, the agency had decided the big push for me would be movies.

*My first girlfriend, "Ronnie" Schune Hartnell at her parents' summer home in Paddock Lake, Wisconsin. We were 13 years old.*

*My first show on Broadway was* Gentlemen Prefer Blondes, *starring Carol Channing. Here I am with fellow cast member, Judy Sinclaire.*

*Me with another cast member, Candy Montgomery.*

*A photo of Smoke Rise in Butler, New Jersey, a private 5,000 acre estate 45 minutes from Manhattan which was owned by my uncle. A replica of a 17th Century English Cotswold Mansion, it was built in the early 1930s. This was my home away from home for 15 years.*

*The chapel on the island as seen from Smoke Rise. Nikki and I were supposed to be married here.*

*My silver "mystery" convertible. (l. to r.) Dean, me, Nikki, Doug, and Charlotte at Smoke Rise.*

*Some of the singers from* Make a Wish *in front of the chapel. (l. to r.) Dave, Nikki, me, Dean, and Charlotte.*

*Nikki under the awning of my apartment at 820 Park Avenue.*

Make a Wish *starred Nanettte Fabray. I'm the top hat on the right. This photo made* Life *magazine.*

A previously unpublished photo of Elizabeth Taylor on the French Riveria. I know, because I took it. She was on her honeymoon with Nicky Hilton, another good friend of mine.

The world-famous ballerina Margot Fonteyn with me in a row boat at Smoke Rise.

*I took this photo of Shelly Winters and Farley Granger and a friend at Granger's Malibu beach house.*

*My old time friend, Tab Hunter.*

*Two of my publicity shots from 20th Century Fox.*

*Back to Broadway for my third show,* Wonderful Town, *starring Roz Russell. The caption reads: "To Mike Mason, all luck to you and great gratitude from me—Rosalind Russell." (Guess as an understudy, I didn't do too bad.)*

*My fourth show on Broadway, Fanny, starring Florence Henderson and Ezio Pinza, I am standing behind them.*

*With Nikki in the library at Smoke Rise planning our wedding.*

*Nikki and I looking out of the rear window of my limo on our way to our wedding in Conneticut.*

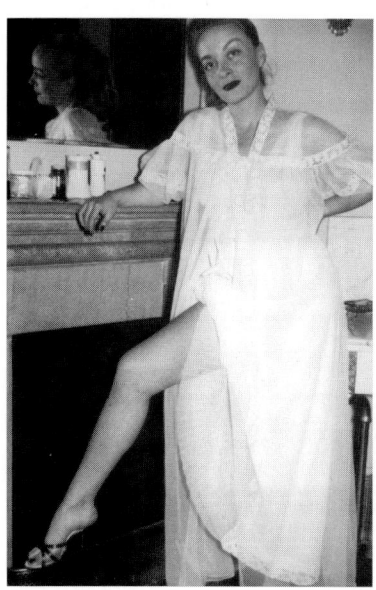
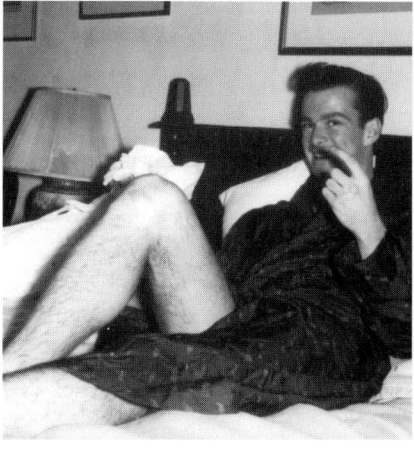

*The legs have it! After a short stay at the Plaza Hotel, we spent a few nights at Smoke Rise, and then went on to our European honeymoon.*

*On our honeymoon, dining with Aunt Maude and Uncle Eli at Ciro's in Paris.*

*Our close friends, Jack and Dianne Washburn. This photo was taken during one of their many fabulous parties at their home "Glenn Gables" in New Hope, PA. Jack and I were in Fanny together.*

*George Kalarsarinis living "La Vida Loca" following his favorite pastime of cruising the Caribbean. George is not only a good friend, but my personal trainer.*

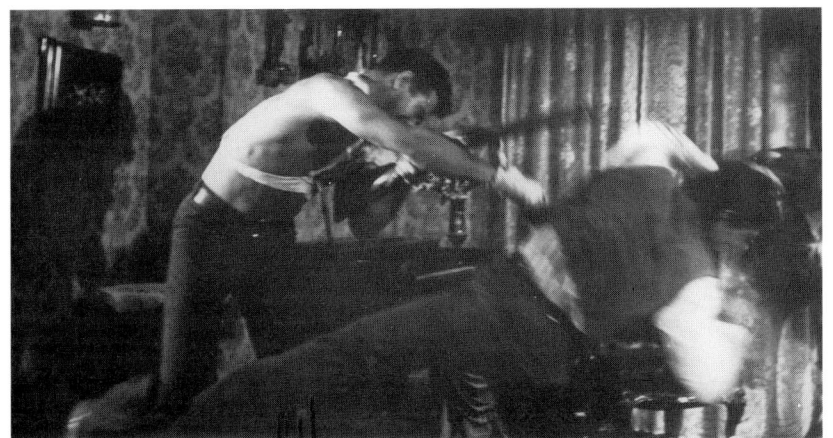

Back to Hollywood. My first movie, Showdown at Boot Hill, *starring Charles Bronson. In this photo, I am knocking Charlie out in a fight.*

*Another scene with Charlie Bronson in* Showdown at Boot Hill, *a 20th Century Fox picture.*

My first Hollywood "preem." I'm in the middle with my date Ginny Gibson. Bill Hayes is on the right.

*My favorite summer stock show,* South Pacific. *I played Lt. Joe Cable and stopped the show singing "Younger than Springtime" and "You've Got to Be Taught."*

*Our dearest friend, as she looks today, the former (and last) Mrs. J. Paul Getty, or "Teddy" as she is known to family and friends.*

*George Cukor rehearsing a scene with Rex Harrison (on the right) during filming of* My Fair Lady. *They are sitting in George's spectacular garden at his home on Cordell Drive in Hollywood. The picture is inscribed "To Nikki and Mike — with love, George."*

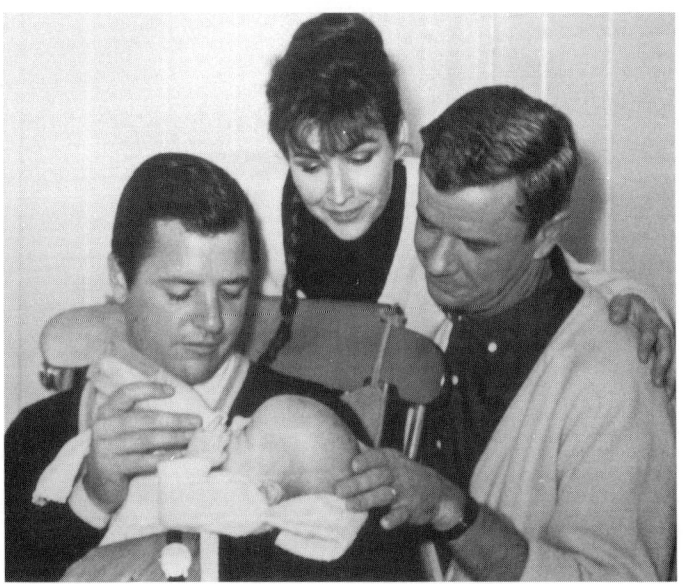

*Richard Long holding my newly born son, Richard. Long's wife Mara Corday is looking on, along with Marshall Thompson. Marshall was married to Richard's sister Barbara.*

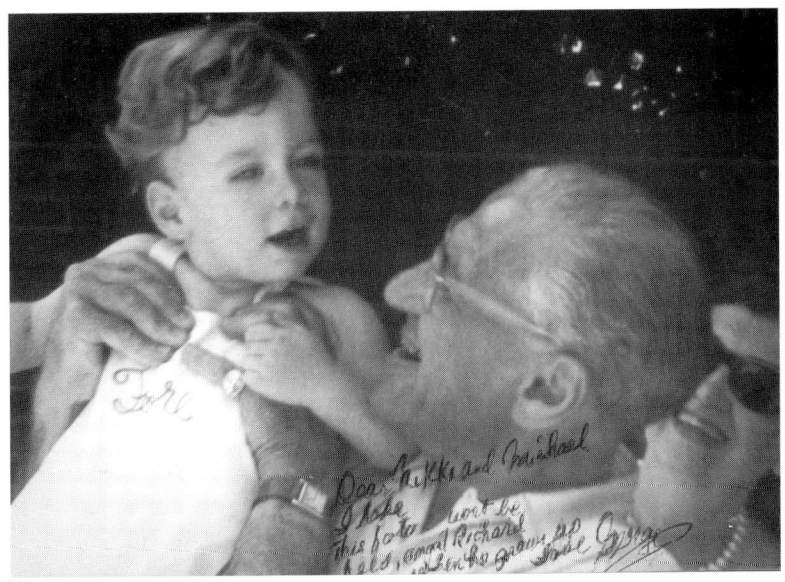

George Cukor, holding Richard, with my mother-in-law Kathleen in the background. The caption reads "Dear Nikki and Michael—I hope this foto won't be held against Richard when he grows up —Love— George.

Richard with me and our guard dog Lady in the court yard of our Encino, California home. Our house was next door to John Wayne's eight acre estate.

*Christmas at St. Moritz, Switzerland. Nikki and Phil Long's (now ex) wife Nancy decorating the tree in our villa.*

*Nancy and Phil's three boys with our son Richard. Brian is in the back, left, and Scott is on the right. Richard and Kevin are standing in front. Kevin and Richard are still good friends.*

*Our four-legged Rolls Royce. I was driving Nikki, Richard, and Kevin Long outside our Villa in St. Moritz.*

*We traded the horse and sleigh for a Mercedes in St. Moritz and drove to Paris. Richard grew out of his cashmere overcoat, but I still have mine.*

*Nikki waiting for me to finish dressing in our suite at the Ritz in Paris on New Year's Eve.*

*Richard and I waiting for Nikki on New Year's Day. We shared the holiday with the Long family and then went on with them to England.*

Lady Nancy Oakes with me at the "mother of all jet set watering holes," The Palm Bay Club, Miami, Florida.

My son Richard and me at the Palm Bay Club.

My dear friend Eva Gabor at a birthday party I gave for myself. She is sorely missed by all who knew her.

Phil Long and me in my Bel Air, California, house. We're still the best of friends after all these years.

Richard Long playing the piano at one of our favorite bars in Encino.

Zsa Zsa and I are calling her mother, Jolie Gabor, in Budapest.

Peggy Lee with me in Laguna Beach California, at a party I gave for her daughter Nicky, a talented artist.

My friend William Durfee with me and Elgin Baylor and William's date, Jan, at a party for the Clippers in Beverly Hills, California.

*Debbie Reynolds, my pal from my acting days.*

*Me today at my lake front home in southern California.*

My son Richard and his wife Stephanie at their wedding in Palm Springs, California.

My three grandchildren, (l. to r.) Robert, Nichole, and Eric.

*My wife, Nikki, looking like Marlene Dietrich. Even Dietrich recognized the resemblance when she met Nikki at Longchamps Restaurant in New York.*

*My last and most important movie, Let's Make Love, starring the one and only Marilyn Monroe.*

*Me with Milton Berle. I played "Yale," his sidekick, in Let's Make Love.*

*A publicity picture of my wife Nikki, shortly before we were married. Among her many roles, she starred on stage in* Light Up the Sky, *played Billie in* Born Yesterday, *and Joan in* Joan of Arc.

*Here I am enjoying the Bahamas, my favorite hide-away.*

*Poster for* Let's Make Love.

GEORGE CUKOR

November 13, 1964

*Dearest Nikki, Mike and Richard —*

Grateful thanks for your sweet wire about the picture...the one I did recently...the name of which escapes me for the moment. I understand it has made a kind of favorable impression.

How's that for being cool?

I won't insult you by going through the routine of 'what wonderful material I was dealing with... what glorious artistes I had to work with...what a generous producer I had'...All of this is true enough, but it was your little ole pal that was right in there punching.

Darn it - I am getting the big head, so I'd better stop here and now and thank you again and send you all loving regards.

*Always,*
*George*

Mr. and Mrs. Michael Mason and
Mr. Richard Mason
17204 Rancho
Encino, California

*Letter from George Cukor referring to his production of* My Fair Lady, *for which he received his only Oscar.*

*Frank sent me this photo after I commented on an article he had written. The caption reads, "To Mike — Thank you for your very kind words about the July 4th piece. — I meant every word — all the best to you and yours—Frank Sinatra, '91."*

## CHAPTER TWELVE
## Undersea Girl

The William Morris Agency swung into action, getting down to work for me in a hurry. They found me my first role in a Hollywood film, a fabulously tacky little "B" picture called *Undersea Girl*.

*Undersea Girl* was filmed on location at Paradise Cove in Malibu. I'd like to tell you about the plot, but it was pretty hard to find. Let me put it this way — have you ever been unable to sleep, it's 3:00 AM. and you have to be at work by 8:15? There's nothing good to munch on in the fridge, so you turn on the TV set and watch some hideous '50s movie that looks like it was made in Spain during the Inquisition and dubbed by a couple of geese with loose dentures? Now you understand — only *Undersea Girl* wasn't good enough to make it to TV.

Mara Corday was the star and the irony of her undersea role was that she was afraid to take a bath without a buddy. Not only couldn't she swim, but she was afraid of the water. However, the producers didn't know that when they hired her. They found out later much later. She was, of course, expected to swim underwater in the movie. Fat chance.

We did numerous scenes on and around the pier at Paradise Cove. Mara, the male lead, and I would be there in the chilly early mornings. The cold didn't bother me because I wore a wet suit for my part in the film, but poor Mara was out there in a skimpy bathing suit full time, even when the crew was only setting up. We sat, waited for the less-than-professional crew to get

*177*

their act together, and listened to the surf and the birds and the noise of the fishing poles on the dock.

"How the hell will they be able to hear our dialogue?" Mara demanded. "Those fishing poles are making a racket."

I shrugged and didn't think about it as we played the scene. When we saw the rushes, I remembered her words. We couldn't hear one word of dialogue in any of the pier scenes, only the clack-clack-clack of the fishing poles in the wind. You'd think the fellow with the tape recorder would have rewound the tape there on location and checked to see how the sound was. No way. We dubbed it later, just like those movies rnade in Spain during the Inquisition.

The lead actor was impersonating a movie star, even though it was just a B picture. Everyone else just wanted to get it over and done with. Mara, however, was a wonderful lady. She had been an Earl Carroll girl and then became the model for all the Vargas girl pinups. If you go back to the paintings by Varga in old *Esquires* and *Playboys,* that's Mara. She had a fabulous body and a great face, but her talent didn't stop there. She had a marvelous sense of humor — I suppose anyone with breasts that large would have to. She put *all* her talent to good use with the leading man.

He was getting on everyone's nerves and giving Mara, in particular, a bad time. He couldn't find one thing right about her — according to him, she wasn't getting her lines right or she wasn't putting enough expression into the scene — Mr. Irritating probably didn't like her figure, either. Her basic reaction, was, "Fuck you. We're in a B movie, so let's get on with it and go home."

We had a short shooting schedule, maybe ten or twelve days' work. With three-quarters of the filming done, one of the most important scenes was coming up — it was to take place in an old car that was a shot of the leading man and Mara plotting how a murder was going to take place.

She came over to me and said, "I'm going to fix that son of a bitch and I know just how to do it."

I leaned closer. "Oh yeah?"

"I'm going to tell the cameraman, who's an old buddy of mine, to film from my side of the car and shoot my profile. Our star can lean forward and get his full face in the frame."

"What, the hell are you doing that for? That's a great shot for him."

"Ah, but it won't be, Michael, my boy — see this sweater I've got on?"

"Yeah."

"This sweater will be his downfall."

"How's that?"

"Watch and learn. All I have to do is put my shoulders back and stick my tits out." She demonstrated. My eyes were glued. "I'll upstage the little bastard and he'll never know a thing. Besides, I know the guys in the cutting room, so I know what it'll look like when it hits the big screen."

Sure enough, he had no idea what she was doing. He leaned forward for the camera to get the full benefit of the shot. He was so proud that he was upstaging the undersea girl herself. She kept looking at him adoringly, tilting her head back, her breasts sticking out a mile. He was so pleased, he even complimented her acting afterwards. The rest of us were standing around watching her work while the great actor was emoting up and down the coast. It was beautiful. The boys in the cutting room were proud to leave it in the film.

They had done the land shots for all the scenes where Mara was dry. Then came the morning when she had to get wet. It was cool that early morning, a little overcast and good for filming.

"Okay, Mara, Michael," the director said. "You'll get in the lifeboat just as soon as we're set up, so get your dialogue ready."

"Michael," Mara said, "what do they mean, get in the lifeboat? I'm going to go down there? I'm going to get in that boat?"

"Don't worry about it. When we do the scene I'll hold your arm the whole time. Nothing's going to happen. See, the boat is tied to the pier; it's not going anyplace."

The less-than-competent crew set up . . . and set up . . . and set up. Four-and-a-half hours later, Mara was so nervous she was shaking. The overcast morning had turned to noon sunlight, the worst light in which to film. Direct sunlight causes too much contrast on film. Finally the director told us to get in the lifeboat. We descended the ladder. Mara was genuinely frightened and I held her as we cautiously went down into the boat.

"Okay, Mara," the director said once we'd gotten in the boat. "We've gone over the scene and it's going to work better with you in the water hanging on the side of the boat, talking to Michael."

"You're out of your mind!" Mara cried. "I'm not getting in that water!"

"What do you mean? That's what it calls for. Then you swim around . . ."

"Swim? I don't swim!" screamed Mara.

"Wha-at?" said the director.

"Wha-at?" said the producer.

"Fu-uck," said the incompetent crew who had been setting up for four-and-a-half hours.

Surprise, surprise — their undersea girl couldn't swim. They cut the entire scene and arranged for a double to do her water scenes in long shots. They'd already filmed all of the dialogue, as well as all the major land scenes, so they couldn't recast her; they couldn't afford to.

I was in a serious blood and thunder scene with three other guys, pounding out of the crashing surf in black wet suits, vicious bloody fishing harpoons at the ready, snarling and tough. From the water we waited for the director to give us the signal. We saw his arm come down, "ACTION!" and we came running as fast as we could through the water to the beach. I was ahead, the toughest of the snarling toughs, and the other guys were following close behind me. I heard laughter behind me as they broke up one by one, falling back with laughter into the surf. The director turned red in the face and yelled "CUT!" I turned and asked what was going on. One of the guys, laughing so hard he was spitting up foam, pointed to my rear end. I looked behind me and saw that I had snagged the back of my rubber suit — it had ripped open so my bare ass was hanging out. The shot was ruined and so was my wet suit. But at least my old Broadway reputation hadn't changed.

They used actual strips of film from previous day's shoots to compare setups for continuity. Continuity is necessary in film so that, from one cut to another, parts of scenes will match and can be filmed on different days, sometimes weeks apart . . . that way someone wouldn't suddenly have a cigarette in his mouth when before, in another shot, he was chewing gum. Using strips of the actual film was unique to this picture as far as I knew. Usually someone on the set takes notes or snaps pictures for continuity's sake, but this was low budget and they had their own perception of how to save money.

We were sitting at a picnic table on the beach one afternoon and I looked up to see some small, oddly shaped objects flying down the beach along the sand. "What the hell is that?"

"Jesus Christ," cried the producer, "that's our continuity!"

We jumped up, the entire cast and crew, and ran down the beach grasping at the small bits of flying film.

Somehow the picture was finished, edited, dubbed, printed and screened, but I never saw it. Mara did. She said it was horrendous.

# CHAPTER THIRTEEN
## The Long Goodbye

Mara Corday went on to marry a close friend of mine, Richard Long. Mara was Richard's second wife and there is a story to be told about his first.

Suzan Ball, a very talented twenty-two year old with a great future ahead of her was becoming a big star in a short time. Her last picture was *Indian Princess* with Victor Mature.

I had met Richard Long once during my first journey to Hollywood, in Laguna, through his brother, Phil, so I only heard about the Suzan Ball tragedy when it happened. When we met, Richard was in the army and had come home on leave for a weekend. Through his brother Phil, I had gotten to know his sister and his parents, and they practically adopted me. Richard's sister, Barbara, later married Marshall Thompson of MGM and *Daktari* fame. It was at Barbara and Marshall's house in Santa Monica that the fantasy of a lifetime came true for me.

Barb and Marsh always gave fabulous parties. Every star in Hollywood eventually passed through their door. But one party in particular was most important to me. Elizabeth Taylor was there. She and Barb were very close friends. Elizabeth came alone to the party and I immediately reminded her of our brief encounter some time ago. I'm not sure she remembered, but she said she did. We ended up sitting on the floor enjoying our buffet dinner and sipping our favorite champagne. Now I realize why Barb had so much Dom Perignon available. It was an incredible evening. Elizabeth was in casual clothes, no gown or jewels. There I sat, totally enraptured by one the most beautiful women in the world.

Hollywood has always been the home of beautiful women. At the time I first met Richard, I was sitting on the beach with his girlfriend-of-the-moment. She and I were jabbering away and he approached and said, "What are you doing with her?" Then and there began the tradition of Long's insecurity about his women and me. We got on well that afternoon, but he always had a nagging uncertainty about me when it came to women, especially his women.

When I was in New York, before I got married and went to Europe, I heard that Richard was engaged to Suzan Ball. I also heard that she had become ill on the set of her newest film. She had apparently fallen down during filming and was having trouble with an infection in her knee. It was at that time that the doctors discovered she had bone cancer in her leg. They were faced with a dilemma — here was a beautiful Hollywood starlet with great career opportunities before her and they had to tell her she had cancer.

Her doctors felt they could save her life if they amputated the leg.. They cut it just above the knee. Then the doctors had a talk with Richard, telling him that Suzan probably had less than a year to live. She was only twenty-two, but her body was totally cancer-ridden. Richard was the only one who knew; the studio, Suzan, and none of Suzan's family or friends were told.

Richard refused to change his plans. He married her, carrying her down the aisle. He intended to give her at least one year of happiness, no matter what.

It was a crazy, scary time before her death, like a surrealistic dream. Fans were sometimes wild in those days, much as they are now, and Richard and Suzan had their share of crazies. Some people would hide in the bushes at night around their house, and without waning, jump out as a group and scream, "Richard Long!" or "Suzan Ball!" Meanwhile, Suzan was using very strong medicines and sedatives, and it scared the hell out of her, hearing strange vices speaking her name, breaking the silence of the night.

The headlines hit London when Nikki and I were there: Actress Suzan Ball Dead of Cancer. That is when Richard's heavy drinking began.

He met Mara Corday about a year later and married her. True to his initial bout of jealousy that first day or, the beach, he was suspicious of me whenever I was around Mara, even though I was married myself. When I realized how paranoid he was about it, I tortured him by saying, "Gee, Richard, any time I get around a black-haired beauty like Mara, 1 go crazy, I can't control myself." You can imagine his reaction.

"Mason," he'd say, "you're married. Cool it."

"Cool what?"

"You know what I mean"

"Oh, you mean Mara? Hell, Richard, I knew her before you did." And then the jokes would begin. Richard loved a good joke, as long as it was not on himself, so this was a good way to get even for his tricks on me.

"What do you mean?" he'd roar and fly into a rage, which would set me to laughing. I knew how easily I could get him angry. It was so easy to tease him about *Undersea Girl* because there was no way he could punch a hole to the past and check out either Mara's denials or my insinuations. I told him in cruel detail about the skimpy bathing suits she wore for the film and the stories about upstaging the leading man. I drove the poor guy crazy. It was fun.

Richard and Mara lived near us and I'd drive over there for a few drinks with him. After a while we'd be three sheets to the wind and Richard would say, "Mason, you're too drunk to drive. I'm gonna drive you home." He was just as plastered as I was, but I'd grin in agreement, and then we'd pile into my car and he'd drive me down the road to my house.

Nikki would greet us and we'd have a few more drinks and pretty soon I'd say, "Richard, you're much too drunk to drive. I'll drive you home." And we'd get back in my car and I'd drive him back to his house where Mara would greet us, and we'd have some more drinks. We went back and forth like this all night long, until either Nikki would make up the bed in the library or Mara would put sheets on their living room couch and tell us, wherever we happened to be passing out at the time, that nobody was driving anybody ever again.

Once, Richard and I were leaving a restaurant called Tail To' the Cock one night, bombed out of our minds as usual, and I left my wallet there, although I didn't realize it until I hit the sidewalk. I tried to go back to retrieve it, but the owner had had more than enough of our rowdiness and wouldn't let me back in. I looked around for a weapon and saw a small metal newspaper stand. I lifted the entire thing up and tossed it through the stained glass window of the restaurant. Richard and I stood there laughing our heads off, when all of a sudden we heard sirens. My chauffeur had gone home because he didn't feel like watching a couple of drunks tear up the place. We jumped into the limo, thinking we were going to have a high-speed chase, gunned the engine, and pulled out into the street. The cops went right by us. They weren't looking for a limousine; they were looking for some lower-class slobs who were damaging property. We thought this was all great fun, but it was really just a sign of Richard's and my shared emotional problems.

Then, there was Tony Curtis. Curtis was the studio threat to Richard. He was the second choice for roles offered Richard, the fellow they dangled in Richard's face to keep him in line. That was tremendously cruel, but there was competition between Curtis and Richard for parts. It was the old story of the studio pitting one actor against another, both under contract, both handsome, the same age, and able to do the same parts. Richard was the first choice for many of the roles Curtis wound up doing.

Mara did go on a boat again, something she'd sworn never to do after *Undersea Girl*. It was when we buried Richard's ashes at sea from his brother Phil's yacht, the Constellation.

The Long family were great sailors. Phil also was, and is, a shipbuilder and has owned many marvelous yachts, including the 110 foot Trenora, the Hirshoff, and the Constellation. He built a 90 foot sister ship to the Ticonderoga, which he called the Whitehawk. It took him three years to build her. Her mast was approximately 120 feet high and the main sail was 87 feet high. The Ticonderoga had held world racing records for some thirty years. When we launched the Whitehawk, the owner of the Ti sailed her all the way from the Bahamas to Northern Maine to give a cannon salute across the Whitehawk's bow. National Geographic filmed the event; it was there I read a poem that Richard had written about the sea.

The remainder of Richard's ashes that weren't buried at sea from the Constellation had been put in a silver box below the mast of the Whitehawk. When the Whitehawk was finally sold, they had to lift the mast, which was five feet in diameter, to get the box out. They didn't want Richard to become a flying Dutchman, never at peace.

In the Long family, perseverance was the key to life. Each one went after what he or she wanted, except for Richard. He was a fine and dedicated actor, but he let too many women and too much booze get in his way and didn't accomplish what he should have. He started heavy drinking after Suzan died and didn't quit until the liquor killed him at age forty-seven. He died on December 21st, 1974, leaving his wife Mara and their three children, Valerie, Carey, and Gregory.

Standing on the deck of the Constellation for Richard's burial, his brother-in-law, Marshall Thompson, read the Lord's Prayer. He then tried to open the box that held half of Richard's ashes in order to cast them overboard, but couldn't do it by hand. We looked around and Steffanie Zimbalist, Efrem's wife, finally found a beer opener and gave it to Marsh. We figured it wouldn't bother

Richard, and perhaps it was totally logical to use this implement, considering that alcohol had filled the last years of his life.

While Marsh was prying the box open with the beer can opener, between the tears and remembrances, Phil was looking worried. Here he had a massive ship at full sail and he was looking for a lull in the breeze so we could set the ashes free. He cut the sails, but it didn't look as if a lull would ever come.

"Why don't you go out by Paradise Cove?" I asked. As we approached Paradise Cove, there was a sudden, total quiet. Not a breath of air stirred. The sails fluttered and we all looked at each other, holding our breaths. Everyone knew it was Richard, telling us that it was time to do what we had come to do. We spread the ashes in silence, all of us feeling that he was standing by us, whispering in our ears.

Richard touched me deeply as a friend. I miss him still.

I named my only son after him.

# CHAPTER FOURTEEN
## The Cukor Connection

With *Undersea Girl* in the can, the Morris Agency pushed me for a role in a major studio picture. Never underestimate the power of the agency, especially a company like William Morris, who can get you almost anywhere. If there was a role on Saturn, they'd set up an interview for their clients. Thus I landed a small part in *Man on a String*, a Columbia picture starring Ernest Borgnine.

What an odd picture it was — an action, adventure, spy story, played deadpan with little action or real adventure. There was a Jack Webb-style voice-over narration, detailing a flat FBI manner a counter-espionage plan to send Russian immigrant Borgnine, a movie producer, back to Russia to spy for the United States Government. The tone was unintentionally camp while the story tried desperately to be exciting. You can see me in a tiny role, sitting in front of monitoring equipment when Borgnine is in Russia collection information.

It was only four or five day's work, but I went on the Columbia lot every day for over two weeks to see how the majors made their pictures. In a way, it wasn't so different from *Undersea Girl*, although more professional and busier. It still was full of ego, waste, and fabricated crises. But this was movies, and I was now part of the industry. I didn't know then how foolish the movie would be, nor did I realize how small my role really was. At the time, it felt just like those first ten days before I went on stage in *Blondes*.

## The Cukor Connection

I was playing down the money, power, and the limousine. I let the chauffeur play houseman and left the limo in the garage during the day, taking it out only at night.

Being on the lot and wandering around looking for famous faces, I realized that I was even more impressed with stars than I had been the first time I had come to Hollywood. It was rather ironic. You'd think I would have been more in awe a few years before, but I couldn't have cared less back then. Now I wanted to be in this world and I was more aware of just what the big stars had to go through to get where they were.

Farley Granger called to invite us to a party at his Malibu beach house. I went alone because Nikki didn't like the beach — too much sand, she said. There I bumped into my buddy, Shelley Winters, along with Katy Thalberg, and Jean Stein. After the usual fun and games romping around the beach, Jean took me aside. She said they were having a small party up at the house on Tower Road and were inviting some old friends of mine — Tab Hunter, Debbie Reynolds, R.J., and a few others — and could I come? I said I'd be happy to. Then she told me she needed an escort for a dinner party at the home of a very important director. I told her I'd be happy to escort her, but my wife had to be invited, too. She said haltingly that she thought it would be all right. She was trapped. Jean hadn't known I was married, and being the gracious lady that she was, she couldn't take back the invitation.

Nikki and I picked up Jean a few evenings later and drove up to 9166 Cordell Drive in Hollywood. The director had lived there on the same piece of property for some thirty-eight years. It was one of the original old Hollywood estates off Doheny Road with a huge ivy-covered wall surrounding the property. There was small door, which looked tiny hidden in the ivy in a twenty-foot wall. It was the entrance to the house and garden. A small telephone box was on the wall by the door. Upon announcing yourself, the door swung wide and quite suddenly you were in a different world with a huge pool, flowing fountains, and enormous grounds leading to an old Colonial house an elegant distance up the walk.

*189*

Around the main house were three guest houses. Katharine Hepburn and Spencer Tracy lived in one, while Somerset Maugham and his friend, Alan Searle, lived in another.

Katherine Hepburn was at the party that night, as were the Jules Steins, Merle Oberon, and Vivien Leigh. She and I renewed our acquaintance from London, where I had met her briefly with her husband, Laurence Olivier. But the most exciting part of the evening was basking in the light of one of the greatest directors in Hollywood — George Cukor. Here was a man who had directed such classic motion pictures as *Dinner at Eight, Little Women, Camille, Holiday, The Philadelphia Story, Gaslight, Adam's Rib,* and *Born Yesterday.* He would later direct *My Fair Lady* and win his only Academy Award for it, a picture that, even in his opinion, is long, slow, and pedestrian.

George Cukor was both one of the most highly paid and most highly respected movie directors in the world. He received a million dollars a picture and he kept the first million he ever made. He could spot a star a mile away, which drew him instantly to my wife. He was very well known for directing women and he loved Nikki's classic voice and elegant manner. Of course, she'd had four years at the Goodman Theatre, but he recognized the something special that is so much a part of her. He wanted to know if she was doing something about her career and she told him she was playing housewife. He laughed and accepted her answer graciously. That dinner party was our entre into what I considered Hollywood Society.

George was a very nice, unassuming man who lived in a grand style. To run his comfortable home and magnificent grounds, he had two full time gardeners, two full time cooks (he loved good food), and upstairs maid, a housekeeper named Myrtle, who had been with him for thirty-five years, and a secretary, who had been with him the same amount of time. No matter how grandly he lived, he was still low key when entertaining small groups of friends.

The pattern was set: dinner parties started at 7 pm and guests were expected to arrive on time. Cocktails were served from 7 to 7:30. No one got more than one drink, except Vivien Leigh and me. At 7:30, we were seated at the table. By 9 pm the dinner and conversation were over and we adjourned to the library for coffee and brandy until precisely 10 pm, when everyone was kicked out. That was it. He followed this pattern throughout his life because he felt that after two hours, everything important had been said. He believes in small, intimate dinner parties, ten people at the most, and he would invite people two or three times a week. Fortunately he liked Nikki and me very much, so we enjoyed the pleasure of his company for many years.

The Cukor dining room had black walls and fourteen foot high ceilings decorated with gold leaf. In each corner was a seven foot tall Moor stature holding lighted candelabra. Silver candelabras and place settings rested on lace. Because everything else was black, the candlelight made the setting luminous.

Conversations at George's dinner parties were about the theatre or his beginnings in New York. The pioneers of cinema in the early days came from different walks of life, seldom from an arts background. Cukor was one of the few who had actually been a director back then; he had directed plays on Long Island. He was supposed to start a theatre project in New York when David Selznick suggested he come to California and work there. He followed Selznick's advice and his first picture was *Tarnished Lady* in 1930. He came out to work with friends and was a part of the closely knit group that tailored the movies in the early years.

Nikki and I were thrilled to meet Kate Hepburn. She's always been one of Nikki's favorite actresses. We were delighted to find out that she's as unpredictable in person as she is on the screen. She is an outrageous lady — her humor was raunchy and hilarious. As we got to know her better, we liked her even more. She didn't act like a movie star and wasn't stuck spinning her wheels patterning herself after the roles she had played the way other

*191*

actresses did. She was wonderful and the only person who could sit at Cukor's table and say, "Now George, please be still."

No one else could tell George Cukor to be still because he literally held court in his home and if you tried to interject anything, he'd shoot you right down. You were to sit and listen. We'd get a vast education about the old Hollywood and days of real glamour. The glamour of the fifties couldn't approach the elegance of the early movie days. George Cukor was one of the last practitioners of that kind of life-style and he held on to it like a miser hoarding gold. He loved to dress up and give ornate dinner parties — that may be why we got on so well.

Kate Hepburn, on the other hand, wasn't much into glamour at all. But she did and does her own thing with such style that you can't help but admire her. We've seen Kate jogging up Doheny Road or driving around town in her beat-up old Chevy convertible, top down, with a scarf on her head, dark glasses, tennis shoes, and sweat pants. She always wears pants of some sort; I have never seen her in a dress.

Years later, through the Cukor connection, Nikki and I were invited to a dinner party in the Beverly Hilton Grand Ballroom, a formal black tie affair. We were at George's table, as was Liz Taylor and the Burton diamond.

Richard Burton had given Liz a fabulous blue Cartier diamond, a two and a half million dollar stone. Liz came to the party in a strapless gown to show off her new jewel. Everyone was gaga over her and the diamond and of course, everyone wanted to see the damn thing. The Brinks' guards were placed discreetly around the room to dissuade anyone from trying to make off with it. One movie star after another came over to her, peered over her shoulder, and then politely asked her to turn around so they could get a better look at it. At first she was pleased, because this is what she was there for, and she was happy to oblige. After a while, though, it got old, and began to interfere with her meal. Liz couldn't finish her soup because every time

## The Cukor Connection

she'd lift her spoon to her lips, someone would interrupt her to look at the diamond.

Finally, Liz tried to hide the diamond. This was not very effective. She went to a dinner party wearing a million dollars between her breasts and tried to hide the jewel with her dinner menu. Obviously, there was no way she could keep it a secret. Cary Grant wandered by, peered over the menu, tapped her on the shoulder, and said, "Elizabeth, may I please see the necklace?" What was she to do, say no? The photographers swarmed again, and we all began seeing green on our plates from the flashbulbs.

George stood up from the table in a rage. "Enough of all this! Those photographers are driving everyone crazy!" The Brinks' guards turned a bit, saw it was only George, and turned back. George continued, "If one more person asks to see that diamond . . . Aha! I've got an idea." He walked around the table to where Liz sat. "Elizabeth," he said, "sit very still."

George took the necklace and turned it around so the diamond was in the middle of her back. Her moved her hair around her shoulders to the front, leaving a clear view of the diamond. After that, everyone went past the back of her chair, oohing and ahhing, and pointing to the jewel. Elizabeth didn't have to turn around anymore and she finished her meal in relative peace.

George Cukor was loved and will be missed by everyone of us privileged to know him. He lived a long, beautiful life, dying at the age of 83.

Some years later, I introduced my son Richard to Richard Burton at a Christmas party. Burton looked at him and said, "Richard, you have been blessed with a wonderful name. And best you live up to it because all we Richards have to be perfect." My son then turned to me, wrinkled his nose, and asked, "Who's that?" I quickly stuffed a copy of *Who's Afraid of Virginia Woolf* into his hands and told Burton that the boy was not really my son, just some kid my wife brought home.

## The Park Avenue Chorus Boy

If by now you are thinking that I was a slobbering, ingratiating puppy in front of movie people, I must defend myself. I never slobbered. No matter how infatuated I was with movie stars, I never had any trouble talking to them as real human beings. I would go right up to them, introduce myself, and begin a conversation.

At Longchamps Restaurant in New York, a nice place to eat in the period just before we went to Europe, Nikki and I saw Marlene Dietrich sitting at the bar. She wore a pair of slacks and sat cross-legged on a stool waiting for Cecil B. DeMille to come in. I did an instant double take from Dietrich to Nikki, went up to Dietrich, and said, "Miss Dietrich, I'm Michael Mason and this. . .," turning her attention to Nikki, ". . . this is Susan McKay."

Dietrich said, "Oh," and they stared at each other.

Before Dietrich could say anything else, Nikki said, "A lady who has such famous, spectacular legs should never cover them up with slacks."

Dietrich smiled and thanked her.

On another occasion, at a reception George Cukor gave at the Museum of Modern Art, Mae West as there, along with Ava Gardner, and Myrna Loy. Mae West was chatting with one or two friends, and there was a small circle of people standing around, staring at her. I grabbed Nikki by the hand and said, "Hey, let's go meet Mae West.

"What are you talking about?"

"C'mon, she won't mind."

So I walked over to Mae West and said, "Hello, Miss West. It's nice to meet you. I'm Mike Mason and this is my wife, Nikki. We're good friends of Mr. Cukor. I hope you don't mind my coming up to you like this and introducing myself."

"Please," she said, "I'm so bored. Why the hell's everyone standing around looking at me like I'm some sort of freak. I can talk, too, you know."

We chatted awhile until George came over. "Ah," he said, "I didn't know you two knew each other."

"Well, we do now," she said. "Michael just came over and introduced himself."

People just stand back in awe and stare and most stars don't like that. Ava Gardner is another star who could stop traffic at a busy intersection. People were afraid to talk to her, too. On the same night at the same party, I stumbled across twenty people to get to her.

"Ava," I said, shoving three accountants and a bartender out of my way, "how are you?"

"Oh, Christ," she said smiling. "Somebody to drink with and talk to. What's the matter with everybody? They just stand and stare at you. What's happened to Hollywood?"

She went on to say that in the old days they would say, "Hey, Baby, let's have a drink." Now they saw the older stars and were afraid to approach them.

The sad thing is stardom can isolate actors and actresses and they don't like it. Imagine a scene on Broadway, if you will, after the play is over, and no one comes backstage to congratulate the star. Actors and actresses always wait backstage with the dressing room door open to greet people and found out first-hand what they thought of the evening's performance. How sad it would be if nobody came. Just because people are on a screen and their filmed images are literally larger than life doesn't mean they don't need feedback and conversation.

# CHAPTER FIFTEEN
## Elmer Gantry Was Drunk

That fine 1927 Sinclair Lewis novel, *Elmer Gantry*, was finally to make it to the screen, written and directed by Richard Brooks. Here was one of the greatest novels in American literature, an intelligent work of satire, the story of the most charming, eloquent, and clever liar ever to preach a sermon, Elmer Gantry. The book was a scandal in its day, the story that exposed the hypocrisy of evangelism.

And who could bring to life the larger-than-life, Elmer? Who was big enough, loud enough, and man enough to portray the great Gantry, a sermonizer whose silvery, slippery tongue swayed thousands of suckers, mesmerized them, and won them over to God? Who else, but Burt Lancaster. But could Gantry remain the cad he was in the body of a hero like Burt Lancaster? Remember this was the Hollywood version, so there would have to be some redemption of Gantry.

The Morris Agency also handled Jean Simmons and Richard Brooks, which gave me my opportunity. I wanted in the film badly. Morris sent me over to meet Brooks. I was willing to take any part that was available. I read, among other things, the role of Elmer Gantry as a young man, or should I say the young Burt Lancaster? Brooks leaned forward as he listened to my reading and said afterwards, "Okay, you'll do. I don't know what part I'm going to put you in, but I'd like to use you."

## Elmer Gantry Was Drunk

I was given the part of the young Elmer Gantry. They told me Shirley Jones was in the film, too. I hadn't seen Shirley since the pavement-pounding days of New York. We had no scenes together, but renewed our friendship and hung out around the set together.

Simmons and Brooks carried on a romance throughout the film which culminated in her divorce from Stewart Granger, a classy gentleman, and her subsequent marriage to Brooks, the wild, tough director.

Brooks was one of those brilliant directors who just seemed to happen to Hollywood, almost as if they bully their way in. He was extremely creative and it was hard not to be in awe of him, especially since he directed at the top of his lungs. There was never any question about what he wanted, and even when he was dealing with Simmons, his own wife-to-be, he could be brutal. In most cases he stopped short of hollering at her, but he ran the show with such a tight rein that the fallout spread like acid rain.

Brooks needed all the bluster and force he could muster for *Gantry,* because it was a bitch of a picture to direct. There was a lot going on the screen all the time, the story was rich and detailed, and there were many crowd scenes, the bane of directors everywhere.

On top of that, he had to deal with Burt Lancaster, the star, an acrobatic, handsome, virile leading man. Hollywood is the capital of ego, the birthplace of inflated self-opinion, the heaven of vanity, and one of the greatest, most infamous egos of all was that of Mr. Lancaster. I, of course, was totally in awe of him and I was not alone. Kim Novak thought he was special, too. She kept wandering onto the set to visit him, still a young girl who would one day be a star in her own right, but now, only beginning to feel her way around. She desperately wanted to get to know Lancaster, but he'd caught a whiff of her intentions and just as desperately wanted to avoid her. She was not his type. He was more interested in spending time working out at the gym, priming his body so that if another picture like *Trapeze* came along he'd be ready for it. He came late to the set after working out, doing his regimen of sit-ups, push-ups, and pumping iron. Novak couldn't understand why he was not interested; she figured everybody wanted her and if they didn't, they should, and ninety percent of the time she was right. Lancaster was part of the remaining ten percent.

I walked past his dressing room one afternoon after filming and he said, "You're Michael Mason, aren't you?" I love Burt's voice, the soft, quick speech, hard-clipped consonants and long, stretched vowel sounds.

"Yes, I am."

"You're playing me as a young man."

"Yes, I am."

"Don't you think you should know more about the young man you're playin'?"

"Hey, I'd love to."

"Well, come on in and let's have a little talk."

So I went in and had a drink with him, then suggested that rather than sitting around the studio. We go someplace and grab some dinner.

"Okay," he replied, "but I don't like having dinner around town. I can't enjoy myself because people mob me and bother me."

"Well, what do you have in mind?"

"There's a great place in Malibu called the Holiday House."

"Fine," I said. So I waited for him to take off his makeup, change out of his wardrobe, and get dressed. We left his car at the studio and took mine. As I drove down Pacific Coast Highway, I began to get a little nervous. Now I'd been around a lot, but here I was out with one of the biggest stars in Hollywood, the proverbial "star of the picture," and I was driving sixty miles an hour along the ocean. Did my insurance cover something like this? I imagined a clause in small print: "You are expressly not covered if you are in an accident doing sixty miles an hour on the Pacific Coast Highway going north with Burt Lancaster in your car."

I'd never heard of the Holiday House in Malibu. It was an unpretentious place up the coast. We went straight to the dining room, Lancaster pausing to say hello to the maître d', the waiters, and the owner. Ava Gardner was sitting in a corner with her sister and Tyrone Power was there with Errol Flynn. It was a perfect star hideaway because it was far from town and were no photographers or fans to bother anyone. In conjunction with the beautiful restaurant clinging to the bluffs overlooking the ocean, there were hotel rooms down the side of the hill.

The inevitable happened. I drank too much and got very loaded. Lancaster was famous for his drinking, so I wasn't loaded alone.

"I tell you what, Michael," he said, "this is ridiculous. It's along trip back into town. Why don't we just spend the night here?"

I sloshed a little to the port side, nodded while propping my eyelids up with swizzle sticks, said that was perfectly agreeable to me and called for a drink. We took a hillside room overlooking the ocean, then proceeded to slurp more champagne and brandy.

Clearing my head a little with champagne, I thought to myself, "How do I stay all night in a hotel room with a man I barely know who happens to be the star of my new picture? I wonder if my insurance covers this?" Somewhere deep inside the gray matter, thousands of cells were being slaughtered every second by the alcohol, but a warning bell was still ringing. It was a little fuzzy, but if I concentrated real hard, I knew I could figure out what it meant. The edge, I thought. That was interesting — wonder what that meant? The warning bell got clearer. "Mason," a voice inside said, "you're dumb; this is the fastest way to fuck up your career you've ever thought up! You've reached the edge. Those guys at United Artists will have your balls on a fence post if they find you kept Lancaster from making his morning call. Then you *will* be called the Bel Air Extra."

After that little talk I had with myself, I realized it was my responsibility to get him back to the studio. It certainly wouldn't be his head that would roll if I didn't.

"I'll tell you what," I stammered, somehow putting a few clear syllables together, "this is stupid — I'll call and have someone pick us up."

"No, no, no," he said. "We're gonna stay here tonight and take a little swim in the morning', boy. Then we'll drive back to the studio together."

So after yet another bottle of Dom Perignon and a little more Courvoisier, he went off to take a shower. I went to the phone, called the house, and told Nikki to have Jimmy pick us up. It was 4:30 in the morning. I knew Lancaster had an early call and no one knew where we were.

Lancaster came out of the shower, naked and dripping and dropped to the floor in front of me to do his nightly push-ups. It was rare to see a man in such top condition; taut biceps stretched as he rose, bulged as he dropped, the rest of him humming like an oiled, alert panther. He had one of the most perfect bodies I had ever seen. No wonder women were in awe of him.

"Listen, Burt, I had to call my house and found out I had an emergency call. My uncle's very ill, so I won't make it to work tomorrow. It would be very complicated for me to drive you to work later this morning, since it's already after 4:30 in the morning and I'm plastered to the gills. So since I'm too drunk to drive, and God knows you are too, my chauffeur's going to pick us up."

"What do you mean, your chauffeur's going to pick us up?"

"I keep a driver and limo."

"You do?"

"Yes, I do."

"Jesus Christ, who are you? What do you mean? You're not under contract to the studio, are you?"

"No, I'm not under contract to the studio."

"Well, what do you mean a chauffeur and limo? You called and hired one?" He started babbling about my hiring a chauffeur and limo, trying to figure it out loud because he was so drunk. Hell, I was high too, and a nervous wreck. Not only could I barely stand up, but I figured if I didn't get the star of the picture to the studio on time, my number would be up, my goose would be cooked, et cetera, et cetera. . . .

"Yeah, I keep a chauffeur and a limousine. I live in Bel Air and I'm super-rich. You're a great guy, Burt, but I'm not going to have it on my head that I finally got you to the studio at 11 am after both of us were out all night drinking. Right now, you don't give a shit and I don't give a shit, but down the line, somebody's going to be very upset, meaning one Mr. Richard Brooks." Brooks didn't like people indulging themselves when there was work to be done.

It was the smartest thing I ever did. Burt started putting on his clothes, pausing only to have another brandy. We sat around and chatted uncomfortably for the longest forty-five minutes of my life, waiting for my driver to arrive.

Jimmy finally got there. I left my car at the hotel and Burt and I got into the limo. Burt was delivered to his dressing room at the studio a little early for make up and I went home. I didn't have any scenes that day, so I spent the day nursing an award-winning hangover. I had told Burt my uncle was ill, so I decided to keep a low profile in case he asked anyone about me. I was concerned about how close I'd come to messing up my career and passed the afternoon in fear. When I finally felt better, I went back to pick up my convertible.

Burt was very standoffish after that. You don't turn down the camaraderie of a big star like Lancaster without suffering the consequences. In the past, I wouldn't have cared less how things turned out. In fact, had I still been the Park Avenue Chorus Boy, I probably would have called the studio and said, "Mr. Lancaster and I are out here on the beach. He's drunk and I'm drunk, and we'll be here for the next three days, so don't bother to call us." But that would have been curtains. I liked him a lot. Things could have been different, and I wish they had.

As the days wore on, Lancaster made little digs at me. He knew I was infatuated with Jean Simmons, another raven-haired beauty, and he saw that I was always trying to sit next to her whenever I could She was probably the sweetest, nicest, most soft-spoken person in the entire world. Lancaster came up to me one day and said, "So, you really dig Jean, don't you?"

"Yeah, I dig brunettes. I think they're fantastic."

About three or four days later, Lancaster, Simmons, and I were together on the set talking and he suddenly said, "Jean, have Michael tell you about this great place where we had dinner the other night. Maybe he'd like to take you and Richard there," and then he laughed.

"Jesus, you don't have to be nasty, Burt," I said, "just because we got too drunk." I started making jokes about it and I think he decided that I had something on him that he didn't appreciate. He pulled me aside and said, "I understand you picked up the tab the other night, so I owe you a lotta bucks." He went into his pocket and tried to push $500 at me.

"Hey, thanks," I said. "Why don't you give it to your favorite charity. But, if you ever want to have a drink again, let me know." Of course, we never did.

About a year and a half later, we discussed what had happened that night at the Holiday House and agreed we were both taking it a little too seriously. I was under pressure and he was doing Gantry, one of the best, but toughest roles of his career, so there was a lot of pressure on him, too.

When the 1960 Academy Award time came around, for their roles in *Elmer Gantry,* Burt was named best actor and Shirley Jones won for Best Supporting Actress. We were all together that night. Shirley was a very sharp lady, and she made a quick assessment of my "friendship" with Burt.

"Why, Michael," she said. "I had no idea you and Mr. Lancaster knew each other so well. It's quite obvious you worked together for a long time on the film."

"Not at all," I said. "Just a few days."

"Well, you wouldn't know it to look at you," she grinned. Lancaster was doing all he could to ignore me.

"Next time Burt and I go out drinking, Shirley, you can come and referee."

The final payoff was that when *Elmer Gantry* finally made it to television, I had been cut out of it completely. Whether or not that was intentional, I'll never know.

There are some good Gantry stories. I'd often come on the set and see Richard Brooks holding Jean Simmons' hand. They were very much in love and were married soon after the picture was finished. She left him while he was doing *Looking for Mr. Goodbar*. She was a very classy lady; in fact, Brooks would never swear in front of her when I knew them. *Goodbar* lowered him in her estimation, and was one of the reasons why the marriage broke up.

Brooks may have had a hot temper and he did scream a lot, but he knew enough about Burt Lancaster to know how to deal with Burt's large ego. I'd see an argument brewing between them on the set and Brooks would halt the filming while he and Lancaster disappeared into a dressing room to finish the argument in private. That way nobody's ego was bruised in public. It was almost like a cartoon scene with noise coming from the closed dressing room trailer as if Wile E. Coyote had finally caught the Roadrunner and was giving him a severe thrashing before the feast. A few times, I expected the dressing room to leap off its wheel base and buck up and down and back and forth. Then there would be quiet and two calm men would emerge from the doorway. Then the scene would be done two different ways: Brooks' way and Lancaster's way. Brooks had a diplomatic streak in him that was pure genius.

If you watch the film, Elmer Gantry redeems himself through heroics. Sinclair Lewis allowed Elmer no such redemption. Burt Lancaster had a lot of power at the studio and over the films in which he starred. It's entirely possible that the hard edge of Gantry was blunted so that Lancaster would not ruin his image as a heroic figure.

# CHAPTER SIXTEEN
## Thin Skin That Wiggles

You would think that with all the contacts I had made and all the small roles I had played, that things would start looking up. Well, they did, a little.

Stan Kamen called to say there was a great part for a young, handsome Western type, a city-slicker, in a film called *Showdown at Boot Hill*. It called for ruffled shirts, string ties, black boots, and black velvet collars. For some strange reason, Stan thought I'd be perfect for it. There were many young men in line for this role and they were presumably going to test the top contenders. He got me a script; I read it and thought I'd be good in it. But I didn't think I had a prayer of getting it because it was 20th Century-Fox and, as you may recall, I had dealt with Fox before. Why would they hire me after my abominable screen test. I didn't want to remind Stan what an obnoxious little shit I had been back then. I even went so far as to plan changing my name before going out to the studio, but I realized that was a stupid idea.

I read for Gene Fowler, Jr., the director. He and his associates thought I was very good, but qualified that by saying they were seeing a lot of actors and would test the finalists. That gave me heartburn because my greatest mental block was still the screen test.

While waiting for a response from the Boot Hill people, I talked about it to Cukor. George said, "It's the juvenile lead in a good picture — "B" movie or not, it's great experience for you and would be great exposure. You'll do lots of scenes and your name will be up there. Tell William Morris you want co-star billing if you get the part."

I called Stan Kamen and told him that, in the opinion of George Cukor, I should have co-star billing. When Stan picked himself off the floor and was able to speak again through his laughter, he said, "What do you mean, co-star billing? You don't even have the part yet. They're auditioning a hundred and fifty guys for that one part and you're talking about billing? You'll be lucky to even get it."

I was ready to tell him I'd do it for nothing — I didn't need the money; I just wanted co-star billing.

A partial cast list was announced. The part I was up for was still not cast. Carole Matthews and Fintan Meyler would be the female leads. John Carradine and Jim Hutton were playing character roles. The male romantic lead was to be played by Charles Bronson. The cabaret girl was to be played by a beautiful young blonde starlet named Jackie Story. We recently re-met and renewed our friendship in Palm Springs where she now lives and works as a writer.

A few weeks went by and I was called back to the studio to read with Carole Matthews and then again to read with Charles Bronson. The producers and director decided that rather than screen testing everyone, they would rehearse the role like a play. I was saved. As long as I didn't have to put my face on the screen for a test, I would get the part. In rehearsals and cold readings, I was exceptionally good. Whenever I auditioned for something without knowing the script, I could take it in hand and give a good interpretation right away. Some of the finest actors in the world are terrible sight readers; maybe I was good because of my musical training, learning songs after hearing them only once. Of course, being a good cold reader doesn't help you down the line when you have to deliver the role to the public. The difference is like asking a guy who has made sandwiches all his life to cook a Beef Wellington for Julia Child from scratch.

Sure enough, after a couple of rehearsals and a few walk-throughs, reading maybe thirty minutes of dialogue in the script, they said, "Hey, you're all right. You've got the part." All this had been done on an empty sound stage with a work-light. The director, Fowler, sat around with the producer and a few of the production people on folding chairs as we walked through the script, just like the early days on Broadway. If they had done the screen test, I would have buried myself out of fear. Instead, they said, "Would you *mind* reading the Bronson? Would you *mind* reading with Carole Matthews?" Would I what? I'd love to! The enthusiasm I brought to my reading worked — I was back on a stage again and I was *safe* there.

Once they hired me, I came in wearing jeans and a western shirt. They told me I was in the wrong type of outfit, that I'd be wearing smartly tailored slacks, grey pin-striped suits, a black coat, ruffled shirt, and a string tie. I was to be a sophisticated kid in the Western, a "dandy." Naturally, I didn't get co-star billing, but I had beaten out a hundred and fifty other guys. I was going to be a serious actor. The costume they gave me included a holster and gun that had been Clark Gable's. It may not seem like much, but it gave me confidence. I figured the minute I wrapped that holster around my waist, I would become the sophisticated Clark Gable type, It was my security blanket. Too bad it couldn't protect me from myself.

We started rehearsals for *Showdown* on the set. A lot of time was spent rehearsing prior to filming because film is expensive. It was a "B" movie with a low budget, but they weren't so "B" as to carry around strips of film for continuity. We rehearsed several pages of dialogue and then shot those pages the next day. The rehearsals were laced throughout the shooting, taking two or three days away from the camera to prepare. The studio system in the late fifties encouraged working that way. They had contract crew members, just as there were contract actors, contract directors, and contract writers. They moved from set to set, doing "B" movies or TV shows.

## The Park Avenue Chorus Boy

Charles Bronson and I became pretty good friends. One day were having lunch together in the commissary and Bronson said to me, "You know, you're a very good-looking guy and you 're very good as an actor — I've watched you rehearse." The only scenes I had with him were late in the picture and he had been watching me work with Carole Matthews. "You're going to be good," he said, "but you know, your skin is too loose."

"What are you talking about?"

"Do you work out? You're obviously in good shape."

"No, I don't work out. I'm a swimmer." Sure Charlie, I work out by lifting champagne glasses and swimming in the grape.

"Well, move the flesh on your arm," he said. He took a pinch of flesh on my arm between his fingers and moved it back and forth showing me how much give the skin had over the muscles and bone. "Look," he said, "it wiggles."

"Isn't that normal? Flesh wiggles if you put your finger on it and move it around."

"No. Feel mine."

I tried to wiggle the flesh on his arm. It was like touching the back of your hand when you've made a fist, it was that tight. He worked out so there wasn't a single layer of fat on his entire body. He was like a molded piece of iron. Later in his dressing room, as he stripped down to change, I noticed his stomach muscles, muscles that rippled, while his abdomen, thighs and calves were as hard as a rock. He looked like a piece of Roman sculpture, carved to perfection out of marble.

I played an arrogant, smart-ass pretty boy in the film which was a setup to the most embarrassing line said about me in any film I had ever done. Bronson (in the film) makes a derogatory comment about my character and Carole Matthews comes up to me and pats me on the back, straightens my string tie, and fluffs out my ruffled shirt. "Well," she said, "he may be dumb, but he's pretty." Inside I was wincing, thinking, "That's cute. Try to live *that* down, fella."

## Thin Skin That Wiggles

They spent half a day setting up a scene in the barroom where I, supposedly a very good hand with a gun, was to take shot glass, down the drink, throw the empty glass up in the air, pull out my gun, and shoot the glass down. No sweat in any of this, except we were using real whiskey, so we were all bombed by the end of rehearsal. Still, I had no idea how they were going to do the actual trick. I turned to Fowler while we rehearsed and wondered aloud about how it would happen in the filming. He told me not worry; it was worked out.

The day we were ready to film the scene, he set up a stunt man under the table where I was sitting. Bronson stood in front of me. The camera was to the left. The time came for me to perform, so I took the shot glass, threw it in the air, and the stuntman underneath the table brought his gun up from nowhere and shot the glass. It took a long time to set up the scene, because it was suppose to be my hand shooting the empty glass. Meanwhile, I was sitting with my legs apart, this guy's head at my crotch, while his hand hung over my right thigh. He was snuggling up next to me so he could get a clear shot. I looked at the director deadpan and said very seriously, "Is this what is known as a Hollywood crotch shot?" The director and producer did not laugh, but Bronson and Carole and I, the crew, and the stunt guy, who gave me a good whack in the balls and got up from the floor saying, "You asshole," were laughing so hard, we held up filming for fifteen minutes. It was the only time during the filming that I saw Bronson, who was usually very serious, laughing.

In another scene, John Carradine was to join a funeral procession as it moved down the street.

"John," I said after watching him do the take, "I just watched that take and maybe you'd better mention something that nobody picked up on."

"What, Michael?" John croaked.

"Well, the character you play has a stiff leg and limps."

"Yeah?"

"Well, you didn't. That whole shot following the casket, you weren't limping. You were just walking normally." No one had noticed it but me.

"Ah, fuck 'em if they didn't notice," said John.

"You better tell them. What if they don't pick it up in the rushes?"

He never told them, no one ever picked it up in the rushes, and, if you watch the film carefully, there's John shuffling along the street without a limp behind the funeral procession and in the next scene, he's limping again. But in "B" movies those are the things that are expendable. The budget is just too small and the irritant value of small slipups like that is equally small.

There was a good fight sequence in the film that pitted me against Charlie Bronson I wasn't much of a fighter and Bronson was (and is) a pretty tough guy. He's a coal miner's son and had worked in the mines himself far a while in Pennsylvania. He was an amateur boxer to boot, which stacked the odds heavily against me. On top of that, his skin didn't wiggle. In our scene we had to struggle for a shotgun. He prided himself on being very strong and you can believe it — the man was an ox. I was a head taller than he was, and I looked big and strong. The skin might not be tight, but the muscles were all in the right places and gave me the illusion of being able to take care of myself. At this point in the film, I'd been shot and had a bloody bandage across my chest. As we struggled for the gun, I was supposed to rabbit-punch him in the back of the neck. Each time we rehearsed, Bronson said, "You're not doing it hard enough. Now when we film this, be a little more realistic. You can't hurt me; just *do* it."

"Well, okay, I'll do it."

The cameras rolled, we struggled for the shotgun, and I punched him with a little muscle, knocking him flat on his back and totally out. When he regained consciousness a few moments later, he staggered to his feet with his head spinning and said, "Yeah, that's sort of what I meant."

I invited Bronson to the house once, but he just wasn't into flash and flair. He was uncomfortable and never came again. We became friends anyway, even though he didn't smoke or drink, and worked hard at his craft.

The picture was finally finished and we saw a rough cut. I realized the movie was terrible. The dialogue was bad, the editing was bad, and the scenes I'd been in turned me into a hateful character without my even being aware of it. We went to the premiere in London and at the end of the film, when I was shot and killed, there was no audience sympathy — in fact, they applauded, hooted, and hollered. I'd thought I was going to be a big star in London, signing autographs in the theater lobby and collecting kudos from the Brits. Then they went and applauded my death. I left the theatre very quickly before the film ended, so that no one would see me when the lights went up.

I did the part well enough to have garnered applause at my demise, but at the time I couldn't separate myself from the role. I was too think-skinned. To make matters worse, I met Dick Clayton for lunch back in Hollywood a few weeks later and got to hear what some other people thought of the film. Clayton was going to try and get me in to see some of his MGM producer pals to parlay my Boot Hill role into some future work. He knew it wasn't a good film, but it wouldn't do me any harm because it was good exposure. Then Pasternak came into the commissary.

"Hey, Mr. Pasternak," I called out, waving. "How are you?"

He came over. "Michael Mason. I been hearing about you for the past few years. I remember you singing for me. By the way, I saw your new release, the one you did for Fox, *Showdown at Boot Hill*."

"Yes, sir, how did you like it?"

"It's not a case of liking it," he said. "Just stick to your singing."

And he walked away.

"Well, Clayton," I said, that kind of takes care of MGM. Don't waste your time." Obviously, he wouldn't be able to do me any favors there.

I was not an actor. I could get by on the personality factor that film demands if the role I was cast in was close enough to me as a person. But I couldn't act in a role that required me to be another person. Unless you're a real actor, you can't do that with any credibility. I was a misplaced singer. Nonetheless, I hadn't expected to be perceived as the villain of the film. I thought there would be some sympathy for my character. I thought the audience would be on my side. After all, I was once the Park Avenue Chorus Boy, in cafe society, and on Broadway — the gladiator with a silver Chevy and a long limousine. Didn't these people understand that I had feelings. How could they laugh at me when I died?

# CHAPTER SEVENTEEN
## Mr. Sunoco Cola Knows Best, Gracie

All right then, maybe things weren't going to work out right away in feature films. There were other things I could do. Television, for instance.

Morris had me doing pilots for TV shows. One was for *Dr. Kildare*, as the young doctor himself. I screen tested with Lew Ayres, who'd played Kildare in nine films for MGM, starting with *Young Dr. Kildare* in 1939. Lionel Barrymore had played the crusty old Dr. Gillespie opposite him. Now Ayres was up for the Gillespie part and I was up for Kildare. They informed me that if they gave Gillespie to Ayres, I'd play Kildare in the show. It looked as if I had a decent shot at it. Ayres had the name recognition with the role; it made sense to cast him. My salary was to be $1,750 a week — not bad, even for a rich kid. I was walking on a cloud. *Boot Hill* couldn't have been too terrible because I was getting close on a lot of new projects. Lew Ayres made a good Gillespie and I enjoyed testing with him, but I kept wondering if his politics, which were unfashionably leftist, would affect the network decision.

In the end, for whatever reason, they cast Richard Chamberlain as Kildare and Raymond Massey as Gillespie. An interesting note to all this is that if I had been given the role of Kildare, chances are my career would have gone in a considerably different direction. I would have been a well-known TV star, a recognizable face with a lead in my own series. It isn't a foolproof way to make it big — the show could have flopped with

*213*

Ayres and me in the lead roles — but chances would have been greatly increased for me. But then, you're never set even if the show is a hit. Chamberlain looked like he was going to be typecast after Kildare, playing only the handsome, romantic young doctor type. He got smart. He took his talent in a different direction once the show ran its course and expanded his horizons. He shucked his image as a teeny-bopper's heart throb and went to England to study Shakespeare. The TV idol smashed his image and created something better and longer lasting — a real career. Would I have been that smart down the road, knowing I'd been typecast and wanting more than that? Or would I have kept on doing the same role over and over?

After losing Kildare, I was then tested for a comedy series. CBS thought maybe they'd found a Fred MacMurray quality in me and wanted to push me as a younger version of him on the tube. Maybe that was my whole problem; I was either another Robert Wagner, James Garner, or Fred MacMurray. No one was looking at me as myself.

I didn't get the second series either.

It's all a matter of timing and luck in Hollywood. If you happen to have the talent when your time arrives, fine, great, and more power to you. But talent alone won't do it. Hollywood is fickle. It was then and it is now. I had everything — talent, looks, contracts, high-powered agents. And where was I? Right on the edge of big success, maybe, but that and a five-dollar bill will get you a cup of coffee at the Bistro Garden in Beverly Hills. I had just been washed out of two TV series which would have established me. I didn't have either the luck or the timing. One has to be prepared for when the time comes, and maybe my time had been when I did my first screen test for Fox. I wasn't prepared then, I had screwed around too much, boozed it up too much, played fun and games too often. If that was my time, then I let it get by me.

So, I went out and did commercials. I was a modern snake oil salesman, a TV pitch man. You name the product, and I did it. I worked with Dinah Shore for Chevrolet; I was a spokesman for Sunoco Gasoline; I did Olympia Beer, Pepsi Cola, Coca Cola, and Kool Menthol Cigarettes, to name but a few. For Sunoco, I did so much work and made so much money, that when I pulled into another gas station, they'd say, "Oh, you're the Sunoco guy. What are you doing here? This is Shell."

Kool was a bitch of a commercial for me because I don't smoke. They called me out to MGM to test for the commercial and I faked my way through the audition. I wasn't about to let any job get away, no matter the price. What if it brought about my big break? I wanted that break and led myself to believe it would come through one of these commercials. I'd watched my wife smoke like a chimney for years, so I was able to fake a drag off a cigarette in front of the producer and have him say, "Hey, that's great; you've got the job. Report next Tuesday at eight in the morning."

The Kool commercial took two full days to film. The first morning, with the camera a foot from my face, the New York ad guy said, "Okay, take a drag from your cigarette, suck in the smoke, *hold* it, then blow it out *very* slowly." I'd never actually inhaled cigarette smoke before. So I was coughing and sputtering like a schoolboy in the john taking his first puff on a dare. After four hours of inhaling Kools, one of the strongest brands around, I was taking my breaks in the can, puking menthol. The producer took me into his office, let me lie down on his couch, and gave me a shot of brandy to settle my stomach. The next day I went back to the set a lovely shade of green. I finished the commercial doing a decent imitation of the green and white colors of the Kool pack. If they'd put pointed ears on me, I could have done *Star Trek* right then and there. The commercial ran regularly on television.

Commercials had cattle calls, too, just like Broadway and feature films. There would be a hundred guys up for two roles in any given commercial. So, I'd lie a lot to get the work. Sure, I smoke. Golf? Of course I golf; doesn't everybody? We'd go on location, they'd hand me a club and tell me to tee off, and I'd think they were talking about putting leaves in boiling water and having afternoon refreshments. Every time they caught on that I couldn't do what I'd said I could do, it was too late to replace me because we were already on location.

The Chevrolet commercial with Dinah Shore was shot out in Palos Verdes. It was a week's shoot, a major production, It was like doing a "B" movie on a big budget; the high production values were inspired by Dinah's involvement. The producers provided luxurious trailers, great meals, and ample breaks. In the commercial I drove a car and two girls were supposed to mount horses and follow me. One girl looked at me in panic and said, "I've never been on a horse before." I wasn't the only one who lied to get into a commercial. "Hew, dummy," I said, "that's something you just can't fake." They had to drive her back to town and bring out another actress. It held up production for two full days.

Every so often I'd do a screen test for a commercial. I did one for Gillette razor blades with another actor who was considerably shorter. To him, I was the typical Hollywood, good-looking 6' 1" winner. We were supposed to be shaving at the same time and be the same height, so they stood him on an apple crate.

"You tall bastards are doing the whole town," he said. "I understand you're doing every commercial going."

This is my second time out, I'm finally testing, and I've got to stand on an apple crate."

"What are you bitching about?" I said. "You're a good-looking guy; you'll make it."

"Oh, bullshit. Maybe I'll be a stuntman instead. My father was a stuntman; there's good money in it. I've got a kid to support." And he went on with his tale of woe throughout the day.

"I'm Michael Mason," I finally said, breaking into his sad story. "What's your name?"

"Bob Conrad."

## Mr. Sunoco Cola Knows Best, Gracie

I decided not to take him up on his dare to knock him off the apple crate. He went from commercials to making $5,000 a week in the series *Hawaiian Eye,* then up to $30, 000 a week doing *The Wild, Wild West, Black Sheep Squadron, The Duke,* and so on. Now he writes his own ticket, and he was telling me I was the right height.

There was a jockey shorts ad I did with Doug McClure, a Vaseline Hair Tonic ad filmed in two days which paid me thousands, and three commercials for Dial Soap which paid me even more thousands. I scored heavily in the money department doing commercials.

Later, the ad agencies got smart and realized actors were being overpaid for what they were doing. As soon as some of the figures got out as to what could be earned in commercials, well-known actors realized there was gold in them thar hills. They moved into commercial territory, six guns a blazing. On commercial cattle calls, I'd start to see well-known faces. Hey, that guy was in *Maverick* the other night, and didn't I see him in an episode of *Perry Mason?* Pretty soon, guys like me who were doing commercials regularly were pushed out in favor of better known faces. How could I possibly compete? If I were in an ad agency executive, I'd want a name actor, too.

None of this ever kept me from trying to pull out all the stops. When I went on commercial interviews, I'd play up my New York experience to the hilt, which really helped me. Most of the guys doing the interviewing for commercial actors were from New York and Broadway was their backyard. They were usually happy to get me. The average Hollywood unknown hadn't had the kind of experience I did, so I was getting damn near every commercial I went out for until the known actors came to town.

I also had a pretty extensive television career at that time, appearing in a guest star capacity on such shows as *The Steve Allen Show* and *The Margaret Whiting Show.*

On *Burns and Allen,* George Burns was infamous for changing dialogue just before a show was filmed. During the first show I did for him, I was sitting in a corner learning my lines when I looked up to see stage hands putting "idiot" cards around the set with script alterations. When I protested that I'd just finished memorizing the script, I was told I shouldn't have bothered because Mr. Burns invariably rewrote the script just before filming.

I went up to George Burns and said, "I might as well tell you right now, I'm nearsighted. I can't see what they're writing on the cards."

"Well," Burns said, "you've got a problem because we don't want you with glasses on."

"Why not? I've worn glasses before doing a car commercial with Dinah Shore."

"That didn't matter then; you were in a car. You're playing a college kid, my son's buddy at school, and we don't want the glasses image."

"What do I do?"

"Go get contact lenses," he said. I listened to "God," and I got contact lenses, which I wore from then on whenever I did TV, movies, or commercials. Most of the shows I did were shot live and occasionally actors would need "idiot" cards because of last-minute dialogue changes. I ended up doing five *Burns and Allen* shows, all thanks to Mr. Burns.

*Father Knows Best* was a show I did many times. I was one of Billy Gray's pals on the show. It was a closely-knit family unit. The people they brought in for small part were a very select few and they kept bringing the same ones in over and over again. Robert Young was very good with his people and wanted to make sure he had the right caliber of people, young and wholesome. Little did he know who was working for him, Michael Mason, a not too upright actor. Young was a total professional, knew what he wanted and how it should be done He was conservative and quiet, a low-key personality. His influence was gentle, but firm, as is the case with many stars of on-going series. Once they are locked into their characterizations, there really isn't that much for a new director to do except maintain the established level and make sure the actors don't bump into each other.

*The West Point Story* was even more fun to do. We were a bunch of rowdy Hollywood actors — including Brett Halsey, Richard Jaeckel, Doug McClure, and Don Durant — who were shipped off to West Point every few months to do our episodes. Don Durant and I became great friends, and he and his beautiful wife Trudy are our very close friends today. We get a big kick out of telling friends at cocktail parties how we went to "West Point" together. No matter where we are, we always celebrate our birthdays together. His wife Trudy was born on May 26, I claim May 27th, and Don and my wife Nikki's birthdays are a day apart, November. 20 and 21st — two Scorpios and Two Geminis. The parties are always great fun, and their two children, Heidi and Jeff, and our son Richard always get together, too, and have as much a blast as their parents do.

After *West Point*, Don went on to star in his own series, *Johnny Ringo*. Just about any young, good-looking actor could do a segment for West Point Story; any guy who would get the proper haircut and looked like a cadet was cast.

I did one episode for the series and the producers like me so much, they asked me back to do two more as the lead. They were great shows to do because the budget was liberal and the actors treated royally. Some the shows were filmed in Hollywood, but some were done at West Point whenever exterior shooting called for a recognizable landmark, like the chapel, dorms, or the Hudson River. When we went to West Point, we were told we must conduct ourselves as if we were young cadets, wear full uniform all the time, buttons buttoned up to the neck, and to salute officers when we passed them on the grounds whether they knew who we were or not.

In the beginning of the series, the producers would shoot one episode at a time at West Point, but then they got smarter and started shooting three at once, thus cutting down on the cost of transporting cast and crews.

I was sent out with Brett Halsey and Richard Jaeckel. We stayed at the West Point Hotel, which was very enjoyable. Jaeckel was a fine gymnast, superior in all events such as the parallel bars, the horse, and the rings, and was in an all around fine athlete. We went to the gym in our West Point track clothes to film athletic scenes with the real West Point Cadets, a number of whom had been chosen to appear along with us on the basis of their athletic excellence. They looked at us as if we were a joke — a bunch of sissy Hollywood actors playing tough West Point Cadets. They were in for a surprise, because apart from Jaeckel, I had been a varsity track star in college, and Halsey had been a swimmer. The cadets snickered and laughed, knowing the actors couldn't hold a candle to America's chosen, soon-to-be officers, the finest of the fine.

Jaeckel went on the rings and made them all look like puppies. He was so impressive, he took your breath away, and you could see the look of awe in the cadet's faces; their guys just weren't that good.

Then it was my turn, a track scene, a few wind sprints around the track. The cadets had nothing nice to say. "Track, huh? The last place he ran was from his limo to a bar'" So the director gathered us together in front of the camera. I was to run against their track star, who told me in a condescending tone that he'd hold back so I wouldn't have to worry about looking bad. The director agreed, thinking the same thing the cadets were thinking — Hollywood wimp, but we'll try to make him look decent for the sake of the home-viewing audience.

"Listen," I said, "just for laughs, let's take off from the beginning."

The track star grinned and faked an apologetic shrug. He was going to show me. We stepped into the starting blocks, the gun went off, and I left him in the dust. My sides hurt, but his pride hurt worse. The director said nothing.

Brett Halsey had his day, too, and although he didn't beat their top swimmer, he gave a good performance. We had earned the respect of the West Pointers.

One day the three of us walked across campus together, having just had our makeup done on the bus. An officer came toward us. It was a hot day and we had our jackets undone, collars folded under for makeup purposes. We were walking like Hollywood slobs, not in that upper class stroll you see at military academies. As we passed the officer, we neglected to salute. He stopped, incredulous. "All right, Mister, what do you think you're doing?"

"We've all gone crazy," I said. "We've just put on our makeup and now we're going over to have lunch."

His eyes widened as we walked away. We got a good chewing out later, but we were not real cadets and they couldn't hang us up by the bootstraps. Don, Doug, and I starred in two more episodes, which we really enjoyed.

Those TV days were all fun — goofing off, having a blast, nothing great happening career-wise, but could I really complain? I was working regularly, eating well, and maybe I was going to break though to stardom.

And then the bad times started.

# PART III
# THE EXORCISM

# CHAPTER EIGHTEEN
## Half A Hero

There seemed to be light years between the star everyone thought I was going to be and the man I actually was. The names of famous people who thought I was going to hit big would make a minor *Who's Who in Hollywood and New York:* Shirley Jones, Liz Taylor, Robert Conrad, Charlie Bronson. Everyone looked me over and said, "buddy, you're star stuff. I'll take ten shares of stock." So I had it figured at this point that my luck was going to change. I was right about the change, wrong about the direction it would go. In fact, my luck was about to go bad.

Nikki became pregnant, which was another reason to think things were going to work out. We were very pleased and excited and decided to phase out Bel Air, get some land, some room, have horses, and get back to Virginia-style roots. I had bought the Bel Air house after renting it, but now literal green pastures beckoned. We started to look in the San Fernando Valley, thinking of either Encino or Sherman Oaks. The Valley was still the location of ranches — the suburban developers hadn't started piling gingerbread houses on the streets — so it was a good place to live. We were in the market for a small ranch.

I'd gotten wind of one that was coming up for sale and someone whispered they thought it was part of Clark Gable's ranch and someone else thought it was part of Ann Sheridan's ranch. All this was enticing, but I figured this was all just the usual Hollywood talk and I ignored it. It could just as well be Joe Grabowski's ranch, so why worry about it? We went out to take a look at the ranch, then drove down Louise Avenue and rounded the corner onto Rancho Street, about two blocks south of Ventura Boulevard. There we came face to face with a high wall, a corral, a couple of horses, and a big ranch house up on the hill. This was not the place we were interested in; it was the main house on a ten-acre estate that was not for sale. The house we were to look at was the gate house for this ranch. As we continued down Rancho Street to the big white double gates, we saw a wonderful Spanish hacienda which had indeed been the original gate house. We drove through the gates, around a huge oak tree which had been there since before insecticide, and into a courtyard.

I heard Nikki holding her breath. "This is our house," she said.

We followed the brick walkway to the front door. The broker gave us a quick rundown of the property as we looked over the living room. It had been the gate house, but had been sold to off by the owner of the main ranch a number of years before. He didn't mention the name of the owner and I didn't ask. He pointed out the wonderful high-beamed ceilings, the fifty-five foot long living room with an adobe fireplace, French doors going to the outer patio with another ancient oak, and about three-quarters of an acre in back with nothing but trees on it. There was a natural stream running through the property with a little bridge over it. I heard Nikki sigh.

"Okay," I said, "we want it."

"Wait a minute," the broker said, "I have to show you the kitchen, the dining room, the bedrooms . . ."

"Forget it, I want to buy it." When I saw something I wanted, I grabbed it. It wasn't always the wisest business maneuver, but it was the way to make sure I got what I wanted. "Where's your escrow office?"

"It's on Ventura Boulevard."

"Fine, do you want to come with us or have us follow you, or what?"

"Mr. Mason, don't you want to . . ."

"I don't want to see the rest of the house. My wife wants it and she's going to have it. And I love it, and that's it, got it?"

"You don't even know what we're asking yet."

"We'll all be fair, don't worry," I said.

So we went to the escrow office and thirty days later I owned the house, although I had to carry two house for a while, since I had not yet sold the house in Bel Air. After signing the papers, we then continued on to Trudy and Don Durant's house which was nearby for a celebration dinner.

I found out that the house had been built sixty years before. The doors were solid hand-hewn oak, made on the property. The tiles had been handmade by Mexican craftsmen. Cantinflas, the Mexican film star, had been a friend of the original owner (who I still didn't know about) and he had sent in his workmen to lay thousands of bricks on sand. These men were artisans and they laid out the inner patio, the outer patios, and the brickwork around the oak trees in a herringbone pattern and it was gorgeous.

"I know why you bought the place," the broker said later. "It suddenly dawned on me that you are in the movie business and you bought it because John Wayne is your next door neighbor."

"What are you talking about? Isn't this part of Gable's or Ann Sheridan's ranch?"

"No, John Wayne lives right next door at the corner of Louise and Rancho."

"Oh, my goodness," I said in my Jack Benny voice, "how nice. The price of our real estate has just gone up."

There was a little guest cottage area near the tennis courts on Wayne's property, within spitting distance of our house. Wayne's makeup man, a fellow named Webb Overlander, lived there. He had been doing Wayne's makeup for thirty-odd years and they were close pals. Every Saturday morning when they weren't on location, Wayne would saunter over to Webb's house for coffee on the patio. They soaked up the morning sun, sipping strong

## The Park Avenue Chorus Boy

coffee, casually chatting shop talk, and before long, Webb would fetch a bottle of booze and the rest of the day would drift by in drinking and discussions.

Well, I wanted in on the fun, so I decided to paint my house. I chose the side of the house that faced the barn, the tennis courts, and Webb's cottage. Ten o'clock in the morning, while Wayne and Webb were boozing, I came around the corner with a ladder on my shoulder and a bucket of paint in my hand. I propped up the ladder, looked busy mixing the paint, then climbed a few rungs.

Pretty soon I heard, "What the hell are ya paintin' yer own house fer — I heard you were rich, kid." It wasn't hard to recognize that voice.

I turned on the ladder and looked at Wayne and Webb and bottle. "I'm not rich; I just pretend to be. Don't let the limo fool you. I'm an out-of-work actor who needs a job. So I'm painting my own house." I turned back to the side of the house and climbed a few more rungs.

Pretty soon, I'd hear, "Well, ya better try a little of this paint remover before ya get too busy."

I climbed down the ladder, left the bucket of paint on the lawn, vaulted over the wall, and sat down with Webb and Duke for coffee and booze. I never did finish painting the side of that house. Of course, the only time I ever tried to paint it was Saturday mornings when they weren't on location. Nikki would come out, see the ladder and bucket of paint on the lawn, and put her head over the wall. "Why don't you ever start on the other side of the house?" she would ask in all innocence. After two or three years of this, I said to hell with it, and hired real painters.

Shortly after moving in, I started remodeling and across the creek that ran through the property, and up on the back property, I built a beautiful mountain lake swimming pool, complete with cabana. It was made of stone and rock, without a piece of tile. George Cukor used to come out to our parties and sit up there by the hour because it reminded him of Lake Arrowhead.

The greatest love of anything or anyone happened in that house when our son Richard was born. We spent many happy years in that house, even if things did go crazy for a while.

Richard was a big baby, although he was born a month early via Caesarian section. I began training two attack dogs, since I became instantly paranoid about my one and only son. Respectability had caught up with the chorus boy.

When Richard was three months old, my life suddenly became crazy. I had been back East on some depressing private business. A collection of things went wrong at once, like collapsing dominos. A good friend had died and I went back to help with the financial arrangements. While at home, I found out there was trouble with my own investments.

I returned to California in a deep depression. No one quite knew what to do with me. Nikki's aunt had come to visit; a nurse was taking care of Richard, but I could be alone if I wanted to. On one particular evening, I was sitting alone in the library, talking to Richard Long on the phone. I was drinking heavily and was very nervous. That afternoon I'd had numerous long distance phone conversations with my lawyers in New York and had found out that my problems were more complicated than they'd previously thought. My finances were looking shaky. Nikki and her aunt decided they had better give me a little room, so they went out to dinner and a movie and weren't expected home until after midnight. The nurse was with my son, so I wandered over to Wayne's. I didn't know what else to do with myself. My lawyers were working late and I was to call them that night and find out what else they knew.

I sat down with the Duke and pretended to be a tough guy and we threw back a lot of belts of whiskey together. When I was around big drinkers like Wayne, I always wanted to play the big shot and keep up with them. I could hold my liquor, in fact I'd always prided myself on being able to drink anyone under the table, but you could not drink John Wayne under the table. He was big and hardy and had lots of experience with liquor. I had started out bombed anyway, so the whiskey was going down soft and making me more and more depressed.

"What's the matter," Wayne said.

"Family business. Pain in the ass."

"You shouldn't have any problems. Ya got this terrific new kid, a great wife, ya got a career that keeps the bottles uncorkin', ya got nothin' to be depressed about."

"Oh, yes, I do. You don't know what's doing on." I was suddenly annoyed with him. Who was he to tell me I didn't have anything to be depressed about?

I asked him if I could his phone to call my lawyers and he sent me over to an extension. I guess he overheard my side of the conversation. I don't remember much of what was said, but the highlights were devastating. It was a blowout conversation: they told me I had a six to twelve month court battle on my hands and they hoped I had enough money on hand to see me though it because my funds were cut completely.

I threw the phone down, turned, and without saying anything to the Duke, walked out of his house. He followed me to the door.

"Where ya goin'? What's yer problem?"

"Never mind. See you later. Go fuck yourself." And I stumbled home in the dark.

I was badly drunk, totally, hopelessly exhausted, and very frightened and desperate when I got home. My feet were shaky and I felt as if the house were going to rise up from around me and fly off, leaving me standing on an empty foundation now that I couldn't afford it. The house was quiet. Nikki and her aunt were still at the movies, and the nurse was with the baby in another part of the house. I was essentially alone.

I staggered into the spinning powder room, wondering who had started the Ferris wheel without my permission. I managed to find the medicine cabinet with only a little bit of fumbling. At that moment I thought I was perfectly aware of what I was doing, but to know what you are doing when you are frightened, in trouble, and stinking drunk is altogether different from knowing what you are doing at any other moment in your life. I took several Seconals. I paused, watched the room stretch, then settle back into right angles, and took several more seconals, thinking I'd go to sleep in the library. I never made it. I came out of the bathroom, the hallway spun fast around me, and the floor came up and bashed me in the face.

Wayne, meanwhile, had been disturbed by my quick exit after what he'd heard on the phone. He collected Webb and they came over to my place, where they found me on the living room floor with a near-empty bottle of pills in my hand. It looked like an attempted suicide. They had no idea how many Seconols had been in the bottle before I had gotten hold of it, and they weren't about to give me the benefit of the doubt. They called the paramedics, who rolled me out to Encino Emergency Hospital and pumped my stomach.

It was pure Hollywood melodrama: if the Duke hadn't come along when he did, the sixteen Seconols would have put me in a deep everlasting sleep. The amount of booze he himself had put away did not detract from his being a concerned, compassionate, and aware person. Had he not been, he would never have thought to follow me home, would never have found me, and I would have died.

I stayed in the hospital two days; it was all explained away as an accident, and we let it go at that. I was very confused and upset by it all. When you're used to having what you want when you want it, it's hard to be told that life won't be that way anymore. I make no excuses for my previous life-style. I didn't choose it, but I enjoyed it, lived it, and it was mine. Perhaps it was a bad way to grow up, but how could I possibly understand that when it was all I knew. How could I possibly know that I was ill-prepared to take on the world without money as a crutch? Expectations are different when you grow up with unlimited money. I didn't expect anyone's eyes to tear when I say there are problems and heartaches growing up wealthy. But the mere fact of money does not make any of those pains or feelings any less important; it just gives you more time to turn them into personal neuroses.

So, as I lay in the hospital bed, I reviewed my life: I'd just bought a new house and was still carrying the Bel Air house, had a new baby, and all of a sudden I didn't have a dime. I had a chauffeur, a Cadillac limo, Nikki's new Mercedes, a maid, and nurse. And I was broke.

Some people can make the transition from wealth to privation more smoothly than others. For me it was to take time and nurturing. Some people remain clam and know that all will be right in the end. Others walk out of seventeen-story windows. Money had created a sense of security in me, but if you don't find security in your own soul, you are lost anyway. Money is transient and doesn't mean very much. I don't want to be without it, but it is only useful for buying material things. What I have discovered is that love and happiness are two things they don't sell over the counter.

The next few weeks, I lived a fragile existence, walking on eggshells while the people around me tiptoed so as not upset my balance. Slowly, very slowly, I got used the fact that my life had changed.

And then it looked as if John Wayne was riding to the rescue again. He told me there was a role in his new film that I would be good for. He was going off to location and would talk to the director and casting people, then get back to me. So I relaxed a little, got myself feeling better and waited for his call.

And waited. Weeks. I didn't understand why I hadn't heard, but I was afraid to call because I didn't want to annoy him. Still, it was getting serious; I was in bad financial shape.

So I did the next best thing — I called Webb.

"Webb, Mike Mason. How's it going?"

"Not bad, thanks for asking."

"Webb, I have sort of a question."
"Why don't you ask it?"
"I think I will."
"I thought you would."
"Duke mentioned something about a part in the film . . ."
"That's funny."
What's funny about it?"
"I don't know anything about a part in the film."
"Well, Duke said it was there. . ."
"Would you take a little friendly advice?"
"Sure."
"Don't count on it."
"Why shouldn't I count on it?"
"Because he's a son of a bitch."
"You mean he won't get me a part in the picture?"
"He hasn't done it for his kids. What makes you think he's going to do it for his next door neighbor?"
"I see."
"I thought you would."
"Well, it's been nice talking to you, Webb."
"I'm sorry Michael, but he does this all the time."
"Goodbye, Webb."
"Goodbye, Michael."

I put my tail between my legs and gave it up. Duke would not be to the rescue twice. The thing that really hurt was not that he hadn't come through, but that he'd offered it in the first place. I hadn't asked him for a favor, he'd offered it, and then when I was relying on him, he swept the promise away, like pulling a rug from under my feet. I felt I was doing a pratfall in a cartoon, except it wasn't very funny.

# CHAPTER NINETEEN
## Let's Break Love

Fox called Stan Kamen at the William Morris Agency and asked that I come out for an interview. I went, not knowing what it was for, but after my experience with Wayne, I was hoping for work. I discovered that they had called at the request of George Cukor who was doing a new film with Marilyn Monroe, Yves Montand, Gene Kelly, and Milton Berle called *Let's Make Love*, and Cukor apparently wanted me in it.

George hadn't called me himself because he did everything officially. "Official channels," as they say, and the routine goes something like this: the director's secretary calls the studio, the studio calls my agent, and my agent calls me. I go to the studio and they tell me I am in the movie. To thank the guy at the beginning of the chain, I'd have to call him myself.

The meeting with the Fox casting office was a formality, and I was hired to play the part of "Yale," a rah-rah Madison Avenue type who was a young business executive and Milton Berle's sidekick. It was a small part and since the shooting schedule for the film was only three months long, I was given an initial contract of only thirty days. I was ecstatic. A thirty-day contract with Fox Studios for a movie with Marilyn Monroe. The first step out of financial hell. Little did I know that thirty days would turn into ten months, ten months that would save my ass financially, ten months because of Marilyn.

## Let's Break Love

By that time I had sold my Bel Air house. The court cases were never resolved about the trust fund, battles that went on for eight years. At the time, though, all I knew was I had to get down to work.

I went home with a script under my arm and a grin a mile wide. I immediately called Cukor and thanked him. He told me my work in *Showdown at Boot Hill* hadn't been that bad. He said he'd only asked the casting department to interview me and hadn't told them I had the job. "Yeah, yeah," I said, "I know, George, but thank you very much anyhow." He didn't want to look unprofessional and be accused of playing favorites. Everything had to look legitimate.

Filming was to start in ten days and in that time I had wardrobe fittings, memorized my part, and prepared in general to go back to work.

The first day at the studio, I wanted to make a big entrance with the limo and impress all the people I was going to see. I always managed somehow to keep a limo in spite of all the money hassles in New York. I was forever trading them in; I'd lease one for a couple of years, then trade it in on a new model, so that when I arrived at the studio it was not in a used, tattletale car, but a beautiful new Cadillac.

There was a drive-on pass at the gate for me, but I informed the guard that my chauffeur would be parking the car. He pondered this a moment, then pointed and said, "Well, why don't you take spot over there, next to Mr. Cukor's, Miss Monroe's, and Mr. Berle's Rolls Royces?" I shrugged nonchalantly. Inside I thought, not too shabby, Mason. The chorus boy's doing it again with the heavyweights. Yes sir, work on the main lot at Fox instead of the dirty Western back lot where the "B" movies are watered. This was an "A" production — elegant and classy. It was better even than *Elmer Gantry* because I had more to do. For *Let's Make Love,* I was a contract player, going to the pay window every week to pick up my check for a nothing, thirty-day part that would build into a bonanza.

I had never expected to see the inside of Fox Studio again. First there had been my disastrous screen test and then there was *Showdown at Boot Hill,* which I didn't think had done me much good. But now, I had eclipsed my whole past; I was at Fox for the third time, and this time in an "A: picture. I was high.

Natasha Lytess was the only person left at Fox from my old screen test days. The casting people had all changed, as had most of the studio executives. The *Showdown* people had been independents, renting one of the Western lots in back. That meant I had a clean bill of health. The head of casting, Gene Reynolds, a wonderful guy who went on to create and produce such marvelous television shows like *M*A*S*H* and *Lou Grant,* liked me and thought I had talent. To my infinite relief, he knew nothing of *Showdown.*

I went into wardrobe the first day and put on my blue suit, blue shirt with button-down collar, and striped tie. The basis of the story was slender — a multimillionaire, Montand, meets and falls in love with a showgirl, Monroe. It was light, nothing story, a romp, as they say. There was a lot of music and dancing throughout, bolstered by big stars in small parts: Gene Kelly as a nightclub owner, and Milton Berle and Wilfrid Hyde-White as millionaires.

The first day was strictly rehearsal and the big excitement was provided by the anticipated arrival of Marilyn. The entire cast and crew waited for the star's entrance.

Natasha Lytess was hanging around, too, and I remembered how she had been Marilyn's private coach for years before Marilyn turned to Lee and Paula Strasberg. Natasha had last seen me ten years earlier, and life had changed for both of us. I was more serious about my work and she no longer worked for Marilyn, having been booted out in New York after *The Seven Year Itch.* It looked to me as if Natasha was wandering around, hoping to intimidate Marilyn when she arrived. I had other worries — she was intimidating me. I hoped she wouldn't recognize me and I hid behind the camera near Cukor as she passed by.

"My God, George," I said, "what if Natasha recognizes me?"

## Let's Break Love

"Fuck her," was his reply. "Who cares? She's a crazy lady."

So I stepped tentatively out from behind the camera as Natasha walked by in the other direction. She didn't give me a second glance.

I renewed my friendship with Yves Montand that afternoon. He remembered me from Paris and as we talked, I realized our previous friendship made me a safe ally in an alien world. He was cautious of Hollywood people, and rightly so. He'd been hired to do a part that was originally offered to Gregory Peck. Peck had gradually backed out of the movie as Arthur Miller rewrote the script, enlarging Marilyn's role and cutting down Peck's. Montand's accent was very thick, his English was not too good, and this was his first Hollywood feature, so he figured he had a lot to lose. But because of the shared times we had in Paris, he trusted me. Simone Signoret joined us and we happily reminisced.

Cukor joined our little group, saying "Well, old home week for you people." He was glad that someone was putting Montand at ease. He started talking to Simone.

"What are you doing on the picture?" Montand asked me.

" A very small part with Milton Berle."

"Ah, good, it will be fun: we will have a good time."

Then he went on to tell me how much he was looking forward to working with Marilyn. Simone glanced over her shoulder at him as he said this, but went on talking to George.

Montand was staying in a bungalow at the Beverly Hills Hotel, a place I knew well. I told him about my roost in Encino, but added quickly that I would probably check into the Hills myself, considering the early calls for shooting.

It was four o'clock in the afternoon. Everyone was there — Jerry Wald, the producer, Cukor, Jack Cole, the choreographer, Montand, and all the rest — all waiting for Marilyn Monroe.

And then — trumpets, fanfare, lights, camera, action — Marilyn. With great pomp, she came in, her mink coat draped over her shoulder. She wore that mink over anything and nothing, summer or winter. She wore the highest spike heels she could find, a pair of Ferragamo pumps. Ferragamo did more for spike heels than anyone else making them, but Marilyn did even more for that footwear by just wearing them.

I turned to look at Simone and she was looking at Montand. Montand was watching Marilyn. Then I knew why Simone was there. Montand was notorious for romancing his leading ladies. It didn't take much for Simone to figure out what it was going to be like this time.

Marilyn hugged and kissed everyone and it was "Oh, darling" this and "Oh, darling" that and it was all just wonderful. George told her they were going to have a wonderful time together, but added they were on a tight schedule. Then he turned to address the rest of the room.

"All right, everyone, it's going to be a big production, but I know we'll all work well together."

George wasn't kidding about a big production; the sets, for one thing, were amazing. The board room for the Madison Avenue tycoons was built of imported oak paneling with solid oak furniture and crystal chandeliers. The conference table was over 40 feet long, a roller skater's dream. Everything was extravagant down to the last detail. There were no phony pictures or imitation oil paintings on the walls — they brought in authentic Renoirs from Cukor's private collection and the security for those paintings rivaled the security provided the President of the United States.

I want to emphasize the aura surrounding this film as work was about to begin. As major a motion picture as *Elmer Gantry* had been (and in fact, it was a more important picture), *Let's Make Love* was something else again. Everything was elegant all the time and it was because of George Cukor and no one else. He created a mood of excellence and professionalism. He was, after all, the great George Cukor, one of the very finest directors in the world, and probably the greatest director of women ever.

The aura on the set was unique. Cukor always dressed in a suit, he did not make small talk or joke around, and business was the most important thing on his mind. Everyone of the set bowed and scraped to him, but he never played it up. He was not an imperious director and there was nothing of the prima dona in him. His reputation preceded him and he created more excitement than most stars hope to do. Even Marilyn knew that. George was the star maker, but he was also the star. Very few directors could demand and get the respect he did.

During the first week, I sat back, listened a lot, watched what was going on, and kept my mouth shut. I'd learned that much. Knowing Cukor as well as I did, I called him at home after the first day and said, "Thank you for a very exciting day."

"Keep it that way."

"What do you mean?"

"Just keep it low-key and speak when you're spoken to and don't get involved with too many people. I know how you can get going, Mason, so just cool it. You're hear to learn. I brought you on the set to learn and give you exposure as to how a proper production is run."

"Yes, sir. I'm extremely grateful and I'll do just as you say, just sit, listen and learn." And that is what I did, at least for the first week.

The next day I was back on the set and Cukor asked if I'd had a chance to go over my dialogue with Milton Berle. As Berle's assistant in the film, I was in every scene with him. I didn't have much dialogue to say, but I was his shadow, always by his side. We had not yet rehearsed together.

Berle was busy playing the star, which of course he was. For instance, he made a big deal about where his Rolls Royce should be parked. He never called it his car: it was his *Rolls Royce*. Of course, I always referred to my transportation as my limousine, so I'm not exactly the one to talk about anyone else. But Berle was pissed off because he didn't have a specific place to park and he raised a stink about it.

To this day, Berle has a magnificent memory. Recently I walked past his booth at the Friars' Club where he holds court, and I said, "Mr. Berle, how have you been?"

He looked at me — mind you, I hadn't seen him in almost eighteen years — and he said, "Michael Mason."

"That's right."

"You were in *Let's Make Love* with me."

His brother looked at him and said, "Jesus, how the hell did you remember that?"

"'Cause the kid was good and we had a lot of good times."

"Hey, thanks a lot," I said. What an incredible memory. Of course, that film left a lasting impression on everyone, especially anyone who had any kind of schedule and was supposed to move on to another film. Forget it. They had to be there for *Let's Make Love* and Marilyn dragged it out forever.

As for Berle, you could understand why he was playing the star. When he walked into a TV studio, people would fall down in front of him. But now he was competing with Marilyn Monroe, Yves Montand, Gene Kelly, and Wilfrid Hyde-White. Berle slowed up production with what he called "schtick," routines that were funny on the small screen, like walking on the sides of his feet. On the big screen, it didn't work, and Cukor cringed. Berle was forever telling George how a scene should be played, not an endearing habit, but understandable since he'd been used to directing himself on his TV shows.

About two weeks into production, with the insanity level rising, I asked Cukor at a dinner party, "How is it you have this great tolerance level? The average director would be ranting and raving and saying, 'Fuck you, it's my movie.'"

"I don't give a damn," said Cukor. "That's how I handle it."

George was unique. He knew that with Berle he was dealing with a frustrated ego out of it normal realm. So he put up with all the nonsense and simply cut it out of the film later. Years after that, I saw him put Jane Fonda in her place in a very nice way. It was while they were filming *The Chapman Report*, before she was a star. She was playing the know-it-all, and he walked over to her and said very simply, "Just remember, you're the star and I am the director. I am the one who directs." Jane was very quiet from then on.

The first weeks of *Let's Make Love* were great. There was camaraderie, fun, and games. Cukor was easy with everyone. Marilyn was happy, she was in her element, had a new audience, a handsome French leading man, and a new film with George Cukor. I wanted to take it all in, so I spent my time hanging around the set, watching, and sitting at Cukor's side. He told me I didn't have to hang around, that he wouldn't need me for a few days, but I told him I wanted to watch him direct. That was bullshit. I wanted to see what Monroe was going to do on this film.

There are stars that are touchable and those who are not. Marilyn was one of the touchables — people on the street would grab at her and she allowed it. Another star, such as Katharine Hepburn, was untouchable. Nobody would dare to grab at her. She created an aura of don't touch me, I'm above that." Marilyn on the other hand was thrilled at the adulation.

It wasn't more than a week or two before I checked into the Beverly Hills Hotel. The story I told myself was that the driving back and forth was making me crazy. It actually wasn't that much farther or harder to drive from home to Fox as it was to drive from the hotel there. But I sent the limo and chauffeur back to my wife and drove my own car to and from the hotel.

One night I asked Montand if he'd care to join me for dinner. I hoped he and Simone would come and chat about old times. He said he could come, but that Simone was going back to Paris to take care of some business. He mentioned that he might bring a friend along, but wouldn't tell me who, only that he would surprise me. We agreed to meet early in the Polo Lounge.

So I waited there, wondering who the friend might be. The maitre d' sought me out, saying Mr. Montand was on the phone and I immediately thought he was going to cancel.

"Can't make it to the Polo Lounge for dinner; we'll order here in my bungalow." He told me which one it was and I walked there through the tropical gardens. The bungalows are little tile-roofed houses, elegantly decorated, with French doors. Every star in the world has lived there at some time, which has made the Beverly Hills Hotel famous.

I rang his doorbell and was told to come in. I opened the door, expecting the usual arrangement: living room, two bedrooms, two baths. I expected the beautiful furnishings and the excellent taste that is a trademark of the hotel. I got all that, and more. I got something I didn't expect — Marilyn.

My God, she was lovely. She was playing kitten for Montand, an act I learned to recognize later. There was none of the sophisticated bitch, which she could also be. I learned about that part of her personality later.

We ordered dinner from room service. I watched the two of them, knowing exactly what was coming. She sat on the couch, curled up around a drink, sucking a little on the rim of the glass, letting Montand gaze at her. He moved around the room casually, very sophisticated and smooth.

Montand was the kind of man Marilyn was attracted to. She was interested in "intellectual" men at that time; she was still married to Arthur Miller, who was in New York.

Marilyn talked about how excited she was to be working with George Cukor. She felt that she didn't have to worry about a thing as to how she looked because Cukor was famous for lighting his leading ladies properly and making sure they were made up properly. She was totally at ease. We talked shop and she asked how long I'd known Cukor. She said she liked working with Montand, and it was all very casual that evening, the three of us just chatting away, except my heart was leaping out of my chest.

## Let's Break Love

"Miss Monroe," I said, " tell me something. . ."

"Call me Marilyn, don't give me that Miss Monroe jazz."

"Well, I understand you have a suite here at the hotel. . ."

"On no, a bungalow. Just across the way. We're all going to be a cozy family here."

And suddenly I couldn't remember what I was going to say.

It was the beginning of the great intrigue, the infamous Monroe-Montand love affair, which was to become very hot and heavy and would bring Simone back from Paris to protect her property. It was also the beginning of Marilyn's downfall. She couldn't put love aside for business; she always had to combine the two.

There would be great drinking bouts later for her, and tantrums when the fun and games turned ugly and the great love affair turned sour. That's why production went on for almost a year before the film was finished. When I look back now at our first social meeting, I realize she was playing a role with the baby voice, the curled up kitten with her mouth always partially open.

Cukor once said, "If her mouth were ever shut with the lips together, you'd see her face isn't all that attractive. You'll notice there is very seldom a picture taken of Monroe with her mouth closed. Everything is pre-planned."

She'd learned a lot from Arthur Miller and Joe DiMaggio and she put it all to work, and it worked well. Whenever you looked at her, you see that she was looking not at you, but at a camera, and seducing you/it with her words and fluttering eyelids.

I could see then that she was out to do a number on Yves Montand, who was vulnerable to beautiful, voluptuous blondes. The kitten was really a cat just waiting to pounce. If he was taken in with that scene, there were even better ones to follow.

This was the first of many dinners the three of us were to have. When we got tired of the hotel food, we called Chasen's or some other restaurant and had dinner sent in. It was nice and for a change, I didn't have to pay for a thing.

## The Park Avenue Chorus Boy

I think Montand liked me because I was young enough not to be any competition to him. We had Paris in common and I was a personal friend of Cukor's. This was Yves' first film in America and he needed all the security he could find, and that made him a sucker for Monroe.

That first evening, Marilyn visually seduced him with every movement, every gesture. She wanted him and she zeroed in and he loved every minute of it.

When dinner was over, Marilyn, Montand, and I had a few brandies and then I said, "Well, I've got to get going." I thanked them both for dinner.

Marilyn jumped up and said, "Oh, would you do me a favor? Yves has to make a call to Paris. Would you escort me to my bungalow?"

She turned to Montand before I could yes or no, picked up her mink, and said, "Good night." Of course, then Mason could tell everyone else that nothing had happened between them because Mason had walked Marilyn home to her bungalow.

So we walked out of Montand's bungalow and I thought I'd take one chance. She was all hopped up from the brandy and obviously nervous, the cat tensed to spring, so I said, "Marilyn, rather than going back to your bungalow right away, how about sneaking in a side door of the Polo Lounge; we can sit in a dark corner and have a brandy."

"Oh, my God," she said, "I'd love it."

So she whipped out her dark glasses, pulled her mink coat up around her face and, in her jeans, with her shoes in her hand, she followed me into the Polo Lounge. Everyone knew who she was, of course, but the nice thing about the Polo Lounge is nobody bothers you. It is an unspoken agreement there. Nobody comes over to say hello. Marilyn and I sat alone at a small table.

"You like champagne," I said.

"How did you know?"

"Who are you kidding? Everybody knows you like champagne." I waved the maitre d' over and said, "The usual, please," and he brought a bottle of Dom Perignon and we sat there for about an hour.

"Mr. Montand's a wonderful man," she said. "It's a shame he's married."

"You're married. We're all married."

We had a nice, off-the-cuff conversation. Her reason for spending time with me was to find out more about Cukor. Everything she did was planned, although it didn't necessarily work out precisely as she had hoped. People said she was devious, but I don't think so; she may have wanted to exert more control over life, but she was not a cold, calculating superintellectual.

She was genuinely excited about the start of filming and the wonderful people she'd be working with. We knocked off the champagne and I walked her back to her bungalow.

I really wanted to turn around, go back to the Polo Lounge and close the place, but I stopped myself. Everyone had seen me leave with Marilyn Monroe. As far as they knew, I was last seen walking down the path to her bungalow. Could I ruin a perfectly good fantasy by returning? Could I let these people down? You mean you didn't stay with Marilyn? You came back to join us for another drink? I went to a back elevator and returned to my room alone. Needless to say, after that night, I had anything I wanted at the Polo Lounge. Of course, once I was back in my room, I immediately called twenty people, rousing them out of bed, and crowed, "You won't believe what I just did."

Marilyn seconded Montand's trust in me and we spent a lot of time together. Cukor asked me how Yves and Marilyn got along and I told him they were getting along beautifully, that it was a budding romance. "Good," he said, "that'll keep our picture together." Little did he know that the romance would be the thing that would blow the picture apart.

Rehearsals went well for a while, although Marilyn had a problem concentrating during dance rehearsals. Like most films, it was going to be shot out of sequence and the lack of continuity bothered her. But it was exciting for me to watch Marilyn work with the choreographer, Jack Cole. The lady was a good dancer and a great comedienne, and she could sing beautifully in that little girl's voice.

I think she really enjoyed the rehearsal phase. She was out from under the gun as far Cukor was concerned, and she was having a good time. Wardrobe fittings come in between rehearsals, but a few months down the line, when it came time to actually film, the costumes didn't fit — she had gained at least 30 pounds. It was a nightmare. New costumes would have to be scavenged and nothing matched. She'd be singing in the nightclub, there'd be a splice, and all of a sudden, slim, singing Marilyn had turned into chunky dancing Marilyn.

The danger signals were all there from the beginning, but we were so used to them we didn't acknowledge their importance . If a makeup call was scheduled for 7 AM, she'd come in at 8:30 or later. She couldn't remember her lines and it soon became apparent she was drinking too much and taking too many pills.

I knew the romance between Marilyn and Montand was heating up, but I didn't know all the details. I had dinner with them numerous times before the first "incident," after which they became more secretive. The incident? The two of them disappeared for three days. No one knew where they were; they were just gone. They could have flown somewhere far away, or simply gone to another hotel. It didn't matter because production ground to a halt in any case. The first day, the entire crew sat around and waited patiently. The only odd thing was that Montand was with her. He wasn't the type to disappear — or was he? The second day, the producer, Jerry Wald, came to the set hopping mad. Cukor stayed in his bungalow, quietly waiting and preparing future shots. The third day, there was talk of shutting down. No one could find them.

Late in the third day, Montand came back and apologized; he said he had been away. That was the only explanation he offered. Naturally he was asked where Marilyn was. He said only that she'd be back the following day.

So Cukor sat there on the fourth day, fuming. You could smell the rage, like a transformer about to blow. There was discussion of postponing shooting for two weeks until she got her head together. Through it all, Cukor sat quietly, outwardly calm, but burning inside, fingernails digging deep into armrests. We kept getting false reports — she was at the hotel, the limo had left, she was still at the hotel, but leaving in a half-hour. This went on all day with rumors that she'd be on the set at noon, then two. At four o'clock, she came flying across the set, crying hysterically, mink coat flying, spike heels clacking. She grabbed George. "I'm sorry, I'm sorry, I'm sorry." It was pathetic.

She sobbed and carried on; George waited calmly through it all, just as he had waited four days for her to show up. The tension on the set was intense as we waited for George to tell her to go screw herself, which he was famous for doing. Everyone focused on him, waiting for him to blow. He held her paternally for a while, then backed away. Here it comes, we thought. He took both her hands in his, then said solemnly: "Darling Marilyn, there's one thing you have to remember: this is your picture and your career. Not mine. When you are ready, let me know." And he walked away and left her standing there. No ranting, no raving. He treated her like a naughty little girl. She was back on the set in an hour and they filmed until 8 o'clock that night.

Simone Signoret was aware of the affair all along and she came back to Hollywood from Paris to see if her marriage could be saved. Marilyn was very insecure with Simone back, but the three managed to maintain a surface friendliness. I joined them a few times at dinner to make a foursome. Simone stayed for ten days, realized there was nothing she could do, and left. It was a losing battle; she and Montand separated and didn't get back together until long after the picture was over.

Along the way, Montand invited me to join him at Peter Lawford's beach house for a party. It had originally been Sam Goldwyn's house and was a natural setting for the kind of parties Lawford and his wife, Pat Kennedy, enjoyed giving. As we drove to Santa Monica, I asked if Marilyn would be there and he said yes. I gingerly asked if their relationship was getting heavy, and again he said yes, but he didn't care to discuss it. Well, I thought, here's an older guy who's just kicked his marriage over the cliff for a crazy, breathy blond — he doesn't have to talk about it.

The party was in full swing and included Angie Dickinson, Sammy Davis, Jr., the Lawfords, Montand, and Marilyn. From the moment I walked in, I could sense that something was off, very badly off. Marilyn wasn't hanging around Montand. In fact, she was obviously staying away from him. She was repeating the routine I'd seen in Montand's bungalow that first night. She had kicked her shoes off and was curled up on a couch, cradling her champagne, once again the vulnerable kitten. She wore a tight sweater and her hair and makeup were perfect. She seemed to be purring, "Are you man enough to protect me?" She preened and waited; I didn't know who she was waiting for, who the victim was to be. All I knew was that it wasn't Yves Montand. He was in another room and the anger emanating from him could peel wallpaper. He knew what was happening, but he wasn't ready to be dismissed so summarily. He began drinking and pacing, and each room he passed through dripped with the steam of the rejected suitor.

We heard the rumble through the floor first, low, deep, and almost indistinguishable from the surf. As it grew closer, we knew it was something else; then we heard the sound of the high, slicing blades and ran to the windows. Lawford was grinning because he knew what was coming. He watched us all as we peered out the windows, drink in his hand, delight on his face. I realized that Marilyn knew, too; this is what she'd been waiting for. Lowering itself on the beach was a helicopter, whining down as the sand kicked up. Out stepped the Attorney General of the United

## Let's Break Love

States, Robert F. Kennedy. Marilyn's eyes glassed over as he strode to the door and was welcomed in.

She continued playing the scene — this was her trap and the new fly was close now. The old one had been eaten to bleached bones and tossed aside. Poor Montand, and poor Bobby; would he be next? Her eyes worked Bobby Kennedy like an animal on the prowl. She used the identical sequence of mannerisms that had worked with Montand, and it worked again. It was the same way she used a camera — she seduced it.

She sat there for a full hour, idly chatting with people as Bobby paced nearby, casing her. At six o'clock, dinner was announced. Kennedy went over to her and said, "Let's have dinner."

"I'd love to," she purred and took his arm to be escorted in to the dining area.

Montand was seething, while all his elegant French manners collapsed into pure and simple hatred. He had become yesterday's news in a matter of hours. Perhaps some of the trouble Marilyn would have later in the picture we were filming was from the difficult times he gave her to get even for this night. Montand was well known to be tough with his ladies if they didn't treat him well. He was not good at taking a back seat while his woman played coy and cute for another man.

Bobby Kennedy and Marilyn got their plates and sat in a corner, talking for another two hours. They ignored Montand completely. To them, he simply didn't exist.

Montand wound up with a group of us in the poker room and blurted, "This is a lot of bullshit."

Sammy Davis said, "You should do yourself a favor and go. Her limo's here, and I'll make sure she's okay."

Montand didn't do any hard drinking, but he had put away a lot of wine and champagne as it became obvious to him that he and Marilyn were through. I volunteered to go back to town with him, but before starting to leave, I went over to Marilyn and asked her why she was ignoring Montand.

"Michael," she said, "why don't you take him back to the hotel? I'm busy, honey, as you can see."

This was one of the few times I saw, first-hand, the hint of her cool, calculating side. She had the electricity of the star, and when she turned it on, it became lightning. There was nothing I could do for Montand but get him out of there as fast as possible.

She was at the top of her profession and she knew it. She could walk over anyone. She worked for that privilege, and maybe she deserved it, but she paid for it. I had been around a lot of stage and movie stars, but never before was I so taken by anyone's personal magnetism the way I was with Marilyn. She was practiced in every gesture, in the way she moved and the way she spoke: "I'm a star, look at me, touch me, love me." God damn, she was good. She needed the approval of everyone, especially her peers, but once she had hooked someone and reeled him in, she couldn't relax with her victory. She had to rebait the hook, because the one she had already caught was no longer a challenge. Once he liked her, wanted her, needed her, he was no longer necessary. Because she didn't like herself, if a man liked her, then she considered him stupid, and so she had to find someone smarter.

It was a long, quiet drive back to the hotel. Montand sat beside me and stared out the window. He knew it was over.

There followed difficult days on the set with hard scenes to film. God knows what was happening behind closed doors, but production slowed visibly. I didn't see Montand and Monroe for dinner after that, but for the sake of the movie, they acted like they were on good terms. Marilyn was having problems and the frayed edges showed. She gained even more weight and could not stay on schedule. None of this was new; it just was worse than before. She was paranoid and a nervous wreck. There was too much pressure handling all the men in her life — Miller,

Montand, Kennedy, and whoever else — and it was taking its toll.

One afternoon in particular, she kept dropping her lines in a scene with Montand. Cukor did a remarkable thing. On a technicolor extravaganza, with maybe a hundred people on the set at all times and the price of filming, even the film itself, running beyond budget, Cukor went up to Marilyn quietly and whispered something in her ear, loud enough for Montand, but no one else, to hear. Montand nodded and walked away, and she nodded. I regularly sat next to George and when he returned to his chair, I asked, "George, what did you say to her?"

"I just told them that if they drop lines, just pick them up and keep going, because I'm going to keep the camera rolling."

It was a good thing that Jerry Wald wasn't on the set that day, but it turned out to be one scene that had continuity. There was about four pages of dialogue and when she finally finished, which took only ten minutes, but felt like ten hours, there was tremendous applause from the crew. Montand showed some irritation with her when she couldn't remember lines, but for the most part he was a gentleman. Marilyn wasn't stupid; she was just crazed. She knew she was going downhill and she began to appeal for sympathy from anyone and everyone who would give it to her. Her weight began to fluctuate even more wildly than before. They went crazy cutting the film together. She had lost control over booze, food, and her emotions.

I didn't understand that it was the beginning of the end for her, but Cukor did. He wrote about it later and said he knew the lady was sliding into madness. In fact, he wrote that she *was* mad, her mother was mad, and Marilyn was destined to kill herself.

Finally, ten months after we had begun it, *Let's Make Love* wrapped.

# CHAPTER TWENTY
## Marilyn And Beyond

Arthur Miller wrote *The Misfits* for Marilyn a few years before they got around to making the film. Gable loved the script, John Huston was pleased with it, and Montgomery Clift agreed to sign on. It would be the last film for both Gable and Monty, and the last completed film for Marilyn. The picture was well-named; never was there such a group of misfits coming together to make a film. It was a noble effort, but not quite worth the final payment. Gable died of a heart attack eleven days after completion of the filming. Some said it was the tremendous heat of the Nevada desert, or it was the work load, while others blamed the scene with the mustangs in which Gable had done his own roping stunt work. Still others said it was Marilyn. She made even the great Clark Gable wait for her.

I called Marilyn twice on the set, wanting to visit her. She told me not to come, that Monty was ill, and so was she. The finished film was indeed a troubled one, but it did not begin to reflect the troubles behind the scenes. Clift and Monroe were both drinking heavily and no one knew what barbiturates she was throwing in for good measure. Lee Strasberg's wife, Paula, was there, whispering in Marilyn's ear and driving everyone crazy, which Marilyn could do well enough alone. Huston was pulling away, not giving the film his best, Clift was going mad, and Gable, the nice affable cowboy, just sat waiting, day after day, wanting nothing more than to get the hell out of there. He told his wife, Kay, how much he hated the whole situation.

Kay filled me in later on some of it. She discovered soon after filming began that she was pregnant. Gable wanted a son badly. He knew he had heart trouble, but he was damned if he wasn't going to stick around to see his boy. Kay braved the desert heat to be with him. She was smart; she knew Marilyn had a thing about Gable, so she was there to put the lid on even the thought of an affair before it could happen.

The second time I called Marilyn, she had good news. She was thinking beyond *The Misfits* to her next picture, which would be with Cukor again. She was disheartened by the evolution of *The Misfits*. It had been a heady concept and she envisioned herself and Miller creating a work of art together. But they had finally split during filming, hardly a surprise after l'affaire Montand.

"I have good news for you," she said. "I spoke with George Cukor and you're definitely going to be in my next picture."

"Great, fantastic," I said, up on a cloud again. I was upset that she wouldn't let me see her, but understood she felt awkward about my friendship with Montand. She was trying to blot a lot of people out of her life.

Cukor verified her statement and invited Nikki and me over to celebrate, although I'd still have to go through proper channels with the casting office. The picture was called *Something's Got to Give,* a title so rife with ironies as to preclude discussion. Sets were already under construction. A few weeks later, I was indeed called by Gene Reynolds, head of casting. I was to play the part of a young Navy Lieutenant. Although I never got a script, I was fitted for wardrobe. Gene said I'd probably get to work for a couple of months, but knowing Marilyn, I could make another career out of this movie, and we both laughed. The sets were impressive, especially the one that was an exact replica of Cukor's garden, complete with pool.

Marilyn came back into town and was fitted for wardrobe. There were many meetings and filming was to hopefully start soon, but she was so exhausted, it was difficult to be specific about a date. Marilyn went to her Brentwood home, and after trying to get her many times, I finally reached her there.

"Hey," I said, "you're gonna have dinner with an old buddy of yours. I'll send the limo for you."

"No," she said, "I'll bring my own and meet you at the Polo Lounge. Get a quiet little corner and we'll chat for old time's sake." She sounded very cool and very down. The fact that she wouldn't let me pick her up was startling because she never wanted to travel alone.

I made sure I was at the hotel early, although even if you were only on time, you'd be earlier than Marilyn. She arrived, as usual, about an hour late. She was grateful that I was standing there, waiting, even though she'd known I would be. She kissed me on both cheeks. Her makeup was good, but her hair wasn't done, and she'd covered it with a scarf. She wore a little skirt, and sweater, and of course, the mink and Ferragamo pumps. She looked as down as she'd sounded on the phone.

As we walked inside, tourists gathered and gawked tastelessly. A couple of photographers had evidently heard she was coming, I don't know how, but they always seem to know, and flashbulbs started popping. She was upset and concerned that I might have called them. I assured her I hadn't.

We settled into the haven of the Polo Lounge. It was good to see her, but there was something very wrong. I'd heard through various people that she was very heavily sedated these days and was drinking in excess of her own usual heavy norm. She avoided talking about Montand. She discussed *The Misfits*, what Gable's death had meant to her, and how sick Monty Clift was. I had only met Clift a few times and didn't really know him, but I had followed his career and, like so many others, was pained at this slide from stardom to drugs and alcohol.

What Marilyn was really doing was talking about herself. Her problems were similar to Clift's: an emotional instability and failure to cope with the world in general. His instability centered on his homosexuality, her on nymphomania. She simply couldn't cope with all the men in her life and it had finally caught up with her. DiMaggio was gone, Miller was gone, and she had problems with her pictures and co-stars. Everything was escalating beyond her control.

The fact that people were seeing her at less than her best made her uneasy, but she went on talking, showing a little excitement about the new picture and working with Cukor again.

"It's fabulous. Cukor wants me again after all the terrible things I did. I figured he'd never direct me again, even if I begged and pleaded. But he was very willing to go ahead, being the gentleman he is."

"Well, Marilyn, I think he feels *Let's Make Love* and *The Misfits* will bring you back up to where you were when you did *Some Like Hot* and *The Seven Year Itch*. Back then, along with *Gentlemen Prefer Blondes*, she had been in top form, the epitome of Hollywood glamour, on and off the screen. Her acting had improved with each picture, even as her personal life crumbled.

We had a pleasant evening and she emphasized wanting to get back to work. I asked her about Bobby Kennedy, and she said, "There is nothing to discuss. I don't want to go into it. You're sweet to ask, and I'm fine."

She went through a bottle of champagne on her own and then we moved on to brandy. She ate very little.

"Well," she said, "everything's going well. I go to the studio tomorrow. The wardrobe looks great, the sets are marvelous, and I can't wait to get back to work."

That was the last time I saw her. I walked her out to her car, she kissed me goodbye, and I watched her drive off. I truly loved her.

They got some film shot and called in Dean Martin for a few scenes. Then the craziness, the lateness, the disappearing act went too far. She was fired from the film a few days after her thirty sixth birthday.

While filming was going on, I was in regular touch with Cukor. "She's a wreck, Michael. I'm surprised you haven't been out here nosing around the studio."

"I don't think it's the thing for me to do."

"I agree. Stay away."

Most of the sets were closed to visitors, but I could have gotten on through Cukor.

After she was fired, she went to New York to do a play with Strasberg. That fell through and she came back to California.

About two months later, the phone rang very early one morning. I don't remember who it was who said, "Hey did you hear the news?"

"What?"

"Marilyn Monroe died last night."

I froze. I was numb. "Jesus Christ, what happened?"

"I'm not sure."

I remained frozen a moment and then let the phone fall to the floor.

The house closed around me, suffocating me. I slammed into walls and windows and finally stumbled outside. The limo was there. I got in and found the keys and the car moved by itself. It always moved by itself, but that was because there was a chauffeur at the wheel. Images tumbled through the air at me. I was driving away from Nikki and Richard, but where to? I remembered a line of James Dean's that Marilyn had quoted to me: "Live fast, die young, and leave a good-looking corpse." Just in case I'm really driving, I thought, I'd better turn the wheel here on Ventura and get on the freeway. Where the hell am I going? The Beverly Hills Hotel? The beach? The tires gobbled up the pavement beneath me and I drove south.

Marilyn was found nude, with nothing in her stomach. It had been pumped. The questions surrounding her death are legendary — whether it was a suicide, an accident, or murder.

All I knew was that she was dead and I was crying at the wheel, driving wildly on the San Diego Freeway heading into the Los Angeles basin. Tears streamed down my face and the road was blurry. Mulholland Drive was coming up at the top of the Santa Monica Mountains. I was going very fast. I checked my rear view mirror and there it was. One glance was all it took. A truck was crisscrossing, weaving across all four lanes of traffic, coming straight at me.

"Fuck," I said aloud. "Now?"

It kept coming fast, even though I was speeding. Cars flew off to the sides of the freeway, scattering and squealing like calves at a roundup. He hadn't hit anyone yet, but I knew he would hit me. This is it, I thought. I'm going to be killed in my own limo, on the freeway going nowhere.

I accelerated, thinking I might outrun him, If I slowed down, he'd hit me broadside. If he hit me in front, I'd spin like a compass. If he it me in the middle, I'd roll.

He swerved right. I couldn't accelerate out of his way and he hit the right rear end, blew a hole in the right side of the car, and I spun like a toy top in the heaviest car in the world. He went over, upside down. I heard the sound of the crash and I blacked out. I came to with my head against the left window. I had a throbbing headache and a lump on the left side of my head. I heard sirens and a voice that kept saying, "Are you all right? Are you all right?"

"What happened?" I asked in a daze.

My car was blocking three lanes, the truck was overturned, with its wheels spinning. Someone said, "The man's dead." I got out of the car and ran over. The poor son of a bitch was caught under the cab, half crushed by his own truck. He was moaning and groaning, obviously not dead, looking at me. Everytime I looked at him, I saw Marilyn's face. Marilyn Monroe, crushed under the truck. Somebody help her. Marilyn, get out from under the truck!

## The Park Avenue Chorus Boy

Two officers ran up on either side of me and grabbed me before I toppled. "Are you all right?"

"I think so." I looked at this face, saw Marilyn, and blacked out.

I woke up in the hospital with a concussion, my head in bandages, Nikki at my side. The police had filled her in briefly. The last thing she'd known was that I was somewhere in the house, then the Highway Patrol called and told her I was in an accident on the freeway. She didn't believe it because I had been home only minutes before. She saw the car was gone and then she knew it was true.

As she sat by my side, she asked me what had happened and I told her I didn't know. All that I remembered was a truck had hit me the driver was an old man of about seventy, driving a Goodwill truck.

Before they removed the bandage from the left side of my head, the doctor said, "I have some bad news for you."

"What's that? The concussion's all right. I'm rested. I feel okay."

"We're going to have to operate. The blow to the head detached the retina of your left eye, so your vision is going to be off, so don't be shocked."

He unwound the bandage, and I could barely see anything through my left eye. I didn't realize the seriousness of it. I thought, all right, so I will have an operation. The doctor assured me I'd be okay afterward; that it was not an unusual event.

I had the operation and sat in the hospital for one week with both eyes bandaged; they cover both eyes because if you use the good one, the other tracks with it, covered or not. A week in the dark, waiting. I was on the edge of the abyss again. There was no reality, only blackness. I figured everything was over — Monroe was dead, I was nearly killed in a car accident, maybe maimed for life, and was having a nervous breakdown, with no money and no hope.

The bandages came off. I had less than fifty percent of my vision in my left eye. "I can't handle this," I bellowed. I raged, threw the nurses out of my room, and made a general ass of myself. I ordered drinks and canapes from a restaurant next door to the hospital and played the complete self-destructive egoist. I had nothing, so I had nothing to loose. Or, so I thought.

When I was ready to check out, the doctor told me to wear dark glasses and give the eye a chance to heal. Eye surgery is not pretty. The left socket was red and pulpy, and I had to wear a patch under the dark glasses which drove me crazy.

I went for regular checkups. The ophthalmologist said at one point, "It's not improving. It's getting worse."

"What are you going to do?"

"I'll operate again."

"No, you won't. I want the best eye surgeon in the country."

"There is someone in Boston you could see, at Massachusetts General."

"I'll go to Boston."

It turned out the guy's credentials were great. I decided to go it alone, and, feeling sorry for myself as usual, flew to Boston, checked into a hotel and reported for tests. The hospital was a dungeon. I was in the best room in the hospital and it overlooked a jail. In the state I was in, I twisted that around until in my mind I believed the room was my jail.

I was already a nervous wreck and worn out, and then the weather became nasty and congestion settled in my chest. The doctor said he was postponing the operation because of possible complications when I was under anaesthesia. I told him I wanted to have it done immediately. He said he would do the operation under local.

I didn't know what "local" was, and if I had, I never would have allowed it. He said I wouldn't know what was going on, which was not true. They stretched me on a table, feet strapped, arms tied to my side, a strap across my chest, oxygen over my nose and mouth, and my head wrapped except for the one area they were going to work on. Through the gauze on good eye, I could see everything that was going on.

I was on that table for three hours and twenty minutes, unable to move or talk, and I thought I was going to go insane. I came out of the procedure with both eyes re-bandaged. Another two weeks without seeing. I was alone in Boston, except for the volunteers who would come by to chat — "Oh, you're from California. Tell me about it."

"Please leave me alone; get out of here."

They thought I was a manic-depressive and sent in a psychiatrist. "What's the matter? You're throwing people out of your room."

"You get out, too. Leave me alone, all right? Just leave me be. I don't want to talk about Hollywood and I don't want to talk about me. I just want to get out of here."

The situation and I became totally unbearable and I told the doctor, "Look, I can sit in a hotel room but I cannot sit in a hospital. I hate hospitals."

"Well, I don't know the results yet, but it doesn't look too promising."

"What do you mean, 'It doesn't look too promising'?"

"It's touch and go. You may never see out of your eye again."

I checked out of the hospital that afternoon, called a limo, and went to see my uncle, who was living in Brocton at the time. The only good thing that came from that trip to Boston was the fact I saw him, because he died six months later. When I got to his home, I told him what had happened.

"Those things you adjust to, Michael," he said.

"Adjust? How can I be an actor and work a camera if I'm blind in one eye? This is insane."

I was feeling sorry for myself. I went back to the hotel, boozed it up, and turned on the TV. I called everyone in the world and then I finally called Cukor.

"George, I know this sounds crazy, but I'm not going to get the eyesight back in my left eye."

"Bullshit. We'll put you in the Jules Stein Institute at UCLA. It is the finest in the world."

"I was told Boston was the finest in the world, and now you're telling me Jules Stein is the finest. Christ, I know the Steins. Why didn't that damn doctor in Beverly Hills tell me that?"

"UCLA has the finest equipment in the world right in your own backyard. Get your ass on a plane and get back here."

So I did. I flew back, sitting in the lounge all the way, chomping on cheese and gulping champagne and brandy, figuring UCLA was a very slim hope at the end of the line.

I went directly to the Jules Stein Institute because I didn't want my son Richard to see me in my current physical and mental condition. The accommodations there were beautiful; it was like checking into a hotel. The rounds of tests started again and took all day. A doctor questioned me, "Do you think you are psychologically ready for this. It's awfully soon since the last procedure."

"Look," I said, "I want to get it over with. Psychologically, I think I can handle it."

"I don't think you can."

He turned out to be the staff psychiatrist. He was right. I couldn't handle it. On the day of the operation, I cancelled it.

"What do you mean, you're cancelling it?" the staff said.

"I'm cancelling it. It's my prerogative. We'll do it tomorrow."

The phone started ringing. The Beverly Hills doctor, the doctor from Boston, Nikki, and they all called telling me I shouldn't cancel the operation. Then Nikki came racing over to the hospital. "What are you doing? You can't cancel the operation!"

"I cancelled it, okay? It'll be done tomorrow."

They rescheduled. That night, I called Nikki at home.

"Send the car. I'm coming home."

"What do you mean, you're coming home?"

"I'm coming home. I'm not having the operation. I can't handle it. I'm not going to sit with my eyes bandaged to a week again. I'll go crazy, if I haven't already. There is no guarantee it will work. I have no vision out of the eye now and when I asked the doctor what would happen after the operation, do you know what he said? He said, "We don't know." After all these tests, these bastards don't know. They're going to use me as a guinea pig. How do I know what they're going to do. When they have me under, they might operate on the wrong eye."

The psychiatrist came back in to see me. "You can't walk out of here against medical advice."

"Fuck you. It's gonna take you and ten cops and ten lawsuits. I'm walking out of here. My wife's coming in the car in fifteen minutes, and if she doesn't come, I'll divorce her and kill anybody who stands in my way."

So I packed up the picture of my son, my pillow, and was ready to walk out the door.

He pleaded with me. "Will you give me fifteen minutes of your time? I think I can help you."

"I don't need your help, okay? I'm not going to be blindfolded again. They're telling me I may not have any vision at all. At least now I have a little black and white going, but totally black?"

"That's how it is going to be, anyway."

"If it is going to be that way anyway, then who needs the bullshit?" We went through it all over again, and when Nikki arrived at exactly 10:32 PM, I left UCLA and went home.

I realized then what my life was going to be like without my left eye. My equilibrium was off, and my peripheral vision was gone. How could I work a camera or a stage? Of course, I was overreacting, but that was how I felt at the time. I had to accept the fact that I would be totally blind in my left eye and I didn't think I could have control in front of a camera. I decided to quit the business. I didn't want to knock my head against the wall. I decided to go into a real business, not show business, and use what was left of my good looks. I could use the bullshit and the acting and personality doing something else.

Some time later, after I'd been sitting around feeling sorry for myself for far too long, someone finally helped me to put my head on straight. Don Moomaw, the minister at the Bel Air Presbyterian Church reached out to me. He is now well-known because he was Ronald Reagan's minister and officiated at Reagan's inauguration, but first and foremost he was and is a spiritual healer. I was in the chapel, bemoaning my fate, not really looking for answers, and indulging in my usual bitterness.

Moomaw ambled over to me. "Mike, what are you doing?"

"I'm drunk and I'm feeling sorry for myself."

"You don't sit in my church drunk and feeling sorry for yourself."

"You don't know what I've gone through."

"Oh? Somebody die?"

"No. Nobody died. It's me. My eyesight." And I told him the whole sad story.

He took my face in his big hands, squeezed, and said, "You're lucky your face is together. Quit feeling so sorry for yourself. You should be ashamed." That was the beginning of his sermon which made me feel like the biggest asshole in the world. "What about the guys who came back from the war with no arms and no legs? How about the people born blind? How about the people going blind who can't afford an operation? You have a problem? Don't make me laugh!"

I got sober fast. I finally pulled my act together, thanks to him. When I went home, I put *La Boheme* on the stereo. I turned it up loud and let it fill the house, as it churned up memories.

Perhaps I was finally seeing more clearly with one eye than with two. I didn't want to be a star anymore, and it really didn't have to do with my eyesight. It was Marilyn and what stardom had done to her. It had eaten her up from the inside out. Who knows if I could have been a star; somehow it didn't matter. I realized I'd been trying *not* be a star as far back as my screen test, may even farther back, maybe even in the days when I called myself the Park Avenue Chorus Boy.

I had played my games, screwed around, and had a good time. What else did I need? The burden of being a star had killed Marilyn and dozens of others who were crippled by their fame, alone and insecure when the lights went out. They turned to booze, drugs, fast cars, and shotguns. Maybe my insistence on fun and games was a defense mechanism, an acceptable adaptation of my will to live in the society in which I found myself.

*La Boheme* echoed through the corridors of the house and my memory, accompanied by flashing images from the past — Aunt Suzanne, Broadway, Fox Studios, Marilyn. . . Marilyn. Although she couldn't help herself, maybe she saved me after all.

# CHAPTER TWENTY-ONE
## After My Fall

One thing we know is after hitting bottom, there's only two ways to go, and that's either out or up. I chose to go up. I decided there were other areas I could fit into. Since I was a "people" person, I decided to put my talent and gift of gab into the real estate business.

One Christmas, a dear friend of ours, the fabulous Peggy Lee, invited us to spend the week with her in her spectacular French Regency Villa in Bel Air. Peggy had been invited to Barbara and Frank Sinatra's Beverly Hills home for a small Christmas Eve dinner party. Nikki was ill, so I escorted Peggy to the Sinatra's party, and what a party it was.

Frank's wife Barbara greeted us at the front door and Peggy walked in with me, all done up on white silk, chiffon, marabou, and spectacular white diamonds to set it all off. Frank told Peggy she looked like a beautiful white snowstorm, breezing in through the front door. What a fantastic man Sinatra was. I truly felt honored to be in his home, especially at such an intimate party — the waiters and waitresses out numbered the guests.

Major, heavy-duty musicians were there; the music never stopped. Quincy Jones, Dean Martin, Dinah Shore (with whom I had worked so many years ago on her Chevrolet commercials), the ever beautiful Angie Dickinson, and my old buddy from 20th Century Fox Studio days, Bob "R.J." Wagner and his gorgeous bride, Jill St. John. R.J. and I had a great time discussing early

## The Park Avenue Chorus Boy

studio days, when he dated Debbie Reynolds and I was with Virginia Gibson.

Steve Lawrence and his wife Edie were at the party, too, as well as Frank Sinatra, Jr.; Mel Torme and his wife; Glenn Ford; Gregory Peck; Lee Minnelli with Louis Estevez; and Milton Berle, with whom I reminisced about how we had worked with Marilyn Monroe in the film *Let's Make Love*. The ever-young George Burns was also there, and although I am sure he didn't remember me appearing on his TV show, he was gracious enough to say he did.

What a party that was, and what a group of people! Not the usual, Hug, Hug, Kiss, Kiss Hollywood party, but a beautiful, elegant, yet down-to-earth Christmas Eve. What a privilege to be a guest in the home of Barbara and Frank with some of their closest friends.

"I don't know you," Frank said to me, "but you must be OK if you are with Peggy Lee."

The Sinatra's estate is one of the most magnificent properties in Beverly Hills. Security was very tight at the front gate, and the long driveway up to the mansion was spectacular. The driveway on both sides had large potted poinsettias and all the trees were covered with small white Christmas lights — thousands of them. The interior was ablaze with the same lights and plants, as were all the trees surrounding the huge swimming pool and guest house.

As this was an enclave of show biz greats, there were no photographers, so everyone was at ease. Originally Peggy was only going to stay a short time, but she was having such a good time, that we didn't leave until three hours later. As we got to the front door to go, Sinatra sang a few bars of "Peg O' My Heart" to Peggy, who is loved and admired by everyone.

My luck in real estate was better than my luck in the movies. I was soon working with major clients such as Ted Field, the Marshall Field heir from Chicago who is now a movie producer, Kenny Rogers, Sylvester Stalone, Peggy Lee, Aaron Spelling, Lisa

Minnelli, Barbra Streisand, the late Steve McQueen, and the former (and last) Mrs. J. Paul Getty, or "Teddy" as she is known.

Teddy has been one of our dearest and closest friends for over 30 years. She is a unique woman and very special. I handled the sale of her colonial mansion on the beach of the Gold Coast in Santa Monica. This was the house that Paul Getty built for her in the 1940s, just below their ranch, which is now the J. Paul Getty Malibu Museum. Her daughter GiGi is a good actress and is already and accomplished writer. I introduced her to George Cukor years ago, and George said, "GiGi, you are an exquisite beauty like your mother and Ava Gardner. Keep working and you'll make it."

Eventually, I had what I started out to get on Broadway — recognition, friendships with people in show business, a Malibu Beach house, homes in Bel Air and Palm Springs, trips to Europe — all the trappings a star would have, but not the pressure.

As I said to R.J., you can take the person out of show biz, but you can't take the show biz out of the person. Do I miss the business? I can honestly say, I don't know. Now that the Park Avenue Chorus Boy is no longer, *maybe* I will make a comeback in top hat and tails singing under the billing of "Mr." Park Avenue.

• • •

My wife Nikki and I spent a special New Years Eve, December 31st, 1999, at the Beverly Hills Hotel to welcome in the year 2000. Yes, Dom Perignon was served all evening.